EDENVILLE

Also by Ivan Ruff

THE DARK RED STAR
DEAD RECKONING
BLOOD COUNTRY
THE ORPHAN SOLDIER

Ivan Ruff

EDENVILLE

HEINEMANN : LONDON

William Heinemann Ltd
Michelin House, 81 Fulham Road, London SW3 6RB
LONDON   MELBOURNE   AUCKLAND

First published 1990
Copyright © Ivan Ruff 1990

A CIP catalogue record for this book
is available from the British Library

ISBN 0 434 77979 2

Printed and bound in Great Britain
by Richard Clay Ltd, Bungay, Suffolk

To Wisia

ONE

The 737 from Majorca banked in off the sea, winked its lights as it dropped over a few miles of British town, and steadied comfortably on to the deserted tarmac of Edenville International. Only the shadowy outlines of a Handley Page freight carrier and a couple of private lightweights, a Chipmunk and a Piper, with the silhouette of a windsock stiffened by the sea wind, indicated an airport. The passengers trailed into a flimsy-smart customs shed, then entered the wipe-clean brown plastic surface of a low-ceilinged foyer. Outside, beyond a narrow hedge-lined road, evening sun still shone on green fields.

A thin man in a beige suit, with powder-blue shirt and gold chain at his neck, dark glasses concealing his eyes, effortlessly carried large oxblood leather cases over to the uniformed car-hire girl who addressed him as 'Mr Salway?' and indicated the baggage trolleys. He shook his head and followed her to the waiting BMW.

One of the cars along the meagre row would give the girl a lift back to town. Sometimes the customers offered the lift themselves. Then they usually tried for more than just the girl's company, assuming that a uniform meant available for business. Sometimes they were right.

But this time the car-hire girl knew there would be no drive round the scenic route, dinner date for the evening, room number of a good hotel. The thin man with bad acne scars under his hollow-cheeked tan did not once look at her chest, her legs or her bottom. Even from behind his black glasses she could tell. She checked his licence and quickly returned it. He put his case into the trunk with a kind of violence, took the keys as she held the door open, then ignored her. As he drove away, the girl gave the polite little wave that was part of her job. She shuddered. Of all the creeps to meet off a plane.

The country road looped into an expressway that ploughed through Edenville's outskirts, splitting streets that ended on one side and continued the other as if they had been planned like that. Long mounds of earth curved against the sky to form the ramps of new flyovers. Elsewhere the cratered tawny subsoil, patched with ferro-concrete, slipped the throughway under the old roads like a knife through a ribcage. Buildings were new too, reflector-glass offices that seemed to drift with the motion of clouds, a block shaped like a jukebox made of chocolate and cream fudge. The traveller's name was Reece Deacon. For this trip he was Salway.

Everyone came to Edenville for dreams. Dreams were good for real estate prices. People solaced wakeful nights with the hundreds of per cent their houses had appreciated since they took on the mortgage. Living in Edenville showed good commercial judgment. The town oozed self-congratulation. The real good-lifers also wanted their chalets or timeshares in the sun. Only by selling people dreams could you make strong money. Thinking of the fortune he had made in this market gave Deacon his only respite from the grisly errand which had brought him back to Edenville.

The next day, from his sea-view hotel suite, Deacon rang a private clinic. He had an appointment with Dr Bedell, still under the name Salway, just checking. The receptionist told him Dr Bedell had not been in as expected, they were still trying to contact him. Deacon was about to ask something more, got a nervous feeling, hung up.

The local phone book gave two R. H. Bedells. One was a doctor, with a Firglen address. As Deacon remembered Edenville, Firglen was the right place. Downstairs in the hotel he bought a street map and headed out.

On the edge of a golf course, Bedell's place was called *Avila*. A brace of whitewashed stone lions on the gateposts arched their backs against yellow cypress. The low white house, hacienda style, stood beyond well-trimmed lawns. Bellied black iron railings and sea-green roof-slates were sharp-edged against the white. Above each lace-blanked window the sunshades were still rolled in. Deacon peeled on fine Spanish calf gloves and pressed the bell. It rang deep inside the house. Nobody answered.

Through a rounded arch in the white rough-finish wall, Deacon saw a double garage housing a current-registration Mercedes. The patio led to a rear door which he found locked. The pines of the golf course screened the property's seclusion. A lace curtain rippled and drew Deacon's notice to a crack where the aluminium slide window had been left ajar. He eased it further, lifted the curtain aside, and climbed into an empty room.

Deacon found himself in a study. A leather-inlaid desk, mahogany shelves crammed with books. *Principles of Genioplasty*, *Corrective Rhinoplasty*, *The Cosmetic Surgeon*. Deacon recognised the R. H. Bedell he had called long distance from Spain. He went through into a tiled hall. A stair led up to a smaller upper floor, only two rooms and a perfumed area with a moon bath.

From the first bedroom, Deacon looked over the adjacent property. On its terrace a fat middle-aged blonde in a pink baby doll sprawled on a sunlounger. Her face was an angry burnt mask. Her hand hung limp towards a glass of red liquid. On Bedell's own sheltered terrace four white chairs waited round an empty white table. In the second bedroom Deacon found Bedell himself.

The open wardrobe suggested a mature professional man and a large but much younger woman. But if there was a wife around she had not been in this room for at least twelve hours. Or if she had, Bedell hadn't seen her. He was dead, in monogrammed pyjamas.

The pills had taken effect before he could get through the bottle of Jack Daniels. He was twisted over, like someone uncomfortably asleep. Deacon's pitted, unfeeling face stared for a full minute. Bedell had shaved before taking to his bed. Dried blood from an unstanched cut formed a hard blob under his left ear.

The bedside phone rang. To kill the sound Deacon lifted it. About to say wrong number, he heard a female voice with a Gaelic accent say, 'Hello, is that Big Balls?'

Deacon answered softly, 'Yes, speaking.'

'You remember me?'

Deacon thought how Bedell would say the word and answered, 'Absolutely.'

'I've got the directions you want. Have you got a nice long pencil?'

She was Scottish. Just her voice was a seduction.

Deacon purred, 'Yes, go ahead.'

'Take them down then.'

Deacon returned immediately to the hotel and phoned from his room.

'Dr Bedell, please.'

The same receptionist's voice, more anxious now. 'We still have no contact from Dr Bedell.'

'My appointment was eleven. It's now almost twelve.'

'I'm sorry −'

(So they hadn't called back while he was out.)

'I've been waiting here all morning.'

'I do apologise, Mr Salway −'

'My operation's scheduled for tomorrow.'

'I'm sure there won't be any problem. All we −'

'If Bedell's out of action do you have a replacement?'

'Well, I'm afraid − Look, Mr Salway, I'm sure there's a simple explanation. We'll come back to you as soon as −'

'You've tried his home number?'

'Yes. There's no answer.'

(They hadn't rung while Deacon was on Bedell's phone. Good.)

'If Bedell can't operate tomorrow I'll have to cancel. Call me here at four, please.'

Deacon dropped the receiver. He stared at the sea sparkling in the distance and yelled, 'Shiiit!'

Resenting any intrusion on his programme, Deacon kept Bedell's date that night. By then he knew that the clinic had discovered the surgeon's death. Their operating schedules were now in chaos. Bedell's clinic was a secretive place. They could not give polite, bemused Mr Salway a firm reappointment for his operation. Deacon wanted to know more about Bedell. He took his death personally. He took everything personally.

The Scottish voice had said wait for a car. They'll take you where you want to go. Out in the night Deacon heard an engine.

He had left his own car where the voice directed. From the signpost, easily identified by its unique clutch of placenames and distances, he followed a narrow lane. Here the banks were steep, width for only one car. Deacon stopped at the first passing-place, a small inlet cut into the bank, and waited. He pressed his watchlight. A minute before eight. The headlamps.

The engine noise grew louder, then idled. The lights came on full then dipped. Deacon walked towards them. In the car he expected to find the owner of the Scottish voice, maybe alone but he didn't care. Somebody he could slap and start getting an explanation from.

The car was fifty yards away. Deacon trod the brightening channel of the headlamps. The car moved. For a moment it was rolling forward to meet him. Then it was at twenty, thirty, coming to hit him.

Deacon turned and ran. The car's lights rose and flooded the lane. The passing-place, Deacon thought. But that tiny scoop would never save him. The car was old. Metal banged under its hood. Deacon could already feel its prow lifting him, breaking him, tossing him through the air.

Deacon leapt up at the bank. His hands clawed at weeds. Nettles stung his face as his feet skidded. He scraped against crumbling soil till his hand caught a root, gripped the knotty wood. Hand overlapped hand as he ignored gashed flesh and hung on panting while below the saloon shot by.

Ahead, the lane bent. Only the junction gave space to turn. Deacon clung to the hedge above, waiting for the car to reverse and try to hit him again. But the rattletrap kept going. Deacon dropped to the road.

He chased the car. The driver didn't seem to want another shot. When Deacon reached his BMW the other car was still visible, specks of light in the distant dark.

The BMW eased forward on to tarmac. Gas pedal butter smooth, it glided to eighty. Deacon knew the terrain out here. Roads wandered or switchbacked through miles of heathland which at night became a flat blackness sometimes lit by stray cars. In twenty years it hadn't changed.

Instantly Deacon understood the whole shitty deal. A stranger leaves his car on a dark road for the purpose of physical relief. Is killed by a hit-and-run driver. The car with all its forensic details goes to the scrapyard the next day. And an eminent plastic surgeon takes a headful of danger to the morgue.

The BMW flowed through the dark. The saloon ahead, an old orange Ford, seemed to come back towards it like a reverse-motion film. Deacon turned on full beam and hovered within yards of the Ford's bumper. Then he was alongside, half on the verge, nosing in front. He shaved the BMW over so the Ford gradually left the unkerbed road. Then he lurched, clipping his nearside bumper against the Ford's right front corner. The Ford bounced around as it left the road and scoured the soft heath turf. As the driver's foot lost contact with the pedals the engine stalled. The Ford came to an uneasy rest, heavily canted to one side in the dark.

The Ford's driver was male, young, a thin white face with a moustache, dishevelled hair, terrified eyes. Mentally he was still waiting for the car to crumple around him, even after Deacon had climbed inside and started to pound his head against the window.

TWO

Snow on palm trees. *Well,* Annie Sawbrick thought, *that's* something.

As for Edenville being an open prison for genteel geriatrics, or the biggest sink of money outside London's West End, or the gay capital of the south, or a characterless sprawl built on sleaze and make-believe – well, that depended where you looked. For a poor Scots girl it was the furthest south you could go. After that, swim or drown.

Annie had hitched from London. First she landed a truck whose driver offered chocolate bars, canned beer and sex, in that order. The secret with the sex was to seem interested, let the driver relax through miles of anticipation, then climb out at a service area to make everything nice in the ladies' room, then skip. But this time it was cold and Annie couldn't be bothered. So she kept him quiet with a hand-job in a lay-by. A great name for those places. But then the trucker grew maudlin and told her about the loneliness of these long hauls, his daughter who Annie so much reminded him of. And then, filling the cab with taped country and western, he asked her almost shyly if he could look at her tits. Not touch if she didn't want, just see the beauty of them. Shyly, as if half an hour before Annie hadn't been squeezing him off into a Kleenex. So she pulled the service-area trick, asking in the cafeteria if anyone could help her get to Edenville. The truck, a 16-wheeler rolling frozen sheepmeat, still sat out on the tarmac while Annie drove away in a swish new Honda. When the pink-faced insurance man slid his hand along her thigh

Annie told him about her quadraplegic brother whose ninth birthday she was desperate to get back for. The insurance man's hand winced and withdrew like a wounded mollusc. And that was that, all the way to Edenville.

In the seaside town rooms were easy, off-season. Annie got one for three months. After that the pattern was weekly, then with the tourist bookings and trebled letting rates, eviction. Her money swallowed by the deposit, Annie went straight out and found work. Towns like Edenville sprouted cheap-labour jobs as lively entre-preneurs plugged into the tourist market and the heavy money that basked beyond long private driveways or high security fences. Working in a unisex leatherwear shop Annie met Lewis.

Lewis was a customer who had tried on half the shop, leering at Annie as he paraded before the mirrors, then ostentatiously bought nothing. Lewis hung around after her in lunchbreaks when she sought the muzak of burger bars as a relief from the smell of polished hide, the smell of the shoppers, the high-speed goo of endless disco.

Lewis was a weighty six feet. He didn't want to pull her, he wanted a colleague. With narrowed eyes Annie told him, piss off. No, straight up, he'd been studying her. He liked her style. She was perfect for it. She'd be amazed how many chicks he'd turned down and they didn't even know it. Half the talent on view in Edenville he'd been through. Only Annie was perfect for it.

She asked, 'You a score, or what?'

'No way. That's the rule. Business, no feeling up.'

She looked at his oily hair, blue chin, greenish teeth.

'So what makes me perfect?'

'You're icy cold, babe. Plus every punter in the world wants to get down on a body like yours. And while you're wiggling their dicks, I relieve them of their dosh.'

'Just like that.'

'Right. 'Cause, see, we only take money. No credit cards they'd have to report. Money you can't trace. They go to the police, they have to admit taking a fuck in a public place. Maybe their wives find out. Or maybe they just keep quiet about it.'

'Why should I trust you?'

''Cause, darlin', you got the looks and I got the clout. You'll see

8

me count the dosh out the wallet, then later we split it. I got to rob you too, make it look for real. Also I got to come on a bit unfriendly so they don't tie us in together. I mean, these punters are usually loaded. We are talking two, three hundred a week.'

'I don't think so,' Annie said, looking at the size of Lewis's hands.

'I'll come back tomorrow,' Lewis said. 'You'll tell me yes, I know you will.'

The next day he came back and Annie said yes.

It worked a few times. They used remote spots, out in the forest or in the sand dunes across the bay as the evenings got warmer.

The punter took little persuading as Annie told him to drive to a really nice place she knew where they could turn on in the seclusion. And where Lewis would be waiting. How far Annie went depended how much she liked the punter's body, and when Lewis timed his arrival. But the abuse routine they had worked up was getting too real. Lewis liked it too much as a dessert after emptying the punter's wallet. Lewis said it was to give her a reason to run. But each time he smacked her face or chest it hurt more.

One time in the dunes they turned over a muscular young Londoner who would probably have fought back if he hadn't still been groaning and rolling his eyes from what Annie had done to him with her mouth. Lewis's timing was devilish. Before the punter's heart could slow down, Lewis was on to him, knee across his throat, fingers in his wallet.

Somewhere in the routine they blew it, this time. Maybe it was the way Annie looked a second too long at the twenties and fifties Lewis picked from the tooled morocco. It totalled over 500. Maybe the punter noticed, before he began to struggle and Lewis threw sand in his face and bombed a fist into his belly.

The Londoner drove a truck five days a week, collecting rubble, refuse, garbage wherever it was generated. Which seemed to be everywhere. Building contractors, especially, just wanted to hand on the problem and not be responsible for where it was dumped. Fly-tipping, they called it. Pick up a load, cash payment on leaving

9

site, then upend the lorry in a convenient space. Accredited tipping areas were always too far and in the wrong direction. After dark the tippers went for parks, playing fields, other building sites, sometimes even streets in run-down urban districts where people were used to rubbish. You could make 1500 a week, cash. Every time a load got dumped illegally someone else got paid for shifting it again. Sometimes they were the same person.

The fly-tipper had a friend in the business. Every other weekend they took the train to Edenville, where they liked to hurl money at casino tables, gorge seafood and gulp novelty cocktails, and cut a swathe through the seaside pussy. Sometimes together, sometimes alone.

The one lesson in life that Annie had learnt was that when things went well you got stupid. Only fuck-ups kept you thinking. This weekend's first punter was another Londoner, should have made her think. But he seemed a simple guy, just dying to lie in the dunes and have his brains sucked out.

This time Lewis pounced early. He was slipping the proceeds of a week's fly-tipping, another thick wad, from the dude's wallet, when a fourth figure appeared out of the sandhills. He carried two axe-handles, clean beechwood. The punter on his back kicked Annie away and caught the axe-handle thrown to him.

Lewis fought back. That was what they wanted. Annie took off and ran along the tideline towards a distant village. Eventually the roar of the waves smothered everything. The stained axe-handles went out on the night tide.

Annie never saw Lewis again. The leather shop closed. She stayed low for a few weeks. She worked out how much money she would save if she gave up cigarettes. Every time she thought about it she lit another.

The last but one punter they had pulled was a young local guy, an eager beanpole twitching with lust long before Annie had taken him under the pier, let him feel inside her panties, and slid his trousers and boxer shorts round his ankles. He wore a suit and a slim riverboat-gambler's moustache. In the Roxy gaming club Annie had seen him clear several hundred pounds at roulette. As Lewis relieved him of it he lay miserably on the shingle choking out 'Oh my God! Oh my God!'

A shaft of moonlight penetrating the iron struts of the pier had made his knees look very white.

THREE

His name was Bruce Rabey, and he was still muttering 'Oh my God!' as he pulled his Austin Metro into the onion-shaped cul-de-sac of Lagoon Close.

The moonlit estate of two hundred 'starter homes', flimsy boxes for the freshly married, slept in the spring midnight. The heathland out of which the estate had been carved was so poor that the open-plan lawns, without rain for a week, were turning brown already. The grass crackled under Bruce's feet as he took the quick way to the front door. Emmajane was always complaining about the track he had worn by not using the path. The more she complained the more he did it.

Emmajane had had the name *Falcon's Roost* etched in burnt lettering on a slab of wood which her father had power-tooled next to the picture window. A light was on upstairs. Bruce heard a voice, deep, male, paternal, from the bedroom.

'. . . Let's talk about what we've been through so far. The search for love, for that ideal partner, is a natural human emotion, and we shouldn't be ashamed to give way to it . . .'

Bruce listened to the mature confidential tones. For the briefest of moments he thought Emmajane had someone up there. Then he noticed on the melamine hall-table a woman's magazine proclaiming the free offer of a counselling tape from their own Agony Uncle who would talk to them privately about what made that great relationship. The leading feature was headlined 'Press-on Fingernails – A Woman's Personality Problem Solved'.

Bruce contemplated the black marks on his suit. There must have been tar on the shingle. The thought of another dry-cleaning bill brought on the familiar deep-gut hollowness.

He dropped his trousers and jacket on the floor. In shirt, polka-dot shorts, and shoes, he went upstairs. The house still smelt of fish from two days ago. In the master bedroom Emmajane sat in front of a vanity unit, listening to Rex Mountjoy's taped platitudes and doing things to her face.

Emmajane's hair was beautiful. Thick, blonde, fluffy, alive, a sunlit field of ripening barley. The rest of her, at twenty-six, was ageing fast. Under her eyes the flesh was starting to pouch, and her chin merged too smoothly with her neck. The slight lisp which Bruce had once found so charming now made her sound like a cretin. Emmajane sometimes talked of marriage guidance, but she used the words in threat. Like referring to a branch of the police.

Bruce went for a pee. He reflected on how Emmajane now shut the bathroom door when she peed. In earlier days she had sat and peed unashamed at his presence. They had even had laughs peeing together. Now she had started dressing and undressing behind the bathroom door.

Before they married Emmajane had let Bruce do anything he wanted. Well, almost anything, and Bruce guessed the rest would come with time. Instead, three years of being a wife had seemed to change Emmajane's ideas of what was proper. Her hair still resembled a field of barley, but the rest of her body was like countryside on which the rights of way had been fenced off. She had started telling Bruce it was time he grew up.

'And where do you think you've been?' (The creamed face frozen in the mirror.)

'Oh God, don't you start.'

'*Start* – what do you mean, *START*?'

At this point she would go on for two minutes about his provocative, offensive choice of words. Half dressed, Bruce felt unable to adopt the right level of scorn. He looked at the veneered self-assembly furniture on which the corners never quite fitted. Still shaken by what had happened under the pier, he launched into an unstable giggle.

Irony, bloody irony, he had intended to come straight back from the Roxy with his £200 and shower Emmajane with notes and ideas for a wild weekend. Then he had taken one look too many at the Scottish girl, peroxide crewcut, terrifically stacked, who hung around his table, smiling him on, hotting up at his success. And now he had a story nobody would believe.

'If you're going to bed,' Emmajane said, her face still distorted for the mirror, 'perhaps you wouldn't mind saying goodnight before you fall asleep for once.'

Bruce ripped open the fitted wardrobe door and put on fresh clothes.

Emmajane's voice was shrill. 'Where are you going now?'

Bruce shouted back, 'None of your bloody business.'

'You're working tomorrow. You've got to be up in the morning.'

'Oh bloody dear. Too bad, isn't it?'

'I'm not phoning in with any more stories about you being ill. The last time I did that I could hear them laughing in the background.'

'I'll be late.'

'And after you finish work we're having coffee with my mother in the Orchid Lounge –'

Bruce was halfway downstairs.

'And you're not getting out of it the way you did last time –'

Bruce was taking, silently, the £40 he found in the housekeeping tin.

'My father says I ought to report you to somebody.'

Emmajane prepared for a ten-minute weep before ringing her sister for a good trade in marital outrage. Bruce ground the Metro's gears and swung out of Lagoon Close.

Bruce re-entered the Roxy. Adrenalin made the blood hammer in his ears. Tonight was his night, a rare fortune flowing. He had only stopped at 200 because that was the promise he had made himself. Now, back there with the week's grocery money, Bruce still had that incredible feeling of luck.

He downed a lager and tried to get a grip on his nerves. The

Roxy was a converted cinema, its curved balcony now a restaurant. Where the stairs descended to the gaming pit the screen had once flickered. Bruce checked the crowd for the cropped peroxide head of the Scottish girl, didn't see her, and went down.

The smoke had thickened above the tables. The pink shirts and black bow-ties of the club staff drifted through yellow light and haze. Steel balls rattled on fine wheels. Blackjack cards slapped green baize. Bruce drummed fingers on his slacks and looked for an opening.

The Roxy was the kind of place a rich Arab might buy but wouldn't be seen dead playing in. Midnight gone, the fun punters were cleaned out, left only with a chastened sleeplessness. The activity round the tables slowed down as the serious gamblers and the rich zombies dug themselves in. Reptilian eyes in washed-out faces, some carefully noted on club cards the sequences of the wheel, others quivered hands over the table and frantically shifted chips as the ball dropped and spun. They paused only when the girl croupier muttered no more bets. They didn't use French at the Roxy. Before guilt could well up, Bruce pushed four £10 notes across the table.

It was very warm. Bruce felt thirsty as he watched the play. On the gaming floor drinks were banned. The effects of the lager were already soaking into Bruce's singlet. The croupier pushed Bruce's notes through a slot in the table with a rectangular chrome blade. Bruce's head suddenly cleared as she shovelled his plastic chips.

Rapidly Bruce reviewed his earlier session. His allowance had been £10. Instead of trickling it away on single numbers, trios or quartets at long odds, he had hit straight into the even chances. Colours, straight, minimum stake £5, twenty times the minimum on singles. Feeling good, he had guessed correctly into a sequence, Red Red Black Red. The stake had ridden up to 80. A one-in-sixteen chance. He had left 20 on the black and it came up. Twenty on black again, hit. He had run into a one-in-sixty-four sequence. Without scribbling one number on those tacky cards they provided for the bimbos.

In two minutes Bruce had converted £10 to £125. At this point he had decided to notch 200, then quit. And he returned the smile of a pert crewcut blonde who had been rooting for him. But that was then.

This time, downside of midnight, it was different. Bruce went for even chances on colours again, won some, lost some. Twenty minutes on, his 40 was 15. Black predominated, but the start or end of a run? For every twice Bruce guessed right he failed three times. Down to £10 after a run of three blacks, he jabbed all his remaining chips on red.

On his feet by now, sweat coursing down his face, his teeth bared and tight, arms rigid with tension, Bruce began to sense what death would be like. The ladderman, supervising two tables from a high chair, motioned him to sit down. A thin boy in a pink shirt who nightly watched with dead eyes people facing ecstasy and despair, telling him, Bruce Rabey, what to do. Resentfully Bruce sat. The wheel spun.

Black again. Bruce leapt up, staring in disbelief. The girl croupier redistributed the chips by hand. Bruce's plastic was scooped and rehung, dead turkeys. She didn't ask him if he wanted to play any more, didn't even look at him. Without those dinky tokens he didn't exist.

Bruce began to shake and gibber. 'Can't be right. It's not possible –'

A heavy man in a check suit squeezed Bruce's arm and said, 'Come on, sir, don't want any trouble.'

Hustled through the crowd, Bruce tried to brush the bouncer's arm away. At least leave the club with dignity. But they wanted to make their point. Right down to the humiliating shove the bouncer gave him out on the street.

Bruce began slowly beating his head on a lamp post.

'All right, son, you don't have to do that.'

A fat man with sticking-out feet, thinning hair, meaty amiable grin.

'Come on, son.'

They stepped into the doorway of an adult underwear shop. Neon-lit red crotchless panties revealed the bald pubes of a mannequin's torso.

'Put it there, son.'

Bruce took the extended hand. Its grip crushed him.

'I'm talking thousands, son. Not hundreds, thousands. Wanna know?'

FOUR

Reece Deacon stopped pounding Bruce Rabey against the inside of the beat-up Ford when he realised that he could hit him senseless after he got the information, but not the other way round.

Deacon switched everything off in the Ford. He backed out of the door, pulling Bruce with him by the tie. You're going to run somebody down, you put a tie on first, *British*. In the darkness the shape at the other end of the tie scrambled through the car, tangling long legs with the gear stick. Deacon stood him against the BMW.

'What the fuck was that back there?'

'Oh God – it was an accident. Didn't see you till the last minute.'

'That was an accident?'

'Narrow road, I –'

Deacon reached both hands forward. Within seconds Bruce changed his story.

'You were trying to kill somebody, correct? Am I right?'

Bruce whimpered assent.

'Who the fuck was it?'

'They didn't tell me. Just –'

'Somebody would appear on that road, and you'd tank them. Hit and run, am I right? Am I right?'

'Yes, that's it.'

'What happens to the car?'

'I take it for scrap first thing in the morning.'

'Why you doing all this?'

Bruce switched into the other half of his mind, the chunk in which he was not a gambler or a hit man – something more middle class, urbane, man to man.

'The usual money problems – you know how it is – can't seem to stay ahead of my expenses.'

Deacon slammed him against the BMW's solid steel.

'Listen, scumbag. Only think about one thing. What you owe me. When I'm through with you you'll be glad you're still breathing.'

His fist was in front of Bruce's eyes. Bruce pleaded. 'Please don't hit me again. I've got to go to work tomorrow.'

'So what job does a shithead like you do?'

'I work in a bank, well, a building society, that's a sort of –'

Had he spotted something foreign, Deacon wondered. Did the years in Spain show?

'I'm English, you prick, I know what a building society is.'

'Sorry, sorry –'

'How much you get paid to drive a car at me?'

'Five thousand.'

'Five thousand to kill somebody. And now you won't get nothing.'

I won't go to jail, Bruce was thinking. It had been a gruesome mistake. Things had got tough lately. Now maybe he had struck the upturn. He would go for promotion, maybe make Emmajane pregnant, they both needed a break in the sun, Tangier for instance –

'Listen carefully,' Deacon's voice was like a cold blade in the dark, 'I want to know everything about you. Where you live, work, what car you drive, family details. And then you're going to do a few things. Like show me who set you up. Inside.'

Bruce protested, 'What about –?'

'That heap of crap? Later.'

In Lagoon Close Deacon waited while Bruce fetched out his driving licence, phone directory, cheque book.

Deacon studied then said, 'Tell me one thing, Brucie. You got your office job, this cute little home, a wife spreading her legs for you. So why do you take a pissing five grand to run down a stranger?'

In a tone of dignified hurt, Bruce said, 'I owe finance companies. I can't even meet the interest.'

That month Bruce had taken out a megaloan, one of those seductive portmanteau deals that said, 'Condense all your outgoings into one easy payment'. Every thought of it gave him a cold sweat.

They headed back to the country for Bruce to take up his life again in the shape of the clapped-out orange Ford.

As they parted Deacon asked, 'You got any Scotch friends?'

Bruce said, 'No, why?'

A tremor went through him. Did it show?

'Some young cunt with a Scotch accent? You know anybody like that?'

'No. Why?'

'Forget it.'

Bruce delivered the Ford to the scrapyard. Within the hour it would be a compacted metal cube. At the Ajax and Achilles Building Society he explained his lateness by 'car trouble'. This was the one excuse that always got universal sympathy. He said Emmajane had flooded the engine.

Throughout the day, as he answered phones, smiled at customers through the bullet-proof glass, supervised the counter girls and checked his shirtfront for tell-tale damp spots, Bruce replayed one part of the previous night's dialogue.

'When you meet this guy again?'

'Tomorrow evening.'

'Where?'

'At some shop.'

'What bleeding shop?'

'A sex shop.'

The stranger noted the address and time. Still probing for sympathy Bruce said, 'But what's the point now? He'll just beat me up for not doing the job properly.'

'Your problem.'

'If I don't go –'

'They'll find you.'

'Oh God, oh God.'

Bruce sheltered his face in his hands. Deacon coldly watched the super-wimp performance. Bruce Rabey and his wife Emmajane – he had seen it on their leatherette chequebook cover. Some bag of tricks.

But Deacon knew one thing which Bruce Rabey, who would kiss his own arsehole to get out of the BMW right now, had already pushed into the background.

It was this. They had picked the right man. Whoever had selected Bruce Rabey knew exactly what they were doing. When the Ford shot through that narrow lane it came to kill. There was no hesitation, no last-minute brake or swerve. Whoever stood in the path of that Ford was dead. They had picked their man all right.

And Rabey had no idea who his victim was. Deacon took it personally. His plastic surgeon would have been pulped on that country road. When the time came Deacon would have his pound of flesh, his bucket of sweat, from Bruce Rabey.

But for the moment – easy, easy.

'What you tell them,' Deacon said, 'is this. And make sure you get it right. The guy didn't show.'

Bruce said, 'I don't understand.'

'You waited two hours on that road. Nobody came.'

'They won't believe me.'

'Fucking do what I say. They'll believe you.'

The sex shop sat on one of Edenville's oldest arterial roads, now constantly heavy with traffic as a link between the centre and a bypass. The shop was called FLICK. Foreshortening drew the L and I together, and there was nothing anybody could do about it. The shop squatted between a fishmonger and a hardware store. On its blacked-out windows white capitals declared PRIVATE SHOP, SEX.

Bruce walked past five times. He checked his watch and peered along the street so people would think he was waiting for somebody. Then he dived in.

From the black exterior Bruce had expected a cavern. Instead he found an open room with garish carpet lit by a naked bulb. Around the walls the shelves were stacked with shrink-wrapped magazines, miracle body lotions, uninflated dolls. On one rack thick penis-shaped dildos stood pink, gnarled and sturdy like garden gnomes. A radio pumped out racing commentary. A counter sign at least a year old read 'This Month's Special – Spanking Pants For Men'. The bored assistant smoked, stared right through the walls of patchwork flesh, eking out his thoughts over another long day.

Bruce's skin flushed nervously. All over, it felt like. He approached the counter. He tried not to look at these things whose existence excited him so much when he was in bed with Emmajane.

'I've come to meet somebody –'

The assistant stared through him, leaned back and tapped a door. The door opened.

'Through here.'

The back room was run-down, smelt mainly of rubber. The podgy man whose geniality was so alarming stood by a table on which a Danish bestiality magazine was half covered by the early edition of the *Edenville Clarion*.

'So what happened?'

'Nobody came.'

'Nobody came.'

'I waited two hours.'

'Then what?'

'What you said. All the car stuff.'

'Yeah, I checked.'

Bruce looked down. A headline on the *Clarion*'s front page said, SUICIDE OF PLASTIC SURGEON.

'What about the money?'

'What money?'

'You said –'

The fat man's name was Leo Malin. His eyes prickled in his chubby face. Fingers kneaded his palms. He said, 'Yeah – yeah?'

Bruce said, 'I kept my part of the deal.'

'No you didn't, sunshine. All you did was drive a car. Pardon me while I fart.'

Malin frowned, extruded noisy gas. 'What you waiting for?'

'Don't rip me off, you –'

Malin looked coolly at the same unstable rage he had seen quiver

Rabey's white-lipped face a number of times over unfriendly roulette tables. He assessed with contempt the poncey young-executive moustache, the acrylic suit, the wild eyes. Malin took a roll of notes from his pocket and peeled off the rubber band. Paper snapped under his thumb as he counted ten twenties.

'That's more than fair. Now, don't get any fucking stupid ideas. Or mummy will come and smack you.' Malin thrust the bestiality magazine into Bruce's hand. 'Leave by the street door. We never met, right. You're just another punter.'

Parked alongside the mesh fence of a bathroom and sanitary ware wholesalers, Reece Deacon watched through the BMW's smoked glass the rear entry of the sex shop. He had just thrown away his third cigarette butt and buzzed up the window when there was movement.

The figure who walked, waddled almost, across the demolition lot at the rear of FLICK, looked familiar.

The familiarity interrupted Deacon's thoughts about Bedell. It had taken him a year to get to Bedell, who covered old faces with new, covered everything else with secrecy and silence. Deacon was indifferent to why Bedell had iced himself. Basically people always suicided for the same reason, who cared? But these scumbags had been about to waste Bedell anyway, just when Bedell was about to save his, Deacon's, life. Deacon was taking it personally.

He took it even more personally now he recognised the fat guy who emerged from FLICK. The dumpy powerful figure headed across the waste lot. Ten years changed everything but the essentials. The same greaseball clothes, the same jockstrap lifestyle. Leo Malin. Well, well.

Before he left FLICK Malin dialled a number. He asked the mid-Eastern respondent, 'That Scotch bint, she in yet?'

'I tell her, today on time, or I finish her arse.'

'What shift she on?'

'Five minutes to be here or she better not come.'

'Right.'

At the kebab bar Malin beckoned Annie out back, away from the rotary spit of layered meat sweating fat in the window, the teenage Lebanese processing hummus in the primitive kitchen.

'OK, darlin', what went down?'

'I did everything you said. To the letter.'

They jostled uneasily among black garbage sacks, from some of which cats had ripped the innards. Malin's eyes beetled suspiciously around in their sockets.

'You rang the number?'

'Sure.'

Annie was getting indignant. Fifty, he had said, but no sign of reaching for his pocket.

'And?'

'I gave the message.'

'Who to?'

'I called him –' Annie stretched her face in three directions at once as she recalled the name '– Big Balls. Like you said.'

'Get this right. He said it was him?'

'Yeah.'

'Took the directions, said he'd go?'

'Bloody yeah. I'm telling you. What's wrong?'

'Nothing, I just check things out.'

Annie got her fifty. Money wiped out memory. Malin was crude, but cunning and mean. Bad news gave him like rheumatic pain even before he heard it, an urgent pain that had to be rooted out. Bedell had killed himself and was comfortably chilling in the morgue. Their dicey plan was not about to come back and haunt them.

So, Malin thought, why *was* it haunting him?

FIVE

Emmajane had fallen asleep over *Cosmopolitan*. She had slipped to one side, her head back on a propped pillow. Her upper lip was distorted as if an insect had been crawling on it. The nail-varnish brush in her hand had stuck to a page of the magazine, moustaching a model. Somehow Emmajane had knocked over the bottle on her bedside table. Beads of viscous liquid were slowly trickling on to the carpet.

Bruce ignored it. When she woke Emmajane would be embarrassed and annoyed. Bruce would deny having seen it. If he tried to help she would only complain about him waking her. Bruce obsessively flossed his teeth, sitting rigidly in the glare of a bedside light. He re-read the same page of the paperback thriller he had already read four times. Once again it left no trace on his mind.

The doorbell rang. Emmajane's eyes opened. She started up as Bruce jumped out of bed. Bruce pulled a towel robe round his naked body and fearfully parted the curtains. It was a big car, out there in the onion-shaped close. Anonymous men in big cars. His gut began to stretch. Now they were rattling the front door.

'I'd better go. Probably a mistake.'

Emmajane was outraged. 'Who *is* it?'

'I think you've spilt your stuff –'

Bruce indicated, and left the room. Emmajane's whine of irritation, which would turn to blame, followed him.

A minute later Bruce returned to the bedroom. By now Emmajane was on her knees, attacking the saxon carpet with a box of Kleenex.

Her bottom in the air was bare below her shortie, pussy and all revealed. Bruce looked hard, gulped, prayed, despaired.

He was dressing fast. 'I have to go out.'

Emmajane jerked upright, a rosette of rainbow Kleenex in her hand. 'What do you mean you've got to go out?'

How could someone who looked so gorgeous sound so abysmal? Life was a puzzle Bruce would never complete.

'It's all right, just a small business problem. Nothing I can't handle.'

He was pulling shoes on as he ran. An anguished curve of sound pursued him like a boomerang down the stairs.

'Bru-u-uce!'

Bruce was outside, flashing his nervous persuasive smile at Leo Malin. It always worked with customers. It said, I am going to give you everything you want, please be nice to me.

Malin drove off the starter-home estate with no regard for junctions. Then he slowed and said, 'When I stop, either you are going to tell me the truth, or I kick your fucking head in.'

Bruce told the truth. He failed to recall the type of car the stranger had driven – it was big, might have been a Merc. Or the stranger's appearance exactly – it had been dark, he was scared. The stranger seemed to be a heavily built man with a moustache, but Bruce couldn't swear. He wouldn't be able to identify him again, no.

'So you told the guy it was an accident.'

'Like I said. I never expected to see anybody on that road. It was a wonder I hadn't killed him.'

'You didn't think, like, maybe, who he was?'

'I thought he was the guy I was supposed to hit.'

The tumblers clicked slowly in Malin's mind.

'Yeah, yeah.'

Bruce asked, 'Who *was* I supposed to hit?'

Malin ignored it and said, 'Why did you tell me nobody turned up?'

'I didn't want you to know I'd failed.'

'You thought I wouldn't find out?'

'I wasn't thinking straight.'

'This guy shows again, you contact me through the shop, right? Ask for Leo. Don't piss me about again.'

Bruce nodded gratefully. He had acted stupid successfully. Stupid people were no threat. As he left Bruce to walk home Malin reflected that stupid people were an unacceptable danger.

The Ajax and Achilles Building Society was an overheated cell in the giant hive of a new shopping complex. Its all-over window faced on to a pedestrian mall which was separated by a crash barrier from four lanes of traffic, a mounded roundabout island, and tall glass blocks that shut out most of the daylight.

Bruce Rabey waited ten minutes after the counter girls left, and said his usual goodnight to the branch manager so that his dedication would be noticed.

The hoot of a car horn. The BMW, the lean tanned face and impenetrable black glasses. Bruce glanced towards the nearest subway entrance. The impulse to run died at birth. He got into the car. The BMW slid out into the traffic.

Deacon steered one-handed and listened impassively as Bruce, this time, told the truth.

When Deacon first heard the term 'rhinoplasty' it repelled him. Who wanted to look like a fucking *rhino*?

Then he became converted to the idea of altering his face. When some prick of a car thief broke into Deacon's Audi in Valencia, detonating the car bomb, it had been time to go. Leaving places was no longer enough. He had to quit his body. Deacon had cheated the wrong people and in Valencia he had learned how hurt they felt.

In the Edenville hotel Deacon asked for a local advertising directory.

'Yellow Pages or Thomson?'

Deacon shrugged. The receptionist gave him both. There was no heading 'Plastic Surgery'. The nearest he got was 'Clinics' and once you worked your way through Family Planning, Complementary Medicine, Traditional Acupuncture, Alternative Therapy, Abortion and Cosmetic, not much was left.

It pissed Deacon off. He couldn't go back to Spain and retrace the steps that had led to Bedell. Or start again here without letting somebody else into his plan. But it was not part of his new life to start trusting people.

Deacon kept himself deliberately ignorant of things he paid experts to do. Exactly how they changed the skeleton of your nose and jawline, where they obtained the bone to extend your chin, he did not want to know. Or where the skin would come from to smooth his pockmarked cheeks. The clinic had sent explanatory leaflets which Deacon had trashed immediately. He found reading matter offensive.

He had come to Bedell by a tortuous route of enquiry and recommendation. Deacon had to treat everybody as a potential source of help to his enemies. He had flown over to meet Bedell and been impressed by the surgeon's expertise and discretion. The fact that Bedell required half the fee, a five-figure sum, in advance, reassured Deacon that he was not dealing with an idiot.

Bedell had been a legend who was about to become a scandal, if Deacon read the signs correctly. The whole thing was getting a squidgy, shitty feel that Deacon wanted to back off from. But it had cost him money. Worse, until he found a replacement for Bedell he had no future. His schedule was wrecked already. He would have been in the clinic at least a month, anonymous, sheltered by money. When he emerged, no more Reece Deacon.

Now all this was just a fantasy. It still jabbed at the back of his not too complex mind that the mad bastard who had tried to run him down had in fact been hired to kill Bedell.

Why?

Less than half a mile away in the centre of Edenville Leo Malin was staring at a piece of paper on which was written 'BMW' and a registration number. This was the only objective evidence he had so far on the man who had intercepted his plan to murder Ralph Harrington Bedell.

Malin chewed wodges of toasted sandwich as he thought. He brushed a hand inside his collar to tease out the fringe of hair that grew over his neck to compensate for the wastage on his upper scalp.

He ran through it all again. The birdbrained Scottish tart had called Bedell and talked to somebody else. Somebody who said he was Bedell. From the local press reports Malin had worked out that when the call was made Bedell must already have been dead.

Social visit? Burglar? Burglars didn't answer phones. Or, Bedell had been murdered. But the coroner's verdict passed like shit through a goose – balance of mind disturbed, pressure of work, signs of depression attested by a crew of copper-bottomed witnesses. No foul play suspected. They didn't even pick up all the stuff we had on him, Malin reflected. The drag stuff, the little sex parties where he liked to watch girls perform together.

Down in the street some late-afternoon drinkers were starting a fight. Malin stared at the nude calendar on the tree-bark wall of his office as if somewhere in the room there was a sock filled with the remains of dead shellfish.

He grabbed the phone before it completed its first ring.

'Leo, I see the car.'

'Sure it's the right BMW?'

'Yeah.'

'Where?'

'Clifftop.'

'Where you phoning from?'

'Some hotel, the Exkelsior –'

'Exchelsior,' Malin said. 'Now, listen. Stay with it, cop the guy. Get a real good look. If he don't come back, the car's gonna disappear. You stay there. Sooner or later the boy wants his motor. Don't miss nothing.'

The receiver still in his collar bone, Malin chomped some more sandwich and punched buttons. Movit Autos, 24-Hour Breakdown and Retrieval Service.

'Rick? Leo.'

'Sure, Leo.'

'Got a car locked up, Rick. Lost keys. Needs collecting as of now. Can do?'

A hiss like toothache pain came down the line.

'A monkey in your pocket,' Malin said.

'No sweat, Leo. Where?'

'Clifftop, Excelsior.'

'What's the damage?'

'I want it in your shed, out of sight, get into the car, boot included, and I'll be round. BMW, current reg. I don't want a scratch. Then put it back together and I'll tell you when to drop it off. A misunderstanding, we'll say. Deal?'

'The number, Leo.'

Malin gave it and hung up. A gloating smile softened his rubbery features. The phone went again.

A deep voice, slow, thoughtful, said, 'Leo, we meet tonight, please. Eight.'

Malin said, 'Eight, right,' and waited for the line to hum.

SIX

Deacon stretched his legs in a large V, bent at the knees, and watched the slight wobble of her buttocks as she padded across to the window. He didn't know her name, hadn't told her his. She was in the hotel bar 'waiting for a friend'. In other words him, or anybody else with £100 and an afternoon to throw away.

Deacon had locked the door and slapped her. She protested. But his grip on her arms and the dark fissures of his eyes in which snakes of sadism lay coiled, numbed her outrage. Deacon forced her to her knees and they took it from there.

Humiliate them at first, lay it out that you knew what you wanted and were going to get it by the shortest route, they always came on. This was the sum of Deacon's approach. It couldn't fail. Nothing excited a woman like fear. Terror stripped away inhibitions quicker than anything. Once they realised they were not going to wind up dead or with their flesh marked, Christ, they were so relieved they'd do *anything*.

This one was like all the others. An upmarket Edenville hooker, pushing forty, hunting a class clientele who would savour the contrast between her almost prissy manners and the things she would do behind locked doors. Deacon felt like a racing driver who had cajoled and beaten from the machine performance which even the designer didn't believe.

'Your car's the BMW, isn't it?'

Her voice was cut-glass, her left breast a full shadow against the distant sea.

'Yeah, why?'

'There's one being taken away.'

Deacon swung off the bed. 'What you mean?'

He ran to the window.

'The fuck's going on?'

Deacon was in time to see the spider-clamped BMW disappearing on an unnamed recovery truck. He was only parked on the clifftop because a wedding reception had jammed the hotel space. People strolled by calmly as the BMW sailed away.

'I don't believe this. Don't fucking believe it.'

'Language, dear,' the woman said. 'Call the police. It is yours, isn't it?'

Deacon pointed at the door. 'Get your bleeding clothes on and get out of here.'

'My fee, dear.'

The £20 notes were crisp, new, the world's freshest bedlinen. She riffled them a few times on her way to the elevator. Such a relief after the mean, slimy psycho she had just taken them from. Like making it with a demented conger. At least his mouth, thin lips and gold-filled teeth, had never once touched her. She kissed the notes before slipping them into her bag. The money kissed her back.

Deacon got the hotel reception to phone him a cab. He told the driver to drop him at the station and be back there in half an hour. From the station he walked to FLICK, the private shop whose blacked-out exterior looked as if it had been covered in leakproof sealant.

He walked into an open floorspace of yellow carpet that screamed below a bare light. In one corner a large young man with frizzed hair had his feet on the ramshackle counter and was talking, cigarette in mouth, into a phone above the noise from a ghetto-blaster whose built-in amp had all the clarity of a blocked drain. Deacon gave him a rapid glance then crossed the room and stared at the ranks of waist-deep breasts, male erections and caned rears. The assistant's eyes warily watched his back.

'. . . I told this face no way, mate, no fucking deal, shit like that we

31

don't need, you must think we keep our brains in our bollocks, well, he starts putting it about, one of these tasty fuckers, I told him stick his dick down his throat and take a piss . . .'

Deacon lifted out one of the magazines not cellophane wrapped. In cheaply furnished interiors depressed-looking middle-aged men in suits and ties used kitchen utensils, canes and whips to threaten and chastise supplicant women in various stages of undress. Naff rubbish, Deacon thought, and tried another. In this one giant mammaries were squeezed and thrust at the camera by women who sucked their own and each other's or dropped them over TV sets or furniture like melted cheese.

Irritably Deacon replaced it. He did not object to pornography. On the contrary. But for him it had to be *live*. Leafing through these shitty snapshots, as if he was some pathetic wanker who had to get it through books, insulted the hardness of his male being.

Curly-locks, whose eyes Deacon could still feel on his back, told the phone, 'Right, catch you later,' and hung up. 'Help you at all?'

Deacon turned and said gently, 'Just looking. All right?'

Curly-locks got up and sorted through a new consignment of erotic accessories. 'Sure, long as you intend to buy something.'

Basic rule, get the punter in and make him spend his way out. Deacon gave a slight smile. Curly-locks lit a cigarette, unpacked some sexual technology operated by a rubber bulb and asked, 'You into anything special?'

'Sure am,' Deacon said.

He took down a sealed pack of photographic hard-ons. In the lead photo a grinning Nordic jock with iron pectorals displayed an erection that reached above his navel. Before Curly-locks could suspect a sale Deacon said, 'You know what I see here? A big thick dick. Your identical twin.'

Curly-locks pursed his lips and popped his eyes. Sometimes the punters went like this. The shelves of hard core tipped them over the edge. Not like the normal run – the average clientele were like the plastic surgeon guy, polite timid shoppers who came here to obtain a unique service discreetly handled.

'You don't want no trouble, son,' Curly-locks said.

He assessed Deacon. Guys like this he bounced from nightclubs by the dozen. He had several inches of height, thirty pounds' weight, fifteen years' age advantage. The guy would hit the street so fast his dick would end up in his ear.

Deacon raked his arm along a rack and scattered magazines to the floor. Then he ripped at the shelf and the whole tacky unit came away. Plywood split and mags smacked each other as they fell.

'Fucking watch it –'

Curly-locks moved decisively. His long arms flailed towards Deacon. A leather-gloved hand whipped through them and cracked his nose. Curly-locks rocked back and yelled as blood gushed down his shirt. Deacon's other fist catapulted his gut. Then a glossy-shoed foot hooked his crotch. As he moaned and clutched himself Deacon toppled him over.

Now Deacon took the shop apart. Curly-locks cowered miserably. Not daring to go for the door or the phone, he watched as the mags were heaped on the floor, the jars of stimulant creams hurled at the wall, the veined plastic penises strewn like dead soldiers.

Finally Deacon said, 'Tell Leo Malin when he brings my car back he better come and apologise.'

In the glove compartment of the BMW they found a contract from the car-hire company in the name James Salway. By the time the window was replaced and the car returned to the clifftop, Malin had heard the news from FLICK.

The BMW owner knew him. There was a thing. Also he had a description which was not like the one Rabey had given him. So he owed that prat of a bank clerk a kicking. Later.

Malin asked the reception for Mr Salway. Deacon, still half a jump ahead, grinned at the surprise which Malin could not completely hide.

'Reece! Reecey boy!'

'Leo! Leo!'

In the foyer they beamed and slapped each other's arms.

Malin approached the door of the luxury apartment block half a mile along the clifftop from where he had reunited Deacon with his car. The security guard knew him and pressed a button at his lapel to let Malin in.

'He's expecting me,' Malin said.

The guard phoned up anyway. Malin left the elevator at the seventh floor and went along a corridor cushioned with beige wool carpet. He passed two august panelled doors and rang a bell at the third.

The man who admitted him was in late middle age, slim and fit, with a slight paunch that had been kept under control and a tan which even the exceptional climate of Edenville could not account for. He wore a collarless shirt of fine cotton inside a dove-grey lightweight suit. His socks were silk, his backless slippers maroon Italian leather. Although Malin spent large sums of money on clothes he always felt cheap and ordinary here. Somehow it was right that he should.

Malin accepted scotch. The older man drank *birnenschnapps*. In the window, a telescope was aimed across the sea. He always said he liked to watch the boats, but Malin knew it pointed at the naturist beach the other side the bay. So? A man was entitled. Malin's pudgy face assumed as much respect and gravity as nature would permit. He waited to find out why he was here.

'Bedell got cremated today.'

'Right,' Malin said. He added, perhaps too enthusiastically, 'And that's good for us, because we've got rid of the danger without any smell coming our way. Perfect.'

'That aspect perfect, yes, I agree. However, I now have reason to believe that what I most feared is about to happen. Someone will arrive here, Edenville, looking for me. From the past, you understand. We must plan very carefully what we do about this person. He may already be here.'

As the scotch dilated Malin's capillaries, the image of Reece Deacon warmed his mind.

'Already?' he answered. 'You don't say.'

SEVEN

The house was empty without Emmajane. Her father had phoned that she was run down, she had been advised by the family doctor to rest a while, take something to settle her nerves. Her boss was being very understanding. Her mother was being super and was able to give Emmajane the all-day attendance she needed. Bruce could see her again once she had the colour back in her cheeks.

OK, Bruce sneered at the phone, I can read the code. This is just Emmajane's way of scoring a point. They think I can't learn to use the microwave and the washer. Takes more than that to crack me.

Two days later the hollowness of the rooms was getting to him. Even with all three radios playing it wasn't the same, without Emmajane preening her body somewhere. And during the night Bruce woke to a moment of fearful clarity.

This was the cunning first move in a divorce. Sweat seeped into his pyjamas. Next thing, Emmajane's salary would be diverted by some computer, and that finance house would be threatening him with – oh God, furniture out in the street, he could see it all.

Bruce had always felt intimidated by the Wayce-Dockerells. Marrying a double-barrelled name had been creamy. But he had got both barrels back in the face. Emmajane's parents had furnished the house in Lagoon Close and got them into the housing market with a deposit loan whose repayment they had declined to discuss, so far. But now? The sweet silent power of money.

Depressed, Bruce drank two long glasses of sweet sherry and cut short the rented video he was watching. By nine he was buried in a self-pitying foetal sleep. And now it was just after ten and he was awake again, alone and sweating.

Bruce kicked off the duvet, got dressed, left the houselights on as a burglar deterrent, and drove off the estate. Suddenly he felt good again as the quiet avenues of Edenville drifted past, big floodlit houses solid through screens of trees.

Bruce parked and walked aimlessly. A man's destiny needn't be small time. The shop windows spoke of lifestyles which, by a flick of the imagination, could be his. All he had to do was find the switch. A Vauxhall Carlton which cost twice his annual salary sang to him from a showroom, a feast of rich blue and cream, begging him to find happiness in it. Bruce's heart percussioned a crescendo of affirmation.

Away from the house and the invisible presence of the Wayce-Dockerells, Bruce started to feel sore again about the £5000. The fat man had cheated him. Maybe Bruce had not killed his man. But he had determined to do it, he had aimed the car, he had meant it. If his target was an athlete who had leapt to safety, not his problem. He deserved that money. The fat man had insulted him with a couple of hundred. A wimp who would keep his mouth shut and be grateful, they figured.

They would figure again before long.

Neon shopsigns made gaudy scribbles on the street. Pavements, daytime crowded, now lay empty and littered with trash, blocked only by occasional squads of young people who shouted and guzzled from cans which they then hand crunched and slung into the road. Cars screamed around the one-way system as frustrated drivers uselessly sought parking space. From open doors of pubs human voices and heavy-decibel music, compressed like corned beef, hit the street.

Years ago Bruce had run with a group dedicated to all-night drinking and romps with silly girls. Now he was older, married, looking at thirty, fearful that life's tapering road really did close in to nothing. A man with a winner's needs but the credentials of a loser. Unless he clawed something back soon.

Bruce stared twice into the kebab house. Still half empty, they were waiting for the packs of youth *en route* from pub to disco. On the step a raisin-eyed Lebanese surveyed the street. Bruce stared past the yellowing menu at the waitress. Before she disappeared she looked back, as if she knew he was there. It was her, that bleach-blonde Scottish bitch who had seduced him into a mugging.

Bruce was still wondering why the man he had failed to kill had asked, do you have any Scottish friends?

He went in. She was returning from the kitchen. The place oozed hot fat and scratchy bouzouki. Bruce barred her way.

'Table for one?'

'I want to talk to you.'

'Can I take your order, sir?'

She didn't know him. Or was doing well at the pretence. Her face was pert, tough, faintly mocking. Bruce could not forget that his hand had been inside her bra and down her panties. Deep within him there was an old-style English gentleman who said these things were important. The same old-style gent also burned about his wallet being cleaned out.

'You don't remember me?'

'Which movie were you in?'

Bruce tilted his head in a sort of cocky cool.

'OK, now I know you work here I can go straight to the police. You want me to do that, fine.'

'Look, mister, what do you want?'

The blonde's eyes roved nervously towards the manager, whose head was already twitching at signs of waitress harassment.

'I think we better talk.'

'About what, for Christ's sake?'

'Me or the police.'

'Yeah, OK, OK.'

'When do you finish?'

'Twelve.'

'I'll be outside.'

Bruce turned away. Annie's eyes reached for the sky and she went back to work.

Bruce felt high, really pumped. He went down to the Roxy,

drank a Carlsberg in two throatfuls, bought ten chips for £5, put a single on 19, and it came up. Thirty-six times his stake. Even the paste-faced chick shovelling the plastic, nipples showing through her pink uniform shirt, did a double take. Bruce gave his moustached lip a satisfied curl. Boy, did he feel pumped.

Both Reece Deacon and Leo Malin pretended not to notice this moment of drama on the gaming floor below. In general dismissal, Deacon sneered, 'Punters!'

'The secret of life,' Malin said. 'Every punter is a scumbag.'

'Right,' Deacon said. 'But not every scumbag is a punter.'

Malin was buying Deacon a reunion dinner on the glass-fronted Roxy balcony where once couples had groped in the silver-screen darkness and now gilt-edged mirrors reflected tasselled pink boudoir lamps.

Deacon lit another cigarette while Malin worked on his third salmon mousse and said, 'Wouldn't have thought this was your sort of place, Leo.'

'Not flash enough?'

'That sort of thing, yeah.'

Malin dabbed at his chin. 'Bit down-home, maybe. But they know me here. There are always the big casinos if you want to see guys with tablecloths on their heads throwing money away like men with no fingers. Personally, I regard that scene as rather banal.'

Malin pronounced it to rhyme with *anal*. A bespectacled young waiter, nervously precise, hovered over the table.

'I trust ze meal 'as met wiz your satisfaction, messieurs.'

'Knockout, François, as always. My compliments to André.'

Deacon grinned and said, 'Yeah, and tell André I heard better French accent off a Spanish dog.'

The waiter gave a moue of displeasure and swept away.

'They try hard,' Malin said. 'Give them that, the boys bust a gut.'

'Wankers,' Deacon said. 'You know it, Leo, I know it. Wankers.'

Down on the gaming floor Bruce Rabey, having dropped some lucky money, had steeled himself to go to the cashier's window. Having collected, he took a drink to the TV alcove.

From the balcony Deacon could see the alcove and the exit door. He wanted to talk to Rabey, but not here. Not so Malin would connect them. Deacon allowed for the fact that Rabey and Malin had already been in touch. All the more reason to hide any further encounters. Deacon knew he would have to leave first.

He finished his drink, killed his last cigarette. Malin realised and said, 'No, come on, mate, can't go yet. I got some chicks expecting us at the bar.'

'Got a headache, Leo.'

'Asians, a Thai and a Viet, one of the original boat people. Admit it, you never fucked a boat person, am I right? Skin on these women – like shagging a peach covered in silk.'

'I was in the army, Leo. Two years' national service. Fucking Hong Kong, Kowloon, Bangkok – a name like that, do me a favour. Your Viet, I probably fucked her *before* they put her on a boat. Count me out, son. I get tired these days. Old age.'

When Bruce left the Roxy, Deacon stroked the BMW into action and followed him at sufficient distance not to draw his attention. He watched as a girl, blonde crewcut, trousers that didn't reach her ankles, raggy black jacket, came out of an eating place. Rabey was waiting opposite.

'Aw right, what the fuck do you want?'

'You're still pretending you don't know?'

Bruce stared into her neon-blanched face.

She said, 'OK, so fucking what? You go to the police, I'll tell them you're crazy. I just want you off my back. Come in there again, I'll get the manager.'

'You don't understand,' Bruce said. 'You don't understand why I'm here.'

Bruce weighed the truth. Within the humiliating memory there was a pearl of knowledge, the ecstasy of his hand inside her pants, the eternal wonder of that pouting flesh whose discovery he had relived a thousand times.

'I don't care about what happened. Even the money. I just want to do it with you properly.'

39

Annie looked at him for a long moment and exclaimed, 'Shite!'

Bruce said, 'I mean it. I want to feel you again. I'll make it worth your while.'

'Meaning what?'

'Forty.'

'Show the money first.'

Bruce fluttered the notes. He said proudly, 'Roulette.'

'OK. But I'm not taking any rides.'

'Wherever you say.'

They walked. Bruce tried conversation.

'What part of Scotland are you from?'

'The part where black mould grows on the walls and six lanes of trucks go by outside.'

With the sureness of experience, Annie led Bruce into a dark tunnel between two shops whose window lighting revealed half-made counters and sheets of board. Shop refitting was Edenville's growth industry. The tunnel bent them past an iron gate that nobody locked any more, opened into a long narrow courtyard. The space was crammed with uncollected garbage bags. A long way above there were stars in a slab of black sky. Skeletons of ancient fire escapes zig-zagged up the rough brick backs of old buildings.

'Cash first.'

By the dim starlight Annie counted the four tens and zipped them into a pocket slashed diagonally across her thigh. Then she pulled trousers and knickers round her ankles. She expected lover boy to want a complete strip, a nestle on the plastic sacks. But no, he bared himself as she did, functional. His hand sailed straight into her pussy. He hardened readily to her touch like somebody who had forgotten the feel of anything more exciting than his underpants.

Bruce slit the foil and squeezed out the rubber. She had checked him for rubbers on the way. Bruce was unsure if he had the bubble face out, but there was no time for messing. In one movement he sheathed himself and drove into her dark valley. They both rocked as he pulled her hips, then they were locked together. Bruce clasped as her buttocks tightened, Annie gasped as he went in, in, in.

It was quick, tight, efficient. They swayed as he came, light-headed as the blood drained elsewhere. Annie steadied herself on his arm as she slid herself off. Bruce sucked air into his pounding chest. For a moment he stood there like a carnival statue, impressed at what he had done. His first open-air sex, upright too. A double first. Imagine, twenty-nine years old and never before fucked a woman standing.

They adjusted clothes. Bruce returned to the real world, threw the rubber aside, dispensed with wiping. Annie was ready first. Bruce pulled his zip. As Annie was about to go, Bruce hit her in the belly.

Annie staggered. *What?* Bruce shoved her and hit out again. This time it really hurt. Annie overbalanced into the mounded garbage. Bruce grabbed her leg as she raised it to kick his groin. He twisted the leg so she yelled. He slapped her face. Then he found her pocket and retrieved his money.

Annie spat at him. 'You bastard!' Bruce whacked her face again. 'Fucking bitch, this is only the start. I want all my bloody money back.'

Annie was completely passive now. She lay below him, unable to stop him doing anything. The way he had always wanted Emmajane but never dared ask. *Ask!* From now on he was *taking*. No more timidity. Bruce ripped at her shirt.

He never heard what hit him, or even sensed it.

In the car, Deacon told Annie, 'There's a man gonna do horrible things to you. I'm protecting you from him. Know who I'm talking about?'

Still ashake at being dragged from the alley and bundled into a car, Annie said, 'No, who?'

'Me.'

Deacon had moved out of the hotel for a furnished apartment, month's lease. He drove along hushed roads that wrapped themselves in pine spinneys like stoles of fur. When they arrived Deacon showed Annie the bathroom. He poured drinks. Annie's face still had red marks. The natural pout of her mouth was swelling to one side. Deacon contemplated her with a mixture of attraction and contempt. He had brought her here to impress information out of her. And the violence in the alley had toned him up for the inevitable. The blonde scrubber was his kind of flesh.

'You chicks.' He shook his head. 'Nothing but trouble. Like a fucking punch bag in a gym. Invitation to a work-out. Test your strength, get a coconut.'

Annie stared back. 'What is this shit? What do you want?'

One psycho a night was enough. Any move, she would dive for the kitchen, grab something sharp.

'Sit down, relax. We got business to discuss. Just one thing. Don't tell me a lie. Not even a small one. Because we're going over this again and again, and if you start changing your story I'll have to give you a slap.'

'What's in it for me?'

'Like I said, protection.'

'I work in a kebab bar. What do I know?'

'You know something about a doctor called Bedell.'

'I never heard of him.'

'Lying already.'

'I'm not shitting lying. I don't know the guy.'

'You phoned his house. You called him Big Balls. You made a date for him.'

Annie was silent. How did the pocky creep know that?

'OK, so what?'

'You're saying you didn't know who you were calling?'

'I didn't know his name.'

'You'd met him?'

'Yeah, once.'

'Where?'

'He was into a scene.'

'Scene?'

'He liked to watch girls doing it together.'

'You one of the girls?'

'Yeah.'

'They pay good?'

'OK.'

'You been in a three?'

'Yeah, sure.'

'Who organises it?'

'You get a call, that's it.'

'You know Leo Malin?'

'Is he that fat guy?'

'Do you *know* him?'

'Yeah, yeah.'

'Where you meet him?'

'A place called the Roxy, a club –'

'This piss artist up the alley, who's he?'

'I never saw him before.'

'He just wanted a pull?'

'Right.'

'You were doing sex for Bedell. What did he get out of it?'

'Meaning what?'

'He watched, that's all?'

'He used to mess around with our clothes, flop himself off –'

'Touch you?'

'No way.'

'Paid you direct? No? Through Malin?'

'Uh-huh.'

'You never wondered why you made that call?'

'No.' Pause. 'Money.'

'Secret location was part of the fun, right?'

'Yeah.'

'So you told him where to meet for another show. But you didn't do a show.'

'So?'

'You're an accomplice to murder, you know that?'

'Ah shite, what you talking about?'

Deacon leaned back, sipped his drink. He began to wonder how much he should tell this perky little scrubber, how much he might want to squeeze out of her.

'This town – some place, right? Everybody's out to lunch, you noticed that?'

'Sure,' Annie said, 'I noticed.'

Deacon smiled. 'Out to fucking lunch. The whole lot.'

EIGHT

The old man wanted to talk at dawn. Leo Malin had got used to the practice, come to respect it as not just eccentricity but the working of a brilliant psychology. The old man was deeper than whaleshit.

Daylight came soon after four. Often Malin was around the clubs till then. He would sleep as the traffic was starting to buzz into town. He regularly had a girl in the afternoon, and would catch a few hours then. He had achieved life's ultimate joy, to live without a schedule.

This night he had slept a few hours. In the dawn streets of Edenville flocks of gulls shrieked and swooped for the discarded remains of last night's takeaways. Piloting a course along the vomit-daubed pavements, bouncing on his heels, avoiding the hand-crushed cans, the polystyrene Big Mac shells, Malin climbed the narrowing streets, once the smart residential downtown of Victorian Edenville, to the clifftop.

Only the police were about. They drove white middle-range Fords with orange coach stripes and starry badges transferred on. These summer dawns the centre crawled with them. Malin liked being the only man on the street, liked the way they stared as their cars shot by on their way off-shift. They would go back to the station and say, we clocked Leo Malin prowling his territory, and feel good about it.

The road ahead aimed straight into a white nothing of sky. Then a grey sea horizon lifted above it. Malin took the zig-zag down the cliff through vandalised flower beds. One of the illuminations, a giant butterfly wired to a lamp post, was riddled with holes, the promenade shingled with stones and shattered glass. In the weather shelters dossers lay wrapped in rags, corpselike. The bright blue funicular slept at the foot of its cable.

Sea washed placidly out beyond the breakwaters. The man wore a lined windcheater and a check cap, anonymous English, his usual style. They met and walked in silence across the soft beige sand. All over the beach human footmarks were overprinted by birdtracks. Malin and the man walked down to the flat sand beyond the tideline, firmed and browned by the retreating water. The man watched a cormorant dive in the shallows and reappear thirty seconds later fifty yards away. On the horizon an oil rig took definition as the light cleared.

The man's voice was quiet but sharp through the splash of the lazy breakers. With the trace of German accent he sounded more than ever like a prudent Swiss, a banker perhaps, a multinational finance adviser.

'We have pressure from London again.'

'The usual?' Malin said.

'The shops they want, and the escort agency. No funny business this time, their money is upfront and very good.'

Malin knew the man was winding him up. One day Malin wanted to take it over. The man was just tweaking his insecurity, testing his fitness.

Malin said, 'London's a blocked sewer. Too much dosh pumping in. Now the big companies are moving to places like this, the property market's gone crazy, there's a demand for the services we offer. The strong money's gotta come after it. But we got the law on our side.'

'You think?'

All routine. As he got older the man affected to be more nervous, more tidy-minded about things. Just acting, Malin knew. Wasn't it?

Malin said, 'We got no law trouble now. Everything ticks over. We keep it nice and discreet, give the punters what they want. Face it, Eric, this town all you gotta do is not scare off the holidaymakers or bring down house prices, you're laughing. Plus the law don't want headbangers from town moving muscle here. Next thing it's shooters and dead cops and the streets not safe for punters to walk. Tourist trade down the toilet, they don't want.'

Eric's eyes looked sideways from the wrinkled well-tended skin. He moved his tongue round the back of his denture plate.

'So you think we're all right. Now tell me about this man Deacon.'

Malin's fat ugly face assumed total candour. 'It's bad.'

'What exactly is bad?'

'He knows all about our little plan for Bedell.'

'When you say *all* –'

'The lot. The people I used, he got to them. He was there.'

'What do you mean, *there*?'

'When we thought we'd set Bedell up, Deacon was the guy we tried to kill. A bit slower, he'd be dead. Fucking bad thing for us he's not.'

Eric asked, 'What's the quality of your information?'

Malin summarised, leaving out the kind of detail which tried Eric's patience. Malin had been back to Bruce Rabey again, learnt about the conking in the alley soon after Deacon had followed Bruce out of the Roxy. The alley was the link with that Scotch brass, who Malin promptly hiked out of the greasy-sheep's-eyeball eatery and into his car. After a short drive she told him everything, which included Deacon's new address.

The last words of Malin's reply were, 'It's kosher, boss.'

Eric's left eyebrow twitched slightly at the Hebraism. His hand clawed the air as if seeking a stranglehold. 'Why was this man Deacon at Bedell's house? Did he search for the information we wanted to bury for ever?'

'Could be,' Malin said.

'Was he perhaps the doctor's friend?'

'Unlikely.'

'Tell me about Deacon.'

Malin said, 'Not our kind of person.'

'Specifically how?'

Malin tapped his forehead. 'Loner. Nutter. Demanding with menaces, kind of thing. We did time together on the island.'

Malin nodded towards a shoulder of white chalk, small over the distant sea.

'Deacon dropped out of sight. I didn't see him ten years. Got in with some tasty people. Seems to have grabbed a lot of bread along the way. Less he's working some con.'

'You said you thought he had been abroad.'

'Yeah. I couldn't get him to say where. Speaks Spanish though.'

Eric was alert. 'How do you know this?'

'In the Roxy. Some dago punter and a woman had this fight. Yelling Spanish round the place. Deacon suddenly lays on me a complete translation. He ain't picked that up at the North Pole.'

'A dangerous man, you'd say?'

'I reckon, yeah.'

'Intelligent?'

'No, stupid. But psycho. Sometimes a meathead, sometimes real cunning. Might spot a trap.'

Eric considered. 'From now on, Leo, only between you and me. No sub-contracts, yes.'

'Sure.'

'This Deacon. Anyone would notice his absence?'

'He's alone, moving around. All the charm of a dead rat. His own mother wouldn't miss him.'

But things were going well for Deacon. The plan the two men put together in the seaside dawn rapidly became operational because its second most difficult stage – how to get to Deacon without him suspecting anything – was taken care of by the victim himself.

He came to them.

Deacon had found a new plastic surgeon, the clinic halfway to London. He was out of Edenville now. The one thing that held him there was what he had uncovered about the planned murder of Bedell, the involvement of Leo Malin, and the cute, sneaky itch to rape the whole secret wide open.

Deacon already knew enough to blackmail the fat man. He wanted more, an *in*, a percentage. Malin would know that a genuine operator couldn't be bought out with a one-off few grand. Deacon's knowledge gave him power, the world's currency of last resort, to which all the metal and paper had to bow.

When he sought Malin out and put the proposition to him Deacon was not surprised by the fat man's humbled demeanour. Malin had no leverage, and knew it.

Deacon said, 'Leo, let's tell the truth. You're sweating on me. You're unhappy because I know what I know. I want to take away the pain, Leo. I want on the team. You and me. Put two big ideas together, make a fucking enormous one.'

'You cocksucker,' Malin said, because he knew this was the preliminary Deacon expected. 'Think you can grease into this town and start cutting it. You take me on, you got any idea what force is gonna hit you?'

Slivers of gold gleamed inside the thin lips that parted Deacon's pitted parchment face.

'Leo, I know you're big. You were trying to stiff a very important man. I can feel your power. Don't insult mine. Talk to me sensibly.'

A day later Deacon was not surprised to find himself dining in a reserved room of Edenville's most exclusive restaurant. His host was a well-preserved older man, impeccably mannered, who invited Deacon to order anything, absolutely anything, he wished. On the menu or off.

Throughout the meal the older man, who had only been made known to him as Eric, flattered Deacon. He made no enquiries that might be embarrassing, no offers that might be obvious. They discussed life and business in general, and Deacon got the message. He was in very substantial company.

The old gold Corniche convertible was a layer of silence, comfort, and pure class between them and the ground as Eric drove to the private landing stage where he berthed his motor cruiser.

He explained, 'The yacht club marina is all right, but if you're not back in by 1800 hours they let the space to visiting craft. And an evening sail is one of the great pleasures of living here, as you'll see.'

Eric opened the padlock on a wrought-iron gate. They followed a narrow path down the side of a slightly overgrown garden. Another gate led to an L-shaped concrete jetty the width of the property, from whose view it was secluded by rising banks of orange and white rhododendron.

Before they slipped the mooring Eric invited Deacon to look over the 30-foot cruiser. They both knew why. Deacon read the codes. This is an upfront occasion, an offer of friendship, gentlemen trust each other, the code said. Deacon felt almost guilty about the flick-knife in his sock.

They headed for the open sea. The islands, the miles of yellow beach, the indented chalk coastline, melted away. Eric made brief explanations of the controls to Deacon, who was not a sailing man, in that same casual, direct way that was somehow so complimentary.

Out in a gently running sea, the autopilot set and the speed ten knots, Eric began to question Deacon about Leo Malin – how long he had known him, his impression of the man. Because, Eric let it be known, he was unhappy with Malin. The fat man was gross, an uncouth bully whose only idea of influencing people was to squash them in a soft part of their anatomy. Furthermore, Malin had no feel for money, beyond the wad of banknotes he kept wedged against his podgy backside.

Deacon agreed, not too heavily. He tried to show exactly the right mixture of loyalty and ice-clear judgment.

Then Eric said, 'I believe you speak Spanish.'

'That's right.'

How did he know, Deacon wondered. Take time to work that one out. Not important now.

'You learned in Spain?'

'I picked it up here and there.'

'In Latin America perhaps?'

'I never got down that way.'

'You are sure?'

'Yeah, I'd know if I'd been to South America.'

'Yes, yes, of course you would,' Eric called through the wave noise. 'Of course you would.'

He indicated a shelf. 'You see that file? Inside is a legal document. I'd like your opinion on it. Would you oblige me?'

'Glad to.' Deacon had experience of fixing up shell companies to vaporise other people's money. He was nobody's idea of a banker, but bent lawyers' contracts he was well familiar with.

'Take a seat there. The light is best.'

Deacon placed himself at a table in the space between the control room and the cooking and living quarters. As he began to read the badly xeroxed papers something opened behind him.

It was a veneered panel over a utility cupboard. It looked like a section of wall. While showing Deacon round Eric had stood in front of it. The recess was thirty inches deep and taller than a man. Leo Malin emerged from it with a length of nylon rope in his hand.

The rocking of the boat concealed his movement. Eric's eyes never deviated from the sea, darkening as the sun poured a bloody yolk over Edenville. A moment before the rope flew Deacon sensed a presence and jerked his head round.

The garrotting was botched. As he struggled to free his body from the bolted-down stool Deacon caught the rope. Another hand clawed under the table for the knife. Malin stumbled towards him, trying to get the rope back under control. An animal suddenly confronted with death, Deacon twisted clear and got to Malin, feet kicking, hands tearing.

He drove Malin back into the rolling cabin. The fat man would pay for his momentary failure of nerve. Deacon head-butted Malin's face, lashed with the knife. Malin gripped the knife arm. Under his fat Malin still had a lot of muscle. But he lacked Deacon's rage. Just the two of them, Malin would have lasted three minutes, and after that he would have been very messily dead.

It was the last thought Deacon had. The nylon rope came cleanly this time. Expert hands looped it, drew it so tight it almost disappeared, even in Deacon's wiry neck.

'Hold him, Leo. Do it now.'

In spite of pain and a bleeding nose Malin grappled with Deacon's limbs as they flailed in their last agony. The knife dropped, the eyes bulged, the tongue thrust out. A bad smell filled the air. But there was no doubt in the hands that held the rope.

They dragged Deacon out of the cabin. Malin was given the task of stripping the corpse. They would sink the clothes separately. Malin tried to ignore the bowel-voided contents of Deacon's trousers. He had already lost enough face with Eric, who was back at the controls as if nothing had happened.

Trussed with biodegradable twine and made heavy with training weights totalling 100 pounds, the naked remains of Reece Deacon were lowered into a darkening, deserted sea. The boat turned towards the distant lights of Edenville.

NINE

Bruce Rabey left the bus and walked past long lines of cars which roasted in the heat, engines dead, awaiting the return of the ferry, a floating bridge held on course by mighty chains that ran under the rapid waters of the tidal rivermouth.

The best beaches lay on the other side of the ferry, a mile's walk round a headland. Even in summer there were wide spaces on the fine pale sand which one way spread into dunes and the other shelved gently into a fast-running sea of marbled blues and greens. A wooden sign, small and coy, said that beyond this point 'Nudists May Be Encountered'. It sounded like a granting of permission.

Barefoot, Bruce winced at the jabbing of shell splinters. Across the bay the hotels of Edenville were board-game pieces awaiting play. Flecking the luscious emerald sea, dipping spinnakers cupped the breeze. Against the great space of water and sky Bruce was wrenched by self-consciousness.

His agoraphobia was totally sexual. He had forced himself to come here. The seclusion of the beach was guaranteed by the presence of nudists. Lovers of public nakedness had been coming here for half a century, even before the chain ferry had made the journey easy. The absence of road access had deterred capital investment. The nearest properties whose values might be affected were miles away. Nudity had stamped the place its own. The law had never caught up.

Even the Edenville beaches had finally gone topless. Bruce had done his share of boob-spotting as he persuaded Emmajane into yet another promenade stroll. But that was a demure scene against what he saw now. On the firm sand along the waterline Bruce stepped past the head of a woman who lay with her body in the surf, eyes closed, limbs spread. Her brown skin had no pale patches, her breasts lolled ripely, pubic hair curled in the tide. Bruce's head turned in painful longing. Such audacious beauty he had never seen.

On his way to the dunes Bruce sneaked backward glances at the woman in the foam. Her indifference to people's eyes made him feel guilty and excited. Then, ahead, hints of bodies in bowers of marram grass. Bruce felt desperately conspicuous, trudging along in jeans and tee-shirt, with a bag on which a beaming face said SMILE.

A tremor of panic rose in him as two naked men, bronzed and muscular, strode past. Their laughter as they ran towards the sea stabbed Bruce's mind. On a high sandhill a slim sunburnt man profiled majestically against the blue sky. Even without staring Bruce remarked the rubbery thickness, the pendulous strength, of large genitalia.

Over here solitary men were gay. That was the folklore, the reason people like Bruce stayed off this beach. Suddenly he panicked at the thought that the deeply tanned men with bold eyes would see him as cruise-bait. He knew all the legends. On certain reaches of the dunes men browsed each other's bodies, alternated sunbathing with carnal abandon.

Nearer the sea heterosexual couples were reckoned safe. Bruce turned for one more glimpse of the woman in the surf. But she was following him, now with a male companion, both licking ice creams. Bruce's fantasy of joining her in the water died miserably.

He stopped to let the couple pass. He stripped off his shirt, snatched furtive glances at the woman's every curve and ripple. He bit back a mad envy toward her companion. There was a whole erotic world, Bruce felt, of which sex was only the scaffolding. Like the yachts out on the sea, the bronzed bodies and erotic freedom went with being *rich*. Some had it, some didn't. Those that had it, flaunted it. Bruce would give his life for something to flaunt.

He stripped to swimming trunks. More alone than ever, Bruce spread his towel, keeping an anxious distance from the enclaves of sunburnt nudes. After a few minutes he lost concentration on his paperback, whose pages began to curl and yellow in the sunlight. Bruce's pale skin was burning. He felt exposed, helpless.

Along the beach flesh bounced in the frolic of mixed volleyball. Three women, three men. Brown, naked, confident. Would they let him join in? Bruce would never dare find out.

A yacht glided by, close in, maroon sails majestic. In his whole lifetime Bruce knew he would never even set foot on a boat like that. A woman passed, dripping briny, breasts golden, pubic hair trimmed precisely to her vulval cleft. She slid a finger between her buttocks to brush away the water-beads that ran from her spine. Bruce thought his heart would explode. Hell was the land of desires you could never hope to fulfil. He had never felt so close to hell in his life.

Emmajane always refused to come here. She wouldn't even talk about what went on here. Normal people didn't go to the nude beach. Defiant, Bruce thought, I've made it here now, I'll stick with it. After minutes of argument with himself he slid off his trunks.

He sprawled out, stared up through dark glasses. The sun vibrated like a globe of female flesh. Sweat crept over Bruce's scalp. He must have fallen asleep, because the next thing he knew the sun had moved and two naked girls were watching him.

One of them was the Scottish girl, the blonde crophead. They had woken him by throwing sand at his body. Bruce swept it away.

'Sleeping beauty,' the other girl said.

The Scottish girl said, 'Sorry if we woke you.'

Bruce realised they wanted fun, to humiliate him then walk away laughing. He looked at the Scottish girl. She hadn't told her friend she had met him before. She wanted revenge for the alley. Bruce decided to face it out.

'My name's Bruce. Who are you?'

'Tracey.'

'You?'

'Annie.'

Bruce said, 'Hi.'

To hide confusion Annie got cigarettes from a bag. The girls smoked, Bruce didn't. It had taken him a year and a course of hypnosis to give up.

He surveyed the girls' bodies as they smoked. A nude male walked by, middle aged with a firm paunch and stretch marks on the glutea.

Bruce and the girls all stared hard at the man's dark-honey skin, the pulpy brown penis slapping his thigh, scrotum like two golf balls in a sac of soft leather. Bruce looked down at himself as the girls' eyes turned there too. Normally slim and docile, his penis had not actually changed direction yet, but was large, relaxed, sun-thickened on his groin.

Surprised, he said, 'I'll have that cigarette after all.'

Later they played pig in the middle with a beach ball. Once he chased them into the sea Bruce kicked off his inhibitions. In the sea you could be anybody you wanted. He plunged after every ball, grappled with Tracey and Annie, brushing their bodies in every tussle.

Heaven, already. Sudden, instantaneous paradise of the flesh.

Back on their towels Tracey said, 'I'm dying for a Ladies.'

The nearest one was at the beach huts a mile away. Annie pulled a face and said, 'Christ, just do it in the sand like everybody else.'

Tracey looked towards Bruce and said, 'I can't.'

'Go in the sea then.'

'I don't like to. I mean, I've just swallowed a load of it. I don't like to think of people doing it in the water.'

'Sit and burst then.'

In the end Tracey went back to the sea. She swam for five minutes to deceive anyone who might be watching, then waded up to her chin before relaxing her bladder.

To Annie Bruce admitted, 'I'm dying to go too.'

Annie said, 'Why make hassle?'

She scooped the sand below her public hair. Bruce watched spellbound as water oozed through the hair and quickly soaked away. It excited him, released him. In grateful warmth he jetted into the sand.

Annie lit up again and said, 'Stop gaping at my fanny like that.'

Bruce said, 'It's the most beautiful thing I've ever seen.'

'Aye well, you haven't seen much, have you?'

'Let's go somewhere and make love properly.'

Annie grimaced. 'Aw Christ, forget all that.'

'You think I'm a wimp, don't you?'

'I think you're just looking for a chance to beat me up.'

'That's all over.'

Alone Annie was furtive, suspicious. She glanced with relief at Tracey's dumpy pink form returning across the sand.

'We've got to go,' Annie said.

Tracey, progressively left out of the triangle, agreed. Disappointed, Bruce held his cool. He noted every move as Annie got into her clothes. He called after them, 'See you again.'

He wanted Tracey to think he didn't care, and Annie to know he meant it.

When Bruce got home it was evening. Sun and salt water had reddened his skin. His head was light, his spirit drunk. Emmajane was in the house. She had been there some hours, most of them crying.

The last time Eric Churchill had heard of Lothar Scharfe he, Scharfe, was in Colombia, where he had slowly established a modest position in the cocaine industry. It was no great job, making sure the peasants paid their dues to the barons who operated between the subcontinent and Florida. But all the world trusted a German, and by protecting Scharfe's secret his greaseball employers knew he would work well for them. So Churchill read it.

Over the years letters had come, veiled, threatening, begging. Churchill had always answered them for the simple reason that in the early 1960s, when they still maintained a network for mutual aid, Scharfe had acquired the information that his old comrade was now a prosperous entrepreneur on the south coast of England.

How the information had leaked was to Churchill's pragmatic and ruthless mind of no consequence. His task was simply to keep Scharfe quiet till death or dementia claimed him. Meanwhile, every day was a victory. So Churchill despatched anonymous packages of US dollars, with the briefest of notes on unaddressed paper, mailed each time from a different English town.

It seemed enough. After all, Lothar had as much to lose as Churchill himself. Even out there, living under some dago name in a stinking village with crumbling buildings and goats roaming the streets while ape-faced Indians squatted beneath blankets, even there a life was still a life. So Lothar would always know where to draw the line.

But now this video.

Eric Churchill ran it once again. Dementia or death, Lothar looked close to both. In a wrinkled flannel shirt, stubble covering his hollowed face, Scharfe bore no resemblance to the laughing officer of 1944. Would his own mother have known him? Or the Dutch? The Israelis? Yet, Churchill coolly acknowledged, that was still Lothar Scharfe. He at least would never forget that face.

The video must have been made in one of those public booths. In countries where millions think of little but filth and hunger, everyone can make a video for a few dollars. The way of the world. More surprisingly, Churchill found it fitted his machine. The universal language of Asian electronics.

Churchill watched with cold eyes, occasionally freezing or replaying. It gave him a sort of control over Scharfe, to whizz him around or kill him in mid-sentence, make him stutter and repeat things. But through the maunderings of this sick old man one message was clear. Although Churchill and Scharfe had not met in decades, the hatred was fresh. And he had known where to send the video.

And he had a son.

'Ich habe einen Sohn.' The whole monologue was in German. Apart from some pidgin Spanish, what would Scharfe speak? The *Sohn* was now a man. All those years in filthy tenements or the stinking jungle came out, via the video, in a bitter rattle in Scharfe's throat, the dry eyes burning from Churchill's Swedish TV screen. Poverty, disease, resentment.

'I want my son to have what is rightfully his, what you stole from me.' A mad, haggard face in a dirty video booth somewhere in South America. And stole what, Churchill thought. This madman's life?

The video cassette, cushioned in bubbled polythene, had come to Churchill from the central Edenville branch of his bank. How had Scharfe ever traced him so accurately? The name Eric Churchill Scharfe could have got through the network, way back. The bravado, Scharfe had once written – always with that undertone of envy which life's second lieutenants seemed to be saddled with – the swagger, taking *Churchill* for a name. But the Edenville phone book alone listed a hundred-plus Churchills. What did the fools think he would choose, Adolf Hitler?

Arriving here under the stolen identity of a dead Rhinelander, Emil Goltz had kept his head down, laboured and learned. First naturalisation, then Eric Churchill was born. The mid-50s, before the British invaded Suez, when Vietnam was still a French disaster. Who remembered those days now? The Third Reich itself seemed less dated than that phase of history.

But if Eric Churchill had remained ex-directory and never given his private address, how had the video been delivered to his bank? The manager, taking care of a good customer, wrote to Churchill inviting him to collect from the chief cashier a package which had been left and which they were more than happy to keep, pending his convenience.

The video box carried no postage. It had been delivered by hand.

Troubled by the story's missing link, in the window Churchill swung the Zeiss telescope over the glittering sea on which coloured sails flickered against the eerie sun-bleached white of the chalkstacks. Edenville had been good to Emil Goltz, even better to Eric Churchill. What better place to hide than a town that sold pleasure and tranquillity? He swung the telescope further.

Churchill focused on the nude beach, two miles across the water. His reasons for watching it had nothing to do with sexual craving. Naturally any man who has possessed a thousand women realises how many millions still lie out there defying his potency. But what fascinated Churchill about the nude beach was its innocence. Of course he had never been there in person. But he liked the simplicity of the people who went naked over there. He was also, in his way, a simple man.

Churchill centred on a baseball game being played by about twenty young people. Deep within the German's own cold veins echoed the delicious frenzy of all that young bare flesh. To be young again, have countries and women to conquer!

He watched a young man shower sand, running the bases. While somebody chased the ball into the sea two girls in the outfield caught the runner at second base and in a flurry of breasts and limbs dragged him to the ground. The kid seemed in no hurry to struggle for home.

Eric Churchill moved the telescope along the beach. He would never know, but he had just been watching the son of Lothar Scharfe, the man who had come to Edenville to hunt him down.

TEN

On the nudist beach, Rudi St Paul dragged himself slowly from the tackle of the two amply fleshed Austrian girls, shook the sand from his hair, and gazed at the engulfing beachscape. It would break my heart, he thought. If I had a heart. Across the bay the Edenville clifftop was a chessboard taunting him to move.

In Bogotá Rudi had found a travel agent who repped for language schools in England. For some he even had brochures, pages of carefully angled pictures that lent glamour to the crowded rooms of converted old houses. Some were more modest in their publicity, cheaper. Rudi went for cheap. The school would provide him with a landlady, visa credibility which he could extend if necessary, contacts maybe.

In fact Rudi spoke excellent English, his Colombian accent reinforced with American and something else which a phonologist would identify as German. The language school would put him in an advanced group and have nothing to teach him. Rudi planned to pay the fees and skip most of the classes.

Rudi soon fell in with a group of mainly European students enjoying life away from their wealthy, repressive families. As well as discos and sex by night, they had discovered the nudist beach by day. As the language school brochure said, 'Recreation with international friends in Edenville's unique leisure environment.' Well, Rudi reflected, sure.

★

Eric Churchill called his bank manager and reminded him of the video cassette which they had been so kind as to hold for him.

The manager remembered. Certainly, and no, it had been no trouble. For a respected customer like Mr Churchill, part of the service. An appointment? Wonderful. Any time.

Expansion, Churchill said, relaxing over some fine mocha coffee in the manager's office. Even if you didn't want to, you sometimes had to grow bigger just to stop the other fish eating you alive. Churchill hoped the bank which had always given him such impeccable service would factor the transaction.

The manager was genial, receptive. The previous day he had been promoted to the bank's Los Angeles HQ. His mood was hypomanic. Churchill's guile, the ploys he had armed himself with, were hardly needed.

The video, he said, was a business promo. A foreign consortium. A strange way to do things, but you understand.

The bank manager understood perfectly.

The problem, Churchill said, was urgent contact with the video deliverer. If he waited they would no doubt come to him, but suddenly time had become critical.

In his eager assurance that there was no problem the manager almost bounced out of his chair. No problem, because the manager had been called out by the chief cashier when the video was left, to approve the bank being used as a drop. As it happened, the young South American also wished to open a cheque account. He had all the necessary references and an international banker's order which he wished to deposit immediately. Couldn't be straighter, the manager said.

He remembered the young Colombian's name. Before the manager got worried about the ethical hurdle of retrieving private information from bank records, Churchill withdrew the hook.

'I wonder if you could fix a meeting between the two of us. Inform your client that I'm most interested in the video, and would like to meet him on neutral ground. This office would be perfect, all the more since we already share you as our banker. Any appointment you make will be acceptable to me.'

The meeting was set up. Five minutes before he was due to arrive

Churchill put through a call to the bank manager's secretary regretting that he was tied up by other business and would have to postpone.

Rudi St Paul received the message and the bank manager's apologies, smiling, courteous, cool. When he left the bank's busy concourse he was followed by a young Vietnamese who had been studying the exchange-rate screen since noting who it was the manager ushered into his office.

The Viet was called Trong. He worked for Leo Malin. An ethnic Chinese, he had come to Edenville via an overcrowded boat that survived piracy in the South China Sea to reach Hong Kong, where after six months in wire pens some were accepted for settlement in Britain in the government's gesture of humanity for world consumption.

The Vietnamese were collected in a disused airfield in the country, lodged and fed and given English lessons for several years until the funding terminated. By this time Trong had already left. He had survived alone, he remained alone. He saw how many of the Viets were trapped for life in the camp mentality. So he went to work for the Edenville Chinese who ran a large section of the catering trade. All they required was total obedience.

Trong understood everything that went on around him, but hardly ever spoke. Especially in the cosmopolitan babble of Edenville, words were trouble. Malin had met Trong at the Roxy, impressed by his cool head at the blackjack table. It was as if the almost total absence of conversation in the Viet's life freed all those brain cells for the colder arts of observation and recall. Trong was one useful soldier and seemed to have no ambition to get rich. He understood nothing of the law, and the only thing that rattled him was talk of deportation. Perfect, really.

Insignificant in chinos and a cotton jacket, Trong snapped the milling street with Malin's Nikon. Just another tourist with a camera. Then he followed Rudi to a salad bar. A bunch of assorted foreigners welcomed Rudi and, among other things, called his name and declared that he was early.

For appearances' sake, Trong bought a black tea and drank it quickly. He sat with his back to Rudi and the students, most of whom carried shoulder bags of plastic binders printed with the logo and name of the Ace Language Academy. Trong had already seen that, and that was all he needed to see.

Reece Deacon had left his BMW in the visitors' parking strip behind the clifftop block from which Eric Churchill had taken him to dinner. The same night they disposed of Deacon and relieved his body of the keys, Leo Malin removed the BMW and garaged it. The hire still had several days to run. When the return date came he delivered the BMW in person. The girl behind the desk said, 'Thank you, Mr Salway.' Everything was in order. Malin beamed and waved, in and out under a minute. Fly-by-nights like Deacon came and went, who cared?

Along the street from the car-hire company Trong waited to drive Malin back to his office. The pressing business now was this person called Rudi who they had pinned down to one of those rip-off language places. One thing about Trong, he delivered meat.

'Emmajane!'

All the way back from the nude beach Bruce Rabey had been thinking about Annie. His utterance of Emmajane's name was ghostly.

'Oh Bruce!'

Emmajane raised her tear-smudged face, leapt up, pressed herself against his tee-shirt, wept through the cotton.

She raised her lips to his, skin salty, features pulpy with grief. Bruce clasped Emmajane to him. The parts of him that could get sexually aroused got sexually aroused. The rest of him contemplated her limp body and swollen face and thought, oh Christ!

If Bruce had ever loved Emmajane it didn't count now: he didn't love her at this moment, would never love her again. His heart made its chilling confession. Why? Because he found her misery-stricken face boring. Boring and ugly. And because he was already calculating what he could get out of this reunion.

Emmajane wanted comfort, soft handling. Bruce comforted her. She wanted to be missed and needed. Bruce told her he had missed and needed her. She wanted to be desirable to him. Bruce suggested a shower together and a long evening in bed.

In bed he took what advantage he could. Some of the little things which Emmajane had always refused, she now agreed to. But she didn't participate, just let him use her. Bruce sensed her gritted teeth. And encores were out.

Once, living alone in lodgings, Bruce had sent away for one of those blow-up dolls. The advert proclaimed 'Fully Receptive Bottom With Auxiliary Vibrator'. Less said about that memory the better. But in bed Emmajane was like a dummy. For her, sex and passion were the same thing, a quick aseptic screw. Bruce had discovered the *erotic*. Emmajane thought the word meant *dirty*.

The next morning she started to complain. Complaining and talking about shopping were Emmajane's main routes to self-esteem. Some of the forks were facing the wrong way in the presentation box. Bruce had also wiped up some coffee with a tea-towel which now had a horrid brown stain right across the print of Acapulco, and he hadn't even bothered to put it in for a biological soak.

As they both got ready for work Bruce's chest tightened. His disillusion was total. His head was going down, eyes darting sideways, a cornered animal. The toxic chemistry of marital reunion gnawed him all morning. Leo Malin's appearance in the building society queue was a relief.

They took a lunchtime walk in a decayed pleasure garden peopled by ozone-eroded statues with vandal-amputated limbs.

'Nice little earner for you,' Malin said. 'A young foreign gentleman staying in town for a bit. Where he goes, what he's into.'

Bruce asked, 'Why me?'

Malin said, 'You know these foreign punters. Everybody hates them. First English face lays good news on them, they fall down, wiggle their legs in the air. Wanna give it the business?'

Malin was lumbering and crude, a tough rubbery ugliness with bad skin. Wide pustules prodded the region round his ears. In his waxy right lobe he wore an earring. The only indication of mental activity was his habit of grinding right fist in left palm. Finesse, Bruce thought, you either had it or you didn't. Malin didn't. His fat-rimmed eyes waited for an answer.

Bruce said, 'When do I start?'

Edenville's geography was layer-cake, strata parallel to the coast. First the lavish mansions of the town's founders, hotels now, then a wide strip of plummy redbrick villas in quiet tree-lined roads, the Lucknows and Peacehavens of imperial England. A century later these crumbling residences were saved from demolition by their value as student accommodation and holiday lets. Some people paid anything to be near the beaches. Rapid conversion with hardboard and melamine, polypropylene carpets wall to wall and colour TV in every room turned raddled monstrosities into goldmines.

In one such building the Ace Language Academy conducted the business of TESOL. It meant Teaching English to Speakers of Other Languages. The casual labour force that staffed the Edenville language schools had other versions. In another such building Rudi St Paul had rented a room.

Rudi left behind him the frenetic *Ciao! Ciao!* of the Ace concourse, the peeling entrance of a one-time stockbroker's summer retreat. Along the avenue he yet again went over the bank incident. The manager had been apologetic, but too busy to give anything away.

Churchill had reacted. He had taken the bait, fixed a meeting, cancelled it. Since then, days now, nothing.

As he left the bank Rudi had expected to be snatched off the street, bundled into a car, taken for interrogation or just whacked and dumped on a roadside. Two things, he reiterated to himself. One, this is Edenville, England. At home he had seen, floating in the Magdalena river, headless torsos of men who had crossed the cocaine barons. Things like that didn't happen here. And two, he didn't scare that easily, or he would never have got this far. He guessed he had been watched, but in the cosmopolitan swirl of the Edenville crowds he hadn't spotted a tail. He was sure they hadn't followed him out of the centre. So what, then? But days were passing, and his next move, hell, he didn't know.

'Excuse me.'

The Englishman had approached from behind.

'Charborough Gardens. You wouldn't know where it is?'

'Sorry, I don't live here.'

The Englishman, a tall thin guy with a pencil moustache and twitchy manner, said, 'Well, I know it's around here somewhere. Where are you from?'

'Colombia.'

'Studying English?'

'Yes.'

'Been here long?'

'Ten days.'

'Like the town?'

'Yeah, fantastic place.'

'You speak good English anyway.'

'Thanks.'

'Cigarette?'

Bruce was smoking for real again. Emmajane had got very upset at this infidelity once her back was turned. She insisted they would now have to return the multi-snack toaster, her father's reward for Bruce quitting tobacco. Bruce said he didn't give a shit. This was what Emmajane called *language*. Language always made her cry.

The men lit up two Marlboros and walked on together. They exchanged names. When they came to Rudi's lodging he said, 'Sorry, I'd ask you in but the landlady don't like visitors.'

'Doesn't look much of a place,' Bruce said.

'No, but cheap.'

'You eat here?'

'She does meals, yeah.'

'Any good?'

Rudi pulled a face. 'Normal English food: French fries with everything, lots of grease, you know. Tins and packets. Hey, look, I don't mean to insult your country –'

'No, you're right,' Bruce said. 'I tell you what, my wife's a terrific cook. Why don't you come to supper one evening?'

'Sure, I like that.'

They exchanged phone numbers. Bruce suddenly remembered where Charborough Gardens was and promised to be in touch. Rudi watched the car out of sight and thought, could be. But something about the guy, about Edenville, said, Oh come on, no.

66

Bruce, driving home, had a sudden, gleeful idea that made him shout and hammer a fist on the steering wheel. It was brilliant, neat, magic. The greatest idea he ever had in his life.

ELEVEN

'I lost my watch.'

Bruce thrashed around the house, making irritated noises. He knew he wouldn't find the watch.

Bedtime, it was still hot. Emmajane sat unhabitually naked in front of her vanity unit, flossing her teeth and waiting for her moisturising agents to seep in.

Bruce was naked to the waist. A smart touch, removing his shirt. Good cred point. He slapped his forehead.

'Lunchtime. I nipped into the Roxy. Blast! I remember I just slipped it off. My arm was sweaty.'

He was getting back into his shirt.

'I know exactly where I left it. Won't be long, sweetie.'

Bruce leant over Emmajane. She was suspicious, but by the time she worked out why she suspected him Bruce would be gone. He placed his wide thin palms like scales below her breasts. Frenzy overcame him, the frenzy of unstoppable desire. He fell to his knees, pressed his face to her pubic hair. Emmajane struggled sideways.

'It must be really smelly down there, Bruce. Don't.'

Possessed, Bruce clutched Emmajane's hips, bare, still firm. His mouth slavered into her hair. He tried to pattern his breath while parting her thighs. How could such ravishing flesh be so naive?

'Ow!'

His nose had gone somewhere it shouldn't. Emmajane leapt up and pulled the fully drawn curtains even tighter together. Bruce was left kneeling, humiliated.

He stayed cool, got up, muttered he would see her later, left the house. He got his watch from the toolbag in the boot of the car. He muttered 'Fucking bitch!' twice, then sought variations.

On the radio they were playing Springsteen, meditative heavy rock for the mature lover who had learnt to cock his lip at the world. Bruce sang along, mellow and cynical. At the end he said, 'Nice one, Bruce.' Together they would cream this town.

The problem at the kebab house was that the Lebanese manager had marked Annie down for himself. Even the customers who consumed the full £30 per head menu didn't get to so much as touch Annie's calf without the Lebanese hovering round their table with intimidating politeness. So far he had tried it twice and Annie had fought him off. But they both knew he would get there in the end. Or, she could walk.

The Lebanese watched vindictively as Bruce and Annie talked. He scrutinised her face. Was she happy? Did her heart leap at this milk-skinned suitor? Her rules of employment, made by the Lebanese as he went along, included no fraternising with the clientele. Her infringement of this rule might serve as a lever on her goodwill later. So, behind smouldering hostile eyes, he tolerated it.

The next day was Bruce's afternoon off, compensation for Saturday morning. An oasis in the week, it was the one block of non-work time he was free of Emmajane. She always asked what he did, and Bruce usually told an unverifiable lie so the afternoon off remained totally free.

This time he said he was going to look at shirts. In fact he drove home, shaved and showered carefully, put on his best casual wear, a condom in his wallet. He left the car running and went back in. Make that two condoms.

Annie had said, sure, they could meet. Your place, Bruce said, but she didn't like the idea. Bruce insisted, please, it was important. There could be money in it. He saw the disgust roll her eyes. No, not that. Really, straight up, business. I just want to talk. She'd heard it before, but OK, she muttered an address.

Bruce could not believe it. He was going to see Annie in a room, her room. Not on a beach this time, under a pier or in a greasy kebab bar or a stinking alley. He would see her at home, defences down. She would make him coffee, curl her legs under her, not mind if he saw down her blouse as she leant forward –

Oh God, Annie, I do love you. The words ran repeatedly through Bruce's mind like an electronic newsreel round a city square. Did people who shot heroin feel like this? Life should be so high.

Annie's street sobered Bruce up. Dark terraces, old houses so shoddily built that demolition would be mercy killing. The hall smelt of damp carpet. Annie was only half awake. The sight of her tight bottom stilled Bruce's breathing. What was it about the bodies of some women? In the hall there was a stack of unclaimed mail addressed to departed occupants who were still being pursued by various computers.

Annie's room was upstairs, front. The unmade bed was not inviting. A cheap, scarred sink unit, a two-ring electric cooker that looked like a fire risk, crowded a corner. Annie didn't make coffee, didn't curl her legs. She flopped on the bed, lit a cigarette, threw the packet to Bruce. A stale fug draped the room.

'Amazing,' Bruce said. 'Brings back my bedsit days. Best time of my life.'

'Don't talk shit,' Annie said.

Bruce protested, 'It's true.'

Annie provoked in him a desperate need to unburden mentally as well as physically. He continued, 'Look at me. I've got a steady career, a house, a car, a wife. And I'm going crazy. If I don't change soon I'll do something really stupid. You – you can walk out whenever you want, kick over the traces. That's what I call freedom.'

'You can walk out too. People do it all the time.'

'I know, but –'

'No fucking buts. You think I spent my whole life like this?'

'Of course not, I –'

'Look, sweetie. There are two ways you can be free. Rich and free, or poor and free. Everybody dreams about one and tries to dodge the other. Guess which way round.'

'Well, of course,' Bruce said stiffly.

Annie said, 'What's your wife like?'

'Well, she's –'

'Whatever you say is a lie. Don't even answer.'

'Actually, I'd like you to come to my house.'

'You're joking.'

'No, there's a way. Listen –'

Bruce outlined his plan.

Annie got up. Afraid she would say he had to go, Bruce got up too. In the cramped room bodies were close.

Bruce reached for her and said, 'I want you so much.'

'You want my cunt,' Annie said. 'That's what you want.'

'Be a fool not to,' Bruce said.

'Aye well, watch out, mister. You don't know where it's been.'

Emotionally and physically deflated, Bruce stood back.

'You'll come in the Roxy tonight, then?'

'Unless something better turns up.'

'Twelve?'

'Sure, you're the boss.'

She refused to kiss or be kissed. On the car radio they were playing Springsteen again. This time Bruce didn't sing along.

Before going to meet Emmajane from work Bruce phoned Rudi. Over dinner, a ready-made freezer item whose TV campaign offered you the freedom to live your life, Bruce lied about his afternoon quest for shirts. Then he told Emmajane about an interesting young Colombian who had come into Ajax and Achilles for financial advice.

They established more or less where Colombia was. Then Bruce fed in a few touches about Rudi's charm and probable wealth and the fact that the best foreign holidays were those where you had friends in exotic places.

Then he said, 'I was going to ask you if we could invite him to supper sometime.'

Emmajane said, 'You only met him this morning.'

'Yes, well, actually, I said I'd take him to the Roxy for an hour tonight. He fancied a splurge on the tables.' Bruce held up open palms. 'It's all right, I'm not playing. He just needs a member to get him in.'

Emmajane said, 'Why don't we both go?'

Bruce sucked his teeth as if in pain.

'That was my idea. Then I thought, I don't really want him to meet you there. You know the kind of women hang out in the Roxy. And Latin Americans are very strict about what places are respectable for women. I'd rather he first sees you here. You could wear that long gown, get the candles out –'

And with a bit of luck he'll fall for you, you'll fall for him, with a bit of encouragement he'll come on to you and you'll buy it.

Bruce would catch Emmajane with her legs round Rudi. She would die of shame. He would forgive her in return for a greater understanding of his own needs. He thought of Annie, but the fantasy kept turning him on to Emmajane. Either way he couldn't lose.

'I'll only be an hour. Once I've got him into the club I don't have to stay. OK with you?'

'I s'pose so,' Emmajane said. 'Anyway, my lady's problem's just started, so I think I'll have an early night.'

Bruce reached out and tenderly touched her hand.

As arranged by phone Bruce picked Rudi up at the Colombian's house. He invented an uncheckable story about how when he was in Paris as a twenty-year-old he had been so grateful to someone who had shown him round, someone who (no shadow of a hint) was still his guest from time to time.

A welcome coincidence, Rudi said. He had been looking for somewhere to gamble. My pleasure, Bruce insisted. Only too glad to refute the myth that the English were uptight xenophobes who lived in mausoleums. On which subject, the dinner invitation was definitely on. They could talk dates later.

Then, my wife's very keen to meet you. We need a fourth. Do you have a friend, female friend, that is? No? Well, I daresay somebody will turn up.

They messed around one of the two roulette games operating,

winning the occasional big sum and trickling it away again in smaller losses. Leo Malin was there, foursquare and fat, surveying tables and punters. Malin seemed to know everybody. Bruce had noticed before how many ears Malin whispered in, how many female backsides he nipped, whose owners clearly had no objection.

When he caught Malin's eye Bruce winked, with the side of his face averted from Rudi. Malin's rubbery features unbent slightly as he realised what the wink was telling him. Then he waddled on by.

'Oh hey, look who's here!'

They were ahead on the tables, up in the bar having drinks, when Annie came in. Heads turned. Bruce was amazed. How she had done it between the kebab bar and here he would never know, but she stunned. Her hair was spikes of white gold, her make-up gave her flaring eyes and plum-red lips. She wore calf-length trousers with pointy-toe boots and a big tee-shirt with holes cunningly cut into it. Below she wore a bra, skimpy as they came. Men and some women spent a lot of time looking at the holes to work out whether or not.

'Annie, hi! This is terrific!'

Annie stepped back. Her eyes opened up in near horror. In a husky American accent she said, 'Darling, how unexpected!'

Bruce laughed nervously. The Carlsberg had permeated his body and was running down the back of his ears. He introduced Annie and Rudi, Rudi kissed Annie's hand and said, 'This is not your wife?'

'You're definitely joking,' Annie said.

'For just a moment –' Rudi said. Big white teeth gleamed in his chiselled tanned face.

Bruce gave a worried ratlike grin. Malin had left the club, Bruce felt easier for that. But the club went on till four, and Bruce had to go. Keeping Emmajane sweet was essential at this stage. Annie and Rudi were happily frittering away plastic octagons on the green baize. Bruce felt sick. What they were going to do after he left was suddenly all too bloody obvious.

Driving home Bruce tried to get a grip on himself, afraid the police would stop him. Too much lager had unbalanced his night judgment. Every time he thought of Rudi and Annie he swerved more wildly. He felt a rare relief to be back in Lagoon Close, a maudlin peace at the simple cowlike warmth of Emmajane's sleeping body.

'We're tailing him. I've got a guy buddying him along. We'll soon know everything about him.'

Malin paused. Through the panorama window, lights blinked down on the bay.

'How does your man report?'

'Phone only. He's doing the job. I've seen them together.'

'What does he know?'

'Nothing. He's just an everyday wally who wants to earn. Somebody too smart who's gonna turn us over later? Screw that.'

Churchill seemed vague. It made Malin uneasy. His one fear in life was what would happen when the German started to flake. Since Malin had fluffed the Deacon killing, Churchill had become distant. Even as the old man had tightened the cord round Deacon's neck Malin had felt the space begin to grow. Years could go by, years of trust, loyalty, success, coining strong money. But always a moment came when Malin saw the truth. The truth was that Churchill had always despised him.

'Might help if I knew why we're worried about this spic.'

Churchill was curt. 'No, you don't need that.'

Malin lowered his eyes, the way he had for twenty years. He had come to Churchill's notice through his talent for persuading tenants to quit properties which the German owned and wanted to convert in a booming market. Things had come a long way since then, but always under Churchill's direction. Malin was forty-two. He needed to secure his future before age caught up and some hungry face decided to take a slice out of him. Maybe the time had come, Malin thought. Time to find out who shoves who off the sidewalk.

'A problem, Leo?'

'No, boss. No problem.' Malin got up. 'Anything else I can do?'

'No.'

Malin left. A good breeze was thumping in, that ballsy sea air. Malin loved it. He loved Edenville, the big money, the way people put their bodies and their wallets on the line in the chase for a fun time. He never went abroad, hardly ever left Edenville. He loved England because it threw up nothing he feared. But sometimes this seventy-year-old German spooked the shit out of him.

★

If you excluded the twenty-five per cent geriatric element, Edenville was Britain's most international city. Among other things Eric Churchill had a monopoly of the escort agencies, quality end. Of course there were always the one-taxi-and-a-scrubber outfits that worked on a quick pizza and a fuck in a car park. The low life looked after its own. But now the multinationals were relocating to Edenville, the conference centre and the lifestyle environment sucked in a high-class expense-account market insatiable for women with the necessary attributes and ambition.

Part of Malin's executive role in the escort business was to select for Churchill. Each week he provided Churchill with a list of phone numbers, seven different. The girl in question would be told to keep the evening free. Either Churchill phoned or he didn't.

Tonight he phoned. He just said, 'All right. Now.' The girl understood the message and already had the address. Apart from Malin covering the charge for this visit, for the girl it was just another client.

In his work-out room Churchill lay face down on a couch while the Norwegian blonde massaged his thighs. Bell-like breasts lapped his back. Thinking was easier now.

Churchill had always allowed Malin to assume that one day he would inherit everything. But somewhere along the line Malin had failed to be worthy of it. A man of clay, one of the world's *Sturmmänner*. A born corporal, period. Lacking a natural heir, Churchill had no mind to hand over anything to anybody. Destroy it first. Sometimes things had to be like that. If Hitler had had a son, the Reich would have survived. Without, why should it?

Churchill manoeuvred himself over. He indicated a cupboard and said, 'Put on the uniform.'

The immaculately clean garments came in various sizes. The Norwegian girl had no problems with the concept. She quickly chose the best fit in high black boots, black underwear and garter belt and stockings, Swastika armband and replica SS cap. She faced Churchill, swishing the riding crop and getting into the role.

'So,' Churchill said. 'You interrogate me.'

Without warning he stepped towards her and drove his fist into her belly. Gasping, the girl doubled up. Churchill pulled her hair back and wrenched her face close to his.

'You will find I don't break easily.'

Hate blazed in the Norwegian girl's eyes. This woman was going to be good.

The interrogation started. Churchill always thought more clearly in these sessions than at any other time. As the Norwegian girl ordered him into the bathroom for heavy degradation, Churchill knew he would have to bypass Malin. Before Malin bypassed him.

TWELVE

In the small hours, drained but refreshed, his mind growing sharper as Edenville was finally falling asleep around him, Churchill dictated a message for his secretary to receive first thing. Technology now meant Churchill rarely had to visit the office in person.

The message instructed her to call the number which Malin had supplied, to inform Mr Rudi St Paul that a meeting would now be in order. Churchill specified a venue. Later the secretary confirmed that Mr St Paul had taken the message.

'And he accepted?'

'He made one condition.'

'What was it?'

'Mr St Paul said that before he met you he wished to deliver a separate communication. He asked for an address or number. Naturally I refused. He then suggested that we put a blank cassette in the answerphone, switch off sound, and he would record the message. We would then pass the cassette to you.'

'And this happened?'

'He named a time and rang from a call box.'

'You had the sound off?'

'Yes, and immediately the line went dead I removed the cassette and sealed it in its case.'

'It's with you now?'

'It's here. Shall I get a messenger to bike it over to you?'

'No, I'll collect it myself. I'll be right there.'

The message was brief. It said, 'Mr Churchill, I'm glad you've decided to meet with me. Before we go ahead with this there's one thing you should know. I have deposited with a solicitor here in Edenville all documents and records, including a copy of the video you've already seen, which apply to you and your real identity. They are packaged, labelled and addressed. Each week on a certain day I call by the solicitor in person. The first time I fail to show up there I have paid them a fee to open the package I deposited and release the contents. These go, among other places, to the British and American media, a whole batch to Israel, and of course the Dutch. I want to make all this clear to you so there is no misunderstanding when we meet. And I would like to name my own time and place so that apart from us not even your secretary knows about it –'

Eastwards beyond Edenville the bay curved out to an eroded sandy headland. At seven in the morning the car park was empty. Churchill had borrowed, as he often did for business, one of his company's anonymous Sierras. He turned up his raincoat collar, tightened his scarf against the cold mist.

Churchill followed the path through ancient defence mounds and crossed an area of flat grass. He had never been here before. A kids' day out sort of place. The only way up was a stepped path whose banks were held down with wire to arrest erosion. Visibility was about twenty metres. The sea was a white-out. Churchill kept climbing.

At the crest there was a triangulation point and a garage-like coastguard station. Worn slopes ran down to mist-shrouded waters. The appointed meeting place was deserted. Churchill checked all four sides of the coastguard building. Nobody. Then he smelt cigarette smoke on the air.

Rain began. Simultaneously Churchill sensed an approach across the soft grass. He remained unmoved, lizardlike. He pulled his collar higher, his back to the windblown drizzle.

'Mr Churchill. Yes? I am Rudi St Paul.'

A handsome face, European features grafted on to brown skin and black hair. Blue eyes. Churchill looked for traces of Lothar Scharfe, but whatever Indian blood Scharfe had coupled with was triumphant.

This Rudi St Paul was mid-twenties, manly, with the open grace of the truly intelligent. Churchill looked into his face for a long time.

Then he said, 'I wish to ask you one question.'

'Sure.'

'How did you find me?'

Rudi brushed raindrops from his face and smiled.

'Sometimes you sent my father money, American dollars. Once a pack of notes came, a compliment slip of the bank got left in. My father always kept this. Seemed a good idea to follow it up. So I got the number of this bank in Edenville – not difficult, they got a branch in Bogotá. Then I phoned and asked them to check something in my account – I am Mr Eric Churchill, you understand. I went for the central bank because I figured that's where a man of your stature would do business. And guess what.'

Churchill's eyes narrowed slightly, the total reaction.

'Tell me, how is your father?'

'Your old comrade is fine. Sends his respects.'

In fact Lothar Scharfe was dead, his last days racked with squalor and senile rage. Rudi had no regrets. He had hardly known the man anyway. But on the videotape Scharfe was very much alive. Rudi wanted Churchill to feel that icy hand reaching after him across every stretch of this world.

'Did he tell you what kind of man I am?'

'He told me what kind of man you *were*.'

'People like me don't change.'

'You're old now.'

Churchill shook his head. 'We are the granite around which everything else wears away.'

'Very noble,' Rudi said.

'And you, you have this dago skin. But inside I see a German. Am I right?'

'Sure, *ein guter Deutscher*. Better believe it.'

Grizzled by the rain, Churchill's face looked relaxed, benign even.

'Why make your visit so threatening? I would have been glad to see Lothar's son. My means are modest, but my hospitality would be entirely –'

'Yeah, I remember my father said you always acted poor. Don't give me any more of this bullshit.'

Churchill was abrupt. 'Don't understand.'

'Before we go on,' Rudi said, 'I better tell you what I do. For business. I'm an art dealer.'

Churchill sneered. 'In Colombia?'

'You bet. Ugly people with dirty money really hot for art. Maybe makes them feel good, you know.'

'You are starting to bore me.'

'People can die of boredom.'

'Die, sure. Listen, young man. You bring me all this crap about somebody I was in the war with. Some garbage about documents you have given to a lawyer. You want what, money? What money do you think I have? For that matter, what documents are these that I should even give you the time of day?'

Cool, Rudi said, 'The video I sent you was only a sample. So one, there's more tape. Two, there are SS papers with your name and my father's on them. Lothar Scharfe, Emil Goltz. Photos too, comrades in arms, smiling men in uniform. Maybe you had a face job, but believe me, Herr Goltz, you haven't changed much. You see that Demjanjuk trial? The way they superimpose his now face on the picture from wartime? Perfect fit too. The things that don't change, huh – eye sockets, groove under nose, all this. They even got computers now can spot the resemblances. Eric Churchill meet Emil Goltz, respectable citizen, super thief, war criminal.'

'Until you show me evidence,' Churchill said, 'this is all talk. The Jews run teams full time, worldwide. Forty years, who have they found? All the money they spent, they couldn't even find Mengele.'

'Sure. But *I* have found *you*. And hey man, I'm *nobody*. That's got to worry you.'

In the teeth of the rain, chopping the syllables, Churchill said, 'OK, smart boy, what's your deal?'

'I told you I work in art. I said a dealer. But not really. I worked *for* a dealer. Didn't make much money but I learnt a lot.'

'You make no sense to me.'

'I want to know about the pictures.'

'What are you talking about?'

'OK, OK. My old man, let's get back to him. Why you think he taped this stuff? He's old, sick. Not too sick to put the finger on you. But he gets religion, yeah. Wants to make everything right before ... So he told me about Holland, the lot. The works. He wanted me to go there. Sort of redemption trip he couldn't make himself. He told me about you, maybe still alive. Wanted me to help you make your peace.'

'I have all the religion I need.'

'Me, I had a better idea. How about salvation in this world? At a price. But something's puzzling you, right?'

'And what is that?'

'My father didn't know about the pictures. So how come I do? Yeah?'

'You say so.'

'Remember Grootendahl? You wouldn't know it now. New houses, everything. But I went there, talked to people. The Dutch got good English. Who am I? American journalist, right? And hey, these people aren't lawyers. They didn't ask for money to talk to me. They're still really sore about the things you people did there. And when I mentioned Emil Goltz, boy, they never forgot *him*. Still commemorate the massacre, you know? And here it got interesting. I met this woman whose father was spared because he handed over a collection of pictures, to the SS officer who organised the massacre. Name, you recall, Emil Goltz. I asked if they knew what happened to this Goltz. Turns out they all think he died, early '45. Body was found, tags, papers. Shell-blast victim.'

The rain had slackened. Watery sunlight wavered through raw wet air. The two men stood eye to eye.

Rudi said, 'You got a week to make me an offer. Seven digits. Dollars are fine.'

'Insane. What money I have is tied up in business. I can't raise money like that.'

'The old guy whose pictures you took. I saw his notebook, this private catalogue.' Rudi pointed at himself. 'Art dealer, remember. So don't give me crap. A week, that's it.'

The two figures were small and isolated on the clearing headland. Rudi walked away.

THIRTEEN

That morning the branch manager informed Bruce that he would not be recommended for the executive development scheme. *Yet*, he said. Bruce expressed his indignation non-verbally. Blotches appeared on his skin, his eyes stared, he kept shifting in his chair.

The manager's name was Ardington. Thirties, thinning hair, conservative suit. Bruce hated his manager because life had programmed *him* to be like Ardington. Except that the Ardingtons always did things right, and Ardington was now telling Bruce why he, Bruce, hadn't.

'Feel there's a maturity gap . . . Need a more solid profile, reassure fellow employees and customers . . . Clearer definition of career objectives . . . Prefer greater distance from female staff . . . In the security business we need to come across as reliable, not a bunch of live wires . . .'

Bruce left the interview bitter and angry. Bastards, bastards. He survived the humiliation by telling himself that at least he would never be Ardington. Later, Malin appeared at the Ajax and Achilles office, timed for Bruce's lunch.

Sheets of rain blew through the town. Multicoloured golfing umbrellas fought for space. At rain in Edenville the tourist population took to cars, jamming the streets in search of escape from the traffic and diversion from the wet. Malin headed for the clifftop. A long way below, the beach was drowning under high tide. Silver rain ricocheted off the glistening promenade. The sea was a foam of green waves.

'Got anywhere?'

'Making progress,' Bruce said.

'Like what?'

'Give me a chance. What do you want to know?'

'Why's he here?'

'He's a language student.'

'I copped you with him the other night. No problem situation, far as I could see. What's he do when he's not learning English?'

Bruce had nothing specific.

Malin said, 'I want a result.'

'He's coming to my house.'

'Party?'

'Dinner.'

'Get him pissed. Milk him.'

Bruce said, 'I'll try.'

Bruce was in over his head. Everything he knew would happen, but hoped he could magic away by worrying about it, happened.

He fetched Annie and Rudi in his car. By the time they arrived at Lagoon Close he knew they had been to bed together. Their cool act, pretending they were just friends, was more erotic than if they just stripped off in the car. Bruce burnt at their little outbursts of giggles.

Annie and Emmajane hated each other at sight. Annie wore a white shirt only just lower than her crotch. When she sat down the sight of dark red briefs parched Bruce's throat. Emmajane wore a coordinated skirt and top which in combination with her anxious-hostess manner made her look like a youthful grandmother. Even her vibrant bush of hair, the only non-synthetic thing about her, was somehow put down by Annie's peroxide stubble. Early on the two women stopped exchanging words.

Annie asked if she could contribute a dessert to the meal. She took four nectarines and carved a clean destoned hole through them. Beside each cored nectarine she put a banana.

Bruce and Rudi got the idea and howled with laughter. Annie gave a lascivious demonstration of how to squeeze the banana through the hole then eat it. Tight faced, Emmajane insisted she was full. With added virtuosity Annie ate Emmajane's as well. After that it was all downhill.

Rudi got a little drunk and told anecdotes of exotic places none of them could match. Annie got drunk too and started using what Emmajane called 'those words', the ones Bruce had once used in bed until Emmajane threatened to sleep in the spare room if he did it again.

Emmajane hovered between misery and outrage, her lavender dralon soiled by the coarse speech and exposed knickers of this Scottish punk from – definitely – the wrong side of town. Bruce kept himself together with a frozen grin and exclamations like 'Great!', 'Out of sight!', 'Mindblowing!', washed down with a lot of cheap wine that furred up the inside of his head like a padded cell.

In 14 Lagoon Close every room had its dinky anodysed aluminium No Smoking logo. Annie had the match to her cigarette before Emmajane's eyes commanded Bruce to point out the house rules. Annie pouted and went out to the garden. Emmajane withdrew to the bathroom, tears imminent. Bruce and Rudi gazed at each other over the debris of some *boeuf* which had somehow failed to be *stroganoff*.

'Your wife's very emotional,' Rudi said.

Bruce said, 'You have to read the signs.'

'How's that?'

'It's you. Can't you tell?'

'You mean . . .?'

'I've seen it once before. A Swiss ski instructor. When it happens, that's it. As soon as you walked in, I knew it.'

'No kidding.'

'That's how she is.'

'So how you feel about it?'

'Emmajane and I have a mature relationship. We accept that passion is something you can't control.'

One of the women was returning.

'You don't say,' Rudi murmured.

Bruce gave an adult smile, the oiliest he could manage.

★

That night one of the payroll boys came to Leo Malin and nearly stopped his heart. For ever.

'We know somebody called Reece Deacon?'

He contorted his face at the unlikely name. Malin quickly capped the well of panic inside him.

'Never heard of him. Who is he?'

'Dunno. Some face was asking.'

'Like who? Filth?'

'No way. Guy I never seen before. Upfront dosh.'

'Let's check him out.'

Two hours later he was in front of Malin, in the office of a body work-out club where till ten p.m. nightly Edenville women racked their figures to endless disco. One of the legitimate outlets for Eric Churchill's money. Twice a week Malin looked over the accounts and kept an eye on things.

'Shut the door. Siddown.'

A tidy man, expressionless, compact and muscular, export-only suntan.

'Understand you're looking for a name.'

'What's it to you?'

'So bad you're waving notes around.'

'So?'

'How much?'

'You selling?'

'Who wants him?'

'You don't want to know that.'

'Old friends?'

'Could say.'

'They want to see him again?'

'Absolutely not.'

'Name again?'

'Reece Deacon.'

'Don't know him, OK. Never heard of James Salway either.'

The tidy tanned face looked mildly impressed.

'You're my man.'

'How much?'

'Three.'

'Five.'

'You set him up good, five. Can do?'

'No sweat. Let me get this right, we are talking goodbye Mr Deacon here?'

'Goodbye, sure. Didn't catch the name.'

'Cash now.'

'You got it.'

'What if I don't deliver?'

The tanned man smiled.

'You'll deliver, because if I don't get Deacon I'm gonna come back and get you.'

'You're a scholar and a gentleman,' Malin said.

He held the £50 notes to the light. You had to. That summer in Edenville there was more dud money around than wet pussy.

Annie and Emmajane in bikinis, Bruce and Rudi in swim trunks, in a sun-filled basin of sand on the nudist dunes. Giggling tension in the air, all of them except Emmajane smoking to ward off *the moment*.

Signals in Emmajane's mind kept flashing wrong, wrong, wrong. Every time she searched Bruce's face for something she could recognise all she saw was a mad stranger. Things between them were out of control.

She was only here because at the end of that terrible dinner party the three of them had embarrassed her into agreeing. With her eyes she was trying to tell Bruce not to do it. His duty was to stay covered, shield her from disgrace.

Once a caring husband, the perverted pig was now refusing to consider her needs, her modesty. Every time a naked body of either sex came by Bruce's eyes pinged out on stalks.

Emmajane flashed him anguished looks, shakes of the head. Bruce just reacted with that fixed, over-the-top grin he'd adopted lately. Brushing sand from her carefully shaven legs, beneath a cinemascope heaven, Emmajane knew she was about to die.

'Come on, then,' Bruce said. 'Let's all do it.'

Nobody moved. Bruce hooked thumbs in his trunks. Rudi smiled.

'I think the question is, Bruce, not when but how.'

Bruce said, 'Right. Well –' He avoided Emmajane.

Annie said, 'We all do it with our eyes shut. Easy.'

Bruce guffawed. 'Anybody who doesn't peep is a cissy.'

'I have a suggestion,' Rudi said. He looked at Emmajane. 'Let's you and me go for a swim.'

He reached for her hand. It came to him with grateful ease. They skated down the dune and, hand in hand, ran across the white beach.

'Your wife's a tight little lady,' Annie said. 'What's she like in bed?'

'A tight little lady.'

'Lucky you.'

From his new-found confidence Bruce said, 'I never knew what a hard-on was till I met you.'

He had realised he could say these things to women without a pack of snarling dogs leaping at his throat.

'Well,' Annie said. 'Fancy!'

They stripped synchronically.

Rudi and Emmajane waded into the tide. The water's cold assault soon became warm pleasure ascending the body.

'This is very tough for you,' Rudi said. He gestured at the nude beach. 'You don't have to worry about it.'

Such a gentleman. And his skin the perfect smooth brown which Europeans risked cancer for. He made Emmajane feel apologetic. Even the guilt she felt at the bulge in his shorts was ebbing away.

'I can't,' she wailed. 'I don't know why, but I can't.'

'The secret is do it gently,' Rudi said. 'Under water. Like this.'

He was sliding his shorts off below the waist-high water. Now they were in his hand. Within the mottled-green waves, Emmajane glimpsed pale contours. Her breath came sharply.

'Try if you like it. If you don't, you put them on again, no problem.'

Emmajane scanned the dunes. She felt Bruce staring down the telescope of her guilt. But where Bruce and Annie should have been, all Emmajane saw was – but she couldn't believe it. She squinted against the sun. A man on top of a woman. No mistaking that shape, ever.

She gasped as large breakers, breast-high, caressed her body like playful fish. Below the tide a warm current wove arabesques round her lower body. Emmajane reached down into the water.

'How's it feel?'

Was it shame or sun that pinked her cheeks? But Emmajane could not hold back. All her friends would know from her eyes what she had done. But it was too late to care.

'Nice.'

Rudi pushed towards her. His strikingly blue eyes smiled. He reached to her back and expertly unclipped her top. Emmajane let him.

She would die of shame. Later.

Her breasts floated polyp-like on the water. Their bobbing aroused her. Panic fought excitement. Her friends would never speak to her again once they knew she was the kind of woman who got excited at her own sea-rippled breasts. She would lose her job and her friends and put her mother in a mental home. But excitement won.

Dolphin-like, Rudi suddenly vanished. How he held his breath she would never know. But now the whole sea embraced Emmajane's body till she was open as a beach, washed and tongued and sucked by endlessly incoming waves. She crooned with the moaning water.

When he stripped Reece Deacon's body Malin had kept the keys he found there. From Annie he knew the apartment the keys would open. The lease would be minimum one month. Deacon's ghost was still tenant.

Malin also knew Rudi St Paul's number. Leaving a message, Malin gave his name as Churchill and asked if Mr St Paul could meet him.

The location was where the pleasure gardens ran through the gigantic concrete wedges of a flyover. Rudi was on time, watching tennis on the red clay courts.

'Mr St Paul?'

'Yeah.'

'Please, no questions. In the car.'

They took an alley through ornamental shrubbery and got in Malin's red Granada. Malin refused him an explanation. He had wiped the keys clean and held them in leather-gloved hands. He told Rudi to memorise the address.

'The keys are a sign of Mr Churchill's trust. He wants you to be sure that everything's in order. So before you meet with him there feel free to inspect the premises. There's work being finished off, so tomorrow evening if it suits you.'

'Sure,' Rudi said. 'Tell Mr Churchill I appreciate it.'

Malin said, 'Course, none of this happened.'

Rudi said, 'That's what somebody told me about Edenville. Nothing ever happens here.'

'That's why it's everybody's sort of town,' Malin said.

He leaned across, pushed the passenger door open.

'My birthday tomorrow,' Rudi explained to Bruce. 'And hey, I got a new place, an apartment. One of these short-let places. I got this idea.'

It was easy by phone.

Rudi continued, 'Also, we got to talk. Just you and me. So how about Emmajane comes later? You come at nine, we have our talk, get things ready. Then the girls turn up and we party. Oh yeah, I just had another thought. There's a chance I might get held up. Best thing is I drop the spare key by your office, so if I shouldn't be there you can let yourself in, have a drink.'

Bruce took the bait, seemed flattered even. Something about Bruce that Rudi liked – a man with a buzzing head and a wish to please. Programmed to self-destruct, meantime giving it his best shot.

Users and losers, Rudi reflected. That was the world. He had been a lot of places, and users and losers were all he'd ever seen.

But Bruce was cleverer than that.

'Rudi said we should go in, set things up. He'll be a bit late. Looks like a decent place.'

A tremor went through Emmajane every time he mentioned Rudi. Bruce felt powerful, in control.

They had all finally been naked together in the dunes, steadied by a frozen innocence, a tableau legitimate only because nothing moved. Since then Bruce had swung between inexpressible lust for Emmajane

89

and a mad jealousy at the thought of Rudi penetrating her body. His Emmajane's body. Bruce argued to himself that the sea water was too cold, lubrication impossible, you'd never slide it in.

But *something* had happened. Look at her flushed cheeks and glowing eyes. Once Emmajane would have said, 'I'm not going into a strange man's house on my own.' But look how she reacted now, as Bruce fumbled the key in the apartment door and said, 'Damn, I forgot the wine. Look, you go in, I'll be a few minutes.'

Emmajane, sounding ten years older than she ever had before, said, 'Fine.'

Bruce unlocked the door, took the key, returned to the car. In spite of himself his expression darkened. The little bitch said 'Fine'. Well, if she was enjoying it, so much the better. He would give her enough time with Rudi for something compromising to happen, then catch them at it.

He would be cool, a man of poise, *savoir faire*. Then, when Annie arrived, he would cash in all his chips. The coming sexual binge made his stomach churn.

From the rhododendrons, beyond the lit forecourt of the small exclusive block, Rudi watched Emmajane enter and Bruce drive away.

On the three floors only a few lights burned. All the garage doors were closed. What kind of people lived in these pine-shrouded blocks? Elderly rich, Rudi guessed. He had been there half an hour. In that time, no action.

After Emmajane went in no extra window lit up. Rudi wondered whether to move to the rear of the building. Then a small neat man came out in a hurry. From the way he left, not a resident. He shut the inner and outer doors, steel-framed reinforced glass, carefully behind him. But his eyes and body declared a man who wanted to get out of there.

The stranger left the drive. Rubber shoes made no noise. A minute later a car revved softly several streets away. Rudi waited. The night was warm, but he began to chill inside. Not from fear, but knowledge. Certainty could make you cold like that.

Then Bruce returned and went in. Just as he let himself through the inner door Rudi tapped on the outer. Bruce tried to look pleased, but surprise showed. Clutching the tissue-wrapped bottle, he came back out.

'Hey, coincidence. Where's Emmajane?'

'She's –' Bruce pointed, finger upwards but eyes cast down, thoughtful.

'I lost my bloody keys, man. Listen, you go up, I'll have another look out here. Had them a minute ago.'

'OK, yeah.'

Bruce went up. Rudi drew both doors gently against their locks so they stayed open. Whatever Bruce found up there, Rudi wanted him to come running back down and not go beating on the neighbours' doors.

Bruce reappeared rapidly. One hand still grasped the bottle of wine. His shock of hair mimicked fright. On his white face his moustache was a circumflex of horror.

Rudi said, 'Bruce, what is it, man?'

Bruce's mouth stuttered. 'Got to get out of here –'

Rudi hustled him into the car and urged him to drive away. After some minutes' driving Rudi told Bruce to pull into a dark place.

'Lights too.'

Bruce had to think where the headlamp control was.

'We've got to go back. Emmajane's in there –'

'What's she doing?'

'Doing? She was, you know, she was –'

Bruce thrust at the ignition. Rudi gripped his hand.

'What you see, Bruce?'

'She was on the floor –'

'Dead?'

'Aaaah!' Bruce nodded.

'You can't go back.'

'I've got to.'

'Bruce, be careful, man. How did she get into that apartment?'

'I let her in – oh God!' Bruce covered his face.

'Bruce, be cool. You want to talk to the police about what you did?'

Bruce's head shook sideways.

'You're a prime suspect. How if they say you took her up there, killed her, went to the wine shop for an alibi, then back again and faked the discovery? You know how police think.'

'But I wouldn't —'

'Motive? Why was Emmajane in this apartment? Another man invited her? You got motive, Bruce. Nobody need draw picture.'

Bruce whimpered. 'Oh Jesus.'

'Bruce, listen good.' Rudi clasped Bruce's bicep. 'You're totally clear. I'm your alibi. Emmajane went there by herself. You never went there, you were with me. You were telling me about you suspected she was seeing some other guy. Three a.m. she still didn't come home, you call the police because this never happen before and you got worried. The apartment door was open or shut?'

'I opened it.'

Bruce saw his own miserable plot coming back to haunt him if he ever had to explain it to anybody.

'She had the key?'

'I kept it.'

'That's good. Means somebody opened to her, was expecting, right? Obvious conclusion. That's how it is, agree?'

'Anything you say,' Bruce answered.

He threw the car open and heaved his stomach into the road.

FOURTEEN

'She still hasn't come home. This has never happened before. I'm worried.'

It was three a.m. Rudi nodded as Bruce phoned the desk sergeant at Edenville Central.

The police were soon back on the line. A lieutenant-colonel on his way back from an Old Nairobians dinner-dance had spotted the open door, investigated, bundled his mink-coated wife into their flat, investigated again, then done his civic duty. The body had no i.d. Bruce stammered a fuller description into the phone. The sergeant said, 'We're sorry to inform you, Mr Rabey, we think we've found your wife.'

Early the next day the police were at the house.

'You have no idea why your wife was there?'

Bruce shook his head. Rudi stared firmly at the carpet.

'You've never heard of a Mr James Salway?'

'No.'

'Your wife appears to have been visiting Mr Salway.'

No reaction. Rudi met the detective's eye then looked away again.

'Where did you think your wife was, Mr Rabey?'

'She used to say she was seeing friends.'

'Used to say. So this was a regular occurrence?'

'Fairly regular.'

'You didn't ask for details?'

'I preferred not to know.'

'Is it likely she had her own key to the apartment?'

'She might have done.'

'You wouldn't have known?'

'She could have kept it hidden.'

'I have to tell you the circumstances of death. We suspect that your wife surprised an intruder. That suggests she had her own key. We believe Mr Salway hadn't been there for some time. It could have been a burglar, a panic situation. There were signs of struggle. The assailant then struck your wife with a glass vase. Death would have been instantaneous. We've tried for fingerprints, but nothing's come up yet.'

'Don't,' Bruce sobbed. 'Please don't.'

The policemen apologised and left.

Suspicion poisoned the funeral arrangements. Emmajane's parents, her older sisters who had both married men who now had their own businesses, the extended family of the Wayce-Dockerells, were in collective shock, but even more subdued by the lurking shame of Emmajane's body being found in the flat of a man nobody had yet put a face to.

Bruce clearly knew more than he was telling. But at least his silence protected Emmajane's name. Against all their inclinations the Wayce-Dockerells had to agree that for once he had demonstrated appropriate behaviour.

At the graveside, as young squirrels chased each other up and down the pine trunks and a warm drizzle fell, Bruce howled hysterically. For some of the Wayce-Dockerells, whose grief came in matching coordinates, this was the last straw. For others it suggested that perhaps he had cared for Emmajane after all. A pity he hadn't shown it sooner.

As a recent Christmas present Emmajane's father, an insurance broker, had given them the first six policy instalments on each other's lives. A computer had directly debited their salaries ever since. Bruce now learnt that a cheque for nearly £20,000 was coming his way.

The Ajax and Achilles gave Bruce three weeks' compassionate leave. Even Ardington regretted the impression that he had under-valued Bruce's talents. Ardington assured him that once he was back on his feet career advancement would be on the table again.

Bruce went to stay with his parents for a few days. He told nobody about the insurance money. The Midlands were ugly and boring. His parents spent the intervals between meals clearing up from one and preparing for the next. Bruce let himself blank out, a void against which new shapes of his future, wavering and jagged, were starting to form.

On his return to Lagoon Close, Bruce left a message with Rudi's landlady that he was back. As he put the phone down the doorchime tinkled. A neighbour, bosomy and anxious, with ageing hair rinsed butter yellow, offered to help clear away Emmajane's things, in case Bruce couldn't face the painful memories. She must be the woman whose Volvo estate sticker said I HEART German Shepherds. Bruce said it was nice of her but he hadn't made any decisions yet. After she had gone Bruce wondered what she was really offering. The way her lips quivered when she spoke. Because it was strange, Bruce reflected, how in life you always ended up getting what you wanted. Just the wrapping you didn't have any choice about.

As the day passed Bruce realised he was in trouble. The house was unbearable. Left to himself he couldn't fill a room. Only fantasies about the insurance money produced energy. He combed Emmajane's library of gift catalogues, playing with pictures of what money could buy. But the excitement soon drooped.

In the local freesheet, Bruce read about flying courses at Edenville International. His pulse changed gear. Whatever it cost he could afford it. Being a qualified amateur pilot would significantly upgrade his lifestyle. He was still alight with enthusiasm when Rudi phoned.

'Bruce, how things?'

'Oh, fine. It was tragic coming back here, of course. But I'm trying to make it.'

'That's good. Let's meet.'

Bruce went to collect Rudi. On the way back they stopped for sausages. Somehow you could never ruin a sausage. Bruce did them with oven-ready chips.

'One thing,' Bruce said.

'What?'

'The flat we went to.'

'The flat, yeah?' Rudi acted dumb.

'You said you'd moved in. But the police found it was in somebody else's name. It wasn't your flat.'

'No, Bruce. That's right.'

'But you had the key.'

Rudi rubbed his nose and gave a short laugh that was too controlled to be embarrassed.

'I met this guy, you know how it is. We got friendly, he said, look, he'd be away, I could borrow his apartment a few days. So I got this idea, I mean, living in this landlady place is real pits. I can't have chicks in, every time you go to the bathroom she wants to know what's going on in there, the food is like retextured horseshit. Hey, these dogs really good, by the way.'

'You said you'd moved in.'

'Figure of speech.'

'Why?'

'I thought we could all get together there, party a little. I guessed' – Rudi paused respectfully – 'Emmajane wouldn't feel easy, she knew the apartment was on loan. So I lied, a tiny lie. I'm sorry.'

'And this guy – was that Mr Salway?'

'This is what I can't work out, Bruce. A guy I met in a club, you know how it is.'

'Where is he now?'

'I didn't want you to know, man, but I scored him some dope. We did each other favour, you know. I never see him again.'

'But you had the keys.'

'Deal was, I locked up, dropped the keys through the letter slot on my way out. The police been on you again?'

Bruce's skin prickled. 'No.'

'That's good. You need peace, space to get back together. Nice quiet place here. You sticking round?'

'Yes, matter of fact –'

'What?'

'The things you were saying about the landlady – how about moving in here?'

'You sure?'

96

'I could use the company. It's not a bad place. Oh . . .'

'What?'

'I just thought of something.'

'Annie?'

'I don't think I can handle that.'

Rudi smiled, went over to Bruce and gave him a friendly smack.

'Hey man, she'll take you and me. You just had one of the great ideas of your life. Tell you what, she's working now. Let's go in and surprise her.'

As Annie entered the house, Bruce, by now drunk, made a giggling grab at her clothes. She slapped his face in a way that didn't hurt but just brushed it aside.

'Listen, sonny, if anybody's raping anybody, *I'm* gonna rape *you*. So take your time and get me some of that red Martini stuff.'

They played strip poker upstairs. Sometime after two in the morning the doorbell chimed.

Bruce froze. Frowning he put on pyjamas and a mock-silk robe with a gold lurex BR monogram. Nobody peeped round the curtains. They all thought, Police.

When Bruce opened the front door Leo Malin stumbled, almost fell, in. He grabbed Bruce's robe. Not for support, just to beat him against the wall.

Bruce raised his hands and protested. 'Hold on, hold on. What's the problem?'

Malin was drunk, swaying. Big gobbets of saliva obstructed his tongue and teeth.

'Bastard, what's going on?'

Malin needed a mouthwash. Stubble pushed out from the fat pin-cushion of his face. His eyes seemed to be looking back into his head. Fear had brought him here tonight. Somehow Bruce, although scared himself, knew it.

'Come in and sit down. Drink?'

There was no sound from upstairs. Before he opened the door Bruce had scooped Annie's bag into a cupboard. Nothing else told of company. Bruce lit a cigarette and looked at the fat man casually.

'What can I do for you?'

'What was your wife doing in that place?'

'It's very painful for me to talk about. Why?'

Malin's fingers uneasily massaged his greasy palms.

'You still on to that South American git?'

Bruce knew he had to act natural. Anything else would provoke suspicion. If Malin found Rudi there he would assume betrayal. Rudi and Annie could skip Edenville just like that, but for Bruce there would be no escape from Malin's retribution.

Annie was tied to the double bed, one limb to each leg. Rudi had enough to occupy him in the bedroom. With luck, sex had damaged his hearing.

'We meet occasionally.'

'How your wife get into that place?'

'The police said they don't know.'

'How come *you* don't know?'

'We led separate lives.'

'She meet him?'

'Him?'

'You know who we're talking about.'

Bruce realised that the more confused Malin was, the safer *he* was.

'Once or twice.'

'Night she got killed?'

'What?'

'She with him then?'

'No, I was with him.'

Malin's heavy, flushed face looked unhappy in its bafflement.

'You?'

'The police have got it on file. Ask them.'

'You this spic ever been that place?'

'No.'

'Strange your wife did, then.'

Bruce asked, 'Was it your place?'

'Why should it be?'

'So why are you so interested in it?'

Inside, Malin digestive trauma, alcoholic deep swell, and uncertainty about what time of day or night it was, made clear thought impossible.

'Seemed coincidence, that's all.'

Bruce saw his chance. Malin wanted to leave but was too stupefied and clumsy to do it.

'Well, if you don't mind I'd like to get some sleep. It's been a hard week.'

At the door Malin grunted, 'Time you got me some information, son.'

'I'm working on it,' Bruce said.

Through the curtain, Bruce watched Malin's car leave. Still no sound from upstairs. Bruce wondered if he would recover his sexual appetite. In the lounge he smoked one more cigarette then went upstairs.

Rudi was sitting cross-legged on the landing. With a big grin he aimed both his index fingers and stopped Bruce in his tracks.

FIFTEEN

The country house had been good once, the place to come. An invitation here, you were making it, on your way. Great parties, the days before everything got edgy and mean and suspicious and the old man withdrew like it was a bunker for his last stand. These days a summons here was bad news.

Malin had to wait while Churchill did a few lengths of the indoor pool, dried, put on a hooded robe. The German's solarium-tanned face was so clean of expression it was frightening. Steam was penetrating Malin's clothes. Behind each ear he felt globes of sweat emerge, roll down the corrugated flesh of his nape.

'My study,' Churchill said, 'there's a cheque for £100,000. You think it's too much?'

Malin tried to whip up confidence. 'You're paying the greaseball off?'

'No, Leo. You.'

Nothing disturbed the gentle hum of the pumping plant, the ripple of light on the pool. Malin desperately needed to unload his guts. In his own view of himself he felt ashamed. He was hard as a brick latrine, except with Churchill. The one man who *could* do this to him, *was* doing it to him.

'Nothing to say?'

'*Why?*'

'Why? That's the easy question. The one you can answer yourself, Listen.'

Churchill took a few paces along the poolside. Malin stayed. Churchill's voice was a harsh boom off the tile walls.

'I get a call from this spic who's giving me a problem. He tells me how this story I read in the papers about some girl got killed is all to do with you setting him up for a hit. I'm trying to negotiate an arrangement with this person and behind my back you, Leo, are fixing up some fucking gorilla to do a murder.'

Churchill glanced round, eyes flashing.

'What the fuck game is this, Leo? Lately everything you touch is a screw up. The plastic surgeon, the man on the boat – you can't cut it, Leo. At the critical moment you fail. Fail yourself, fail me. And now you're, what, in business on your own? I'm in the middle of a deal and you're out there organising for this person to get his skull cracked. Instead of which some whore gets chopped down, and how the hell this never comes back to you and me I'll never know.'

At the end Churchill's voice screamed. Malin knew he was finished. A boyish sense of injustice made him protest.

'I did it for you, boss.'

'What is this, you're appealing against the facts?'

'I wanted to get straight with you. I know I let you down on the boat. I wanted to get your trust back.'

'I only ever trusted you to carry out orders, Leo. I never trusted you to think.'

'It was a neat way out the problem. I had to take the opportunity. There was no time to discuss.'

'This dago boy out-thought you, you realise that?'

Malin had still only half washed all that through his mind.

'I dunno –'

Churchill gave a coughing laugh. 'Then permit me to tell you. And not only that. He now believes that all your moves were directed by me. This weakens me in my dealings with him. But the one thing I can't forgive is that it makes me look *stupid!*'

Churchill stripped off the robe and lowered himself back into the water. He swam in slow circles. Malin knew all the signs. Once he climbed out again, that was it. Malin tracked the German along the pool.

'Boss, look, all I wanted was to right things with you. Show you I can operate on my own, not just taking orders. I mean, come on, boss, see it my way. I work for you all my life, sooner or later you got to retire. How do I show you I'm fit to take over some of the action?'

Churchill gave no sign of listening or tiring in the water. Malin began to repeat himself, to stumble, pause, depressed by treading up and down the humid poolside. He couldn't spell or pronounce ritual humiliation, but he knew everything else about it.

Finally Churchill climbed out again, behaving as if alone. Back in his robe he beckoned Malin to follow him. By the time they reached the study Churchill's barely suppressed fury had returned.

'Let me tell you one thing, Leo. I don't plan to retire. The day I die I will still be smarter than you, stronger than you. In the times when we needed muscle you were useful to me. But for years now I've been carrying you. The party's over. There is £100,000 here, plus you get £50,000 per annum as long as you stay away from the business. Better if you leave town. But you make one more problem for me, there won't be anywhere you can go.'

'Boss, boss, please –'

'In one minute, Leo, I tear up the cheque. You're out anyway.'

'Please, boss –'

'You see, Leo, the greaseball, you call him, out-thought you. Right now he's trying to out-think me. Who needs corned beef any more, Leo? Brains are the thing. In a businessman I need the best. Anybody comes all the way from Colombia and wants in that bad, maybe he's the man I need, Leo.'

Malin's face was a pudge of misery. Tears misted his vision. Even Churchill's iron contempt could not stop them.

Churchill glanced at his watch.

'Twenty seconds.'

Malin picked up the cheque. Churchill sneered, turned his back.

The house was as unlike an English country mansion as you could get, given that it was one. It reminded Rudi of a motel, a long flat building with lots of glass facing the sun, wings and annexes tacked on all over the place. Birches screened it, and to the south paddocks spread for some hundreds of yards to the property's tree-lined border.

The kitchen was oak panelled and ultra-modern. Churchill poured coffee.

'Well,' he said, 'the car is OK?'

'Fine,' Rudi said. 'I never expected the loan of a car.'

'Call it goodwill. After the story you told me I had to do something to make up.'

'I appreciate it. This is really nice place.'

'You brought something.'

'Just some xeroxes.'

Rudi unzipped the leather case and handed the papers. Churchill looked them over, registered no emotion.

Gently, almost kindly, he said, 'Enough to hang me, you think?'

Rudi gave a boyish, embarrassed smile. White teeth, brown skin, blue eyes. Handsome, Churchill thought. Inter-racial breeding was degenerate, where had he heard that?

'I don't want they hang you. Where you get that idea?'

'Everybody misunderstands all that wartime stuff anyway,' Churchill said. 'I don't know what your pa told you.'

'He told me that you personally supervised a massacre of a couple hundred people.'

Rudi blew on his bowl of coffee.

'Plus, through the winter '44–'45 the Germans, specially SS, ate well while the Dutch had all the food taken away. I been hearing these stories for years, starving bodies in the streets, cannibalism. I know about how *Sturmbannführer* Goltz traded the life of some old Jew who had somehow escaped the round-ups for the private art collection which this old Jew had built up the last fifty years. Then had the old Jew killed anyway. Trouble is, there's family who survived, some in Holland, some in Israel, and they still remember the old Jew and his pictures, and the smiling SS officer who called one day and said everything would be just dandy.'

'A long-ago war,' Churchill said. 'What's it to you?'

Rudi wanted to smoke, so they went outside. In another part of the property extensive flower and vegetable gardens, greenhouses where tomatoes and grapes ripened, trellises hung with roses, suggested that somebody else lived here.

The peace was ripped apart by the wild howl of a dog, indoors, just as suddenly stilled again. High in the blue sky a light aircraft buzzed down towards Edenville International.

'Don't get me wrong,' Rudi said. 'I didn't come here to judge you. It's strictly business.'

'The war was business,' Churchill said. 'People don't understand. Nations go to war to *steal*, like efficient companies swallow up inefficient ones. The killing is just one of those things.'

'Right,' Rudi said. 'Matter of fact, the SS have always been sort of hero figures to me, *SS Mann, deine Ehre heisst Treue*. Loyalty is honour, on the cap badges, right? If Germany hadn't lost the war they wouldn't have got such a bad press.'

'You know, Rudi – may I call you Rudi? – you surprise me all the time.'

'Well, I guess we got off on a bad footing. My fault, I apologise. How you like me to call you?'

'There is a small group of people who call me Eric. I think it's time you joined them.'

'Feel really honoured you treat me like this.'

A chill entered Churchill's voice. 'Fine. Can we do business now? This is what I propose. First, forget about money. I give you money, you'll soon be back for more. Anyway, I don't have that kind of money. It's all tied up. What I offer you is a job.'

'A job?'

'You've proved yourself a very smart young man. You become my *numero uno*. I fix work permits and everything, no problem.'

'What about the fat man?'

'Yes or no?'

'Absolutely yes.'

'The fat man's out. Gone.'

'What about all the stuff I got on you?'

'You keep it for six months. At the end of six months you either hand it over to me, everything, or leave my organisation.'

'Reasonable.'

'Well, I think reasonable. I want you to take a week, think it over. Then we'll talk again, hard data. You mind if I ask you a personal question?'

'Sure.'

'Have you ever killed anybody?'

Rudi lied, 'Yeah.'

Churchill laughed, 'In Colombia it's easier, right?'

'Happens all the time.'

'Hot blood or cold blood?'

Rudi's blue eyes never moved. 'What you think?'

Cars began to pull in as evening came on, class German makes, Japanese luxury models. It had been a busy, well-orchestrated day at the country house. For a lone wolf, Churchill spent a lot of time with people. But always business. He was a lonely man, in the sense that power set you apart, but the loneliness of power was one of life's great sensual pleasures. It was what half the dumb bastards in the world wanted and couldn't admit.

Sunset over the distant edge of the forest flooded the wall-size windows as in the drawing room a dozen men slowly assembled. Designer silk, lightweight suits, state-of-the-art dental repair in the smiles, all shades of tan from the mild bronze of good health to the swart of two Arab guests, gathered together, making eye contact, seeking messages to read. On the bar were glasses and mineral water. Nothing to detract from the sobriety of the occasion.

A burly man in a chocolate suit with widely spaced stripes stepped forward and said, 'Gentlemen, as Mr Churchill's lawyer may I declare these proceedings open.'

He indicated a long deep-shine table, walnut, with matching period chairs. Before anyone moved he added, 'Let's see if we can put a price on an empire.'

SIXTEEN

Bruce giggled and said, 'Know what I've got in my pocket?'

Rudi said no.

'Three hundred pounds. Know what I'm going to do?'

Rudi laughed. Bruce drunk was amusing, his most likeable.

'No.'

'I'm going to walk in the Roxy and stack it all on red. No, black.'

'Red or black,' Rudi said.

'Definitely one of those. Think I'm chicken?'

'No, man, I believe you.'

Pedestrianised streets wet after rain. Night-time shops, windows lit, sleeping open-eyed. Outside the Edenville McDonalds, groups of French and German adolescents were making insulting gestures and squaring up to fight.

The smoked-glass cubicle of the Roxy entrance was a buffer of darkness between the street and the yellow light of the gaming floor within. Rudi looked about warily as they entered but saw nobody he didn't want to see.

Two tables were playing, half occupied by the usual midweek crowd, glazed down-homers convinced they had mastered the anarchy of chance or out to impress their heavily powdered companions. Hushed rock music played through the smoky air.

Bruce and Rudi watched 36 come up. Hands scratched the number on the in-house tally cards. Then 3 came up, and for the next spin heaps of dinky plastic chips crowded the middle section of the baize. Thirty-six struck again and the mounds of plastic were raked away. Grim silent punters marked cards, quickly rethought their systems. What did it mean, Red Red Red? Bruce leaned across to the girl croupier.

'Three hundred on black, OK?'

The girl turned to the ladderman. Also in the staff uniform of pink shirt with black bow tie, a porky young man with wispy blond hair and dark puddles below his eyes, the ladderman yawned and said, 'Three hundred on black.' A rare bet for eleven-thirty midweek, but his stupor survived.

The croupier recounted the fifteen twenties which Bruce had flamboyantly slapped down, trowelled them into the guts of the table, allocated Bruce three gold-rimmed chips. The other punters held breath, jiggled remaining chips, watched hopes of breaking even recede.

One, two, three. Bruce dropped the counters on black. A long slow spin. Twenty-two hit. BLACK!

Bruce punched the air. His face was like one of those stick-on wobbly-eyed toys. Excitement was loosening his wires. As Bruce bucked his shoulders for a long session Rudi looked round.

He said, 'It's your night, baby,' patted Bruce's arm, and walked away.

Malin could have been upstairs eating, or come in later and spotted them. Whichever, he was at the door. He was talking to people in the crowd round the bar but staring down at the gaming floor. Massaging his right fist in his palm, an unhappy man.

Rudi guessed Churchill had straightened Malin out. He refused eye contact and went to the blackjack tables. Two well-heeled Turks were playing with malign intensity, and a white-haired old man with a lordly presence sleepily watched his chips disappear. A large big-chested girl in pink and black dealt to him like a machine.

Rudi waited. After a minute the old boy finally said, 'Thank you, my dear,' and pushed his remaining chips across as a tip. Rudi stepped in. The judge reshuffled the deck. As the girl handed Rudi the plastic card to insert where he wanted the deck cut, Rudi said, 'Can I get a sandwich and coffee?' He had noticed girls bringing trays to the tables.

The big-chested dealer said, 'Ask her,' and pointed to another pink-and-black girl. Rudi went across. When he was close enough he took out a twenty and whispered to the girl with the tray, 'There a back way out of here?'

The girl indicated a doorway off the gaming area. There were many of these, avenues to differently priced seats from the Roxy's cinema days. Rudi laid the note on the tray and quickly swung the door shut behind him.

He ran along the tunnel. The rear exit was clear, not the usual garbage-filled alley, but an opulent door with marble steps below a classical plaster front, the former picture palace entrance.

The street was a dead-end service road. Trees overhung a solitary lamp. Rudi was halfway along when somebody stepped out. An oriental face, a switchblade click. Other footsteps. They had seen him leave. Then Malin arrived. A car did a zig-zag reverse then squealed away after they all got in.

The driver knew where to go. Nobody spoke. Trong, the Vietnamese, in the back with Rudi, caressed the knife. Malin's silent bulk overspilled the front passenger seat. They stopped at a demolition site, thirty acres of shut-down factory razed for development. Big white hoardings displayed artist visions of home-charm superstores above wire-mesh fences, signs of dogs with bared teeth. The compound stretched away into a dark rubble of spoil tips, twisted wreckage, hollow girder shapes sketching hypermarkets to come. The traffic sound was distant.

They hustled Rudi along to a place the trucks used for turning and came to a stop in the middle of brickstacks and sections of concrete piping. The only light came from a full moon low over Edenville. In its lividness Malin stared for a long time into Rudi's face.

'Want to walk away from here, you're gonna tell me a few things.'

'What I can,' Rudi said.

'What you fucking can, then some.'

Malin signalled the others to move away. Trong and the driver watched from the shadows.

'I wanna know what power you have.'

'What power?'

'We both know who we're talking about. You got power over him. In the next five minutes I better find out why.'

'What I get if I tell you?'

'We just scare you a little bit. You don't tell me, we scare you so fucking bad you're on the next plane back to whatever wog shithole you come from. Follow me?'

'Hey man, you're all wrong. I ain't no danger to you.'

The dumb spic act would only go so far. Churchill hadn't been fooling. Malin was out. In the moonlight his face was ugly and gross. Hurt, too.

Ponderously aggressive, Malin said, 'Why is the man scared of you?'

'He's not scared of me. He's paying me off for some business, man. What's it to you?'

'Don't give me that shit. He's making you his partner, right?'

Rudi changed approach. 'If he is, should you be doing this?'

Malin leered. He was no psycho, just brutal. He needed to be aroused.

'That's right, bastard, fighting talk. Let's really get the fingers in. What you gonna do to me?'

'I don't want no trouble with you.'

'Son, you got trouble. You came to this town for trouble. You didn't want aggravation, you'd stayed in dagoland.'

'Business is business, man. People like you and me shouldn't be discussing in this garbage tip.'

'The whole fucking town's a garbage tip. That's why you came.'

'We gonna deal, or what?'

'Fucking joking.'

Malin gestured sideways. He took something and pulled it on his hands. Rudi watched for the gleam of brass. But they were heavy-duty work gloves, reinforced leather knuckles.

'Just let you know you got no future round here. Don't think the man's gonna protect you. One tiny squeal, mate, he disappears. Got any sense, you're out here pretty fucking quick.'

Malin zipped one big gloved fist into Rudi's belly. Rudi doubled up, making no sound, provoking no gesture. Malin was a pounder, no expert. He thumped out at the dark shape in front of him. Rudi took it. His strong card was silence. He refused to hit back or go down. On the ground they would kick him.

Malin paused, breathing hard, maybe afraid he was getting carried away. Rudi wiped away blood.

He said, 'Everything you do to me you get back.'

Malin piled one last blow into Rudi's body. It made them both gasp, Rudi stagger. Only some smashed brickwork at his back kept him on his feet.

'Get a plane ticket, greaseball, 'cause next time I don't piss about.'

Malin's crew disappeared through the site. Long before their car started up Rudi was crawling about in the rubble. All his suppressed fear now spilt out. His body ached, his face was swelling. The place stank of earth soaked with petrol. He retched at his own blood smell. He levered himself up on some mangled iron, dragged himself towards the far-off streetlights. In the blank bald moon that rode the sky unchallenged, Rudi saw the hard inscrutable face of Eric Churchill.

Slowly and painfully he walked arterial roads till he reached the familiar chalet-type homes of Bruce's estate. On the way people ignored him, a drunk they crossed the street to avoid. Three boys with shaved heads stepped out to mug him, took one look at his face, said 'Fucking hell!' and turned away again. In Bruce's house the lights were on.

Politely Rudi brushed off enquiries and help. In the bathroom he cleaned up, rubbed salve on, swallowed painkiller. A drink and a cigarette, he felt better.

Fascinated, anxious, Bruce wanted to know how. Rudi forced bulging lips into a smile.

'Guy thought I'm somebody else.'

Bruce had not even seen him leave the casino. That was another story.

'Hey, the money,' Rudi said. 'How much you end up with?'

Then he realised that Bruce had been sick enough without an assault victim ringing the doorbell at two a.m.

'I blew it.'

'Whole three hundred?'

'*Six* hundred.'

'Oh man.'

Rudi knew immediately what sort of night Bruce had spent. The wheel had exacted revenge. Bruce had refused to concede till his wallet gaped like a corpse's mouth. There was nothing like the washed-out scorn of the croupiers or the indifference of those who played on while the big loser lurched blindly away from the table.

Bruce shrugged, defiant. 'I can afford it.'

Rudi knew he was lying. It was always a lie. Forget money. *Losing* you could never afford.

Annie was in a corner, sullen. The Scottish girl had a bright side. Faced with two of the night's casualties she would normally try to cheer them up. But she hadn't a bean of cheerfulness for anybody.

Rudi asked her.

'I lost my job.'

Trade is down, the Lebanese had said. Panties not down, he meant. No need for finesse now, he tried to drag her outside the kitchen door and mount her body clothed. Annie hit him in the face with a dish of hummus and left. It was worth three days' wages.

'Hey,' Rudi said, 'some night.'

On the news of the insurance coming in, Bruce had impulse bought six bottles of Mirage. Maybe for an occasion like this. He opened one.

Rudi lay feet up on the sofa. The drink was lifting him pleasantly as the pain diffused. Good aches and bad aches, he thought. Even through the bruises the sight of Annie was still a good ache. Briefly he wondered if Churchill had softened him up in the afternoon and put Malin in for the kill at night. But it didn't add up. Malin was a pig with a sore arse, the wrong style. The German had just thrown the switches then left them to it. For Malin and him, Rudi, to destroy each other, was exactly what Churchill wanted. Rudi saw it with total clarity because if he was Churchill that was what he would want.

Annie could never stand grim silences. Husky from cigarettes and too many damp rooms, mocking, she sang, 'Oh, I do like to be beside the seaside —'

'Bloody shut up!' Bruce yelled. 'For Christ's sake, just bloody shut up.'

Annie grinned. 'Oh, is Brucie angry because he pissed his money away down a drainie-wainie?'

Bruce was floundering through one of his periodic depressions about Emmajane. He had betrayed Emmajane with Annie, and Rudi's manipulations had brought about her death. He should have kept his head down, worked hard, made a decent life for his poor Emmajane.

'Shut up, you fucking cow!'

Bruce screeched the words, hurled an ashtray. The onyx scarred the vinyl wallcovering above Annie's head. Filtertips and grains of ash sprinkled the room.

Rudi said, 'Hey Bruce, Annie lost her job. Don't give her a hard time.'

'Forget it,' Annie said, 'I've had it with this place. Tomorrow I'm out of here.'

'Oh Christ!' Bruce buried his face in his hands.

'Hey Annie,' Rudi said. 'Where to?'

'Just away from this fuck-awful town. Creeps like Bruce grabbing my tits all the time.'

'Don't call me a creep,' Bruce said. 'You scrubber.'

'See what I mean?'

Rudi said, 'Listen, how about I offer you both something really good?'

SEVENTEEN

It was one of those coincidences that either makes your heart pound or your skin crawl, depending.

'How you going, Leo?'

'Coasting, mate. Funny, been thinking about you.'

'How's that?'

'Thought I might come up the Smoke, check you out.'

'For what?'

'Pick up on last time.'

'My recall says not a friendly discussion.'

'Things change.'

'Don't they.'

'Down here for your health?'

'Sort of.'

'Wanna talk?'

'Why not?'

They walked through the lower gardens, past the teddy-bears-for-charity stall, through the crumbling mosaic pillars of the flyover, on to the paved space at the pierhead. Beneath a row of national flags that the sea wind was slapping around, a Salvation Army band played melancholy hymns to the evening crowds. Feathery cloud hung low along the sea front. A hamburger stand's frying onions competed with the universal reek of seaweed, chips and vinegar.

At the end of the pier the force of the wind was like being caught between two invisible sumo wrestlers. The beach, the people ambling along the incoming tideline, seemed far away.

'Nice town. Might get used to it.'

'Bit sleepy for London boys.'

'Not what I hear, Leo. Anyway, you wanted to talk, so talk.'

'Your people still interested in down here?'

'Why?'

'I'm in the market.'

'Buying or selling?'

'Open to bids.'

'Thing is, we ain't down here for the ozone. Know what I mean?'

'How's that?'

'Can't talk specifics, Leo. Work it out.'

'Your outfit buying in?'

'Seen a lot of faces around. Some not nice as yours.'

'I know this place better than my own dick.'

'Sure, Leo. Trouble is, my people import their own talent. Just the way they are. Never take home-grown.'

'Could work,' Malin said, covering up.

'Shit, Leo, a man your talent soon gonna get back. Maybe change towns be smart thinking.'

'What I had in mind.'

'We're staying at that place over there. White one. Got a whole floor.'

Malin said, 'They're all white,'

'Could really get to like this town. Punters looking for holes to throw money down. Air you can bottle at one hundred per cent profit. Cunt on a stick. Sensational.'

The Roxy was the one place Malin habitually went which Churchill did not own. From the others he had removed all trace of his occupancy. Nothing had been put in writing, nobody had said anything, but Malin knew that he would suddenly find entrances barred by muscle-bound punks who had previously leaked in their pants when they saw him coming.

Malin was a cheerful bully. He would whack a guy round the head then buy him a drink. The only thing that boiled him was people laughing at him. It hadn't happened in a long time. He was not about to go looking for it now.

He had his apartment, but he never spent much time there. He didn't know how to spend time there. He also didn't know how to express anger except in physical violence or drink. The Roxy seemed like all he had left.

Even when the bar was jammed they always served Malin fast. This time he took his dry-roast nuts and Irish Cream to the TV alcove. The alcove seats were covered in fake polar-bear fur. The wide screen flickered in a dark corner, low volume, unwatched.

The thought of the 100,000 plus 50K a year was keeping Malin afloat. Moneywise he was set up. He had the contacts, a man of substance in Edenville, exuding power, receiving respect. But one idea burst persistently in his mind like a tray of popping corn. The hundred grand was a scam. The cheque would be delayed, the 50K was a fairy tale. Churchill was stringing him along. Off the payroll Malin had no clout, none of the pull this South American greaser seemed to carry. Churchill wouldn't spit on a man dying of thirst. A pension for Leo Malin, forget it.

Malin smarted at how easily life could take a dive down the toilet. He had started out as a debt repayment enforcer for Churchill's tenement company, then graduated to property manager when the market took off and tenants needed the right kind of handling. From there on, no limit. The German had stroked from Malin powers nobody ever dreamed he possessed. And now he had snapped his fingers to take it all back. Fucking master race, what did you expect? But Malin was sore.

His mouth chewed the last spice-coated nuts to a pulp. His stomach cried for proper lining. Especially under tension Malin's tastes outdid the cravings of a pregnant woman. A seafood pizza packed with mussels should do, washed down with chartreuse, followed by the long slow rape of a sweet trolley.

Malin looked up. That long streak of piss from the bank was standing there. A gormless plonker, like the juvenile lead from some old British movie.

He said, 'Got a minute?'

'Fuck off,' Malin said.

Bruce sat down on one of the polar-bear seats.

'Somebody wants to talk to you.'

'Don't make me laugh.'

'It's true.'

'Who the fuck are you, Al Capone?'

'His name's Rudi St Paul. You beat him up last night.'

Malin bristled. 'Watch what you're saying, mate.'

'It's all right. He's prepared to overlook that. He wants to talk business.'

'Like what fucking business?'

'You want me to go back and tell him no?'

'Where?'

'My car's outside.'

Bruce had parked on the double yellows and not got a ticket. He felt good, like winning roulette on the first stake. Malin's bulk steamed up the windows. Bruce had the fan full on all the way back to Lagoon Close.

The plan was: Bruce and Annie would go out while the meeting took place. Little brochures of paradise kept opening up in Bruce's mind like boutiques in an Edenville high street. But once in the car Annie said, 'Don't want to worry you, but I think I've got clap.'

'Oh Jesus!' Bruce punched the steering wheel. The Metro scraped the kerb.

'Well, it's itchy and pouring out some smelly gunge, that's all I know.'

'Shit, shit, *shit!* I've been itching too. I've been peeling –'

'Peeling where?'

'Off the end of my, you know –'

'Off the end of your *you know!* Well!'

'You don't think it's AIDS, do you?'

'How the fuck would I know? You're the one that reads the papers.'

'Oh God, I suppose this means –'

'That's right, you can't dip your winkie in my honey pot.'

Bruce groaned. Annie added, 'I may be wrong, it might just be thrush.'

'*Thrush*'?

'Yeah. You know, your chest gets spotty and you whistle a lot.'

As Annie went out Malin went in. Anger still bubbled in him and his fists clenched reflexively. As far as anyone could look gracious with a face swollen and purpled, Rudi was gracious as he ushered Malin in.

'Come in. Sit down.'

Malin was reluctant to do either.

Rudi said, 'Forget this, OK?'

'Don't be fucking stupid. You're not gonna forget it.'

'I got a deal for you.'

'Why me?'

'Way I see it, we're in the same position. Same enemy.'

'How come he's your enemy?'

'He's set us up to wipe each other out, you and me. And while we're fighting he's gonna pull some trick leaves us both –'

'Up shit creek,' Malin concurred. 'Right.'

'I'm interested in this country house. You know it?'

'Know it? Seen him build it.'

'Churchill built it?'

'Twenty years ago.'

'When you say *he* built it –'

'Had a company, didn't he? Building sub-contracts – forty men at three pounds an hour, and he paid them two pounds an hour. You work that out. Those days, that was tough money.'

'He's still got this company?'

'Yeah, one of the legits. The iffy loot gets shunted through the front outfits.'

'The house has just the one storey?'

'Yeah. Maybe a basement.'

'A basement.'

While Churchill was in the bathroom Rudi had looked in a utility cupboard. A wiring conduit, heavy cable, ran down through the floor.

'You been in this basement?'

'No.'

'Who looks after the place?'

'Man and woman run things. Live in.'

'Security?'

'Intruder alarms everywhere, two Dobermans, shotgun.'

'They know you, this couple?'

'Should do. I got them the job.'

'I want to get into this place very badly. You interested in the rewards?'

'Sure, why not?'

'OK, we keep in touch. Fine.'

When Malin was leaving Rudi went to the kitchen and then came back. He pointed to his face.

'Problem is, I said I'd get you for this. And you can't trust me, cause like you know I meant it.'

His other hand snaked from behind his back. The razor tip of a four-inch blade gashed Malin's jaw.

Malin gasped, clapped a hand to the pain. Blood spurted. Rudi held the knife extended against any comeback.

'Quits now. That's finished. Accept?'

Malin accepted.

Two hours later the casualty department at Edenville General had laced ten stitches through Leo Malin's jaw – shaving cut, he insisted – and dressed it. Malin drove home and rang Churchill's number, the number very few people had ever been given.

For the German it had been another taxing day of business. Then he had seen his chiropractor, dined well, had a little S-M genital relief, and was thinking of turning in. Malin's voice brought out a steely irritation.

The fat man pleaded to talk. Churchill considered. Malin was no longer family. But the break had been clean, and an outsider with something to trade should always be given an ear. He told Malin to come directly, and rang down to brief the night guard.

When Churchill heard that Rudi was planning against him he showed no surprise. His small twinkling eyes stared hard at Malin. The SS officer in his death's-head cap with total power over helpless subhumans was still running the show.

'What puzzles me, Leo, is your interest.'

'I want back in, boss. To go against you sticks in my throat.'

'The spic is using you, Leo, can't you see that?'

'I know about the solicitor.'

Churchill's eyebrows moved. 'Solicitor?'

'He told me he's blackmailing you, and all the stuff is at some lawyer's. He was out the room, I looked through letters he had around the place. Like this one.'

Malin produced a sheet of headed vellum. It said that Jacques, Dowson and Walsh were changing premises, with dates, old and new addresses, and the assurance of uninterrupted service to their clients. Impassively Churchill noted the details and returned the paper.

'He'll miss the letter?'

'He'll think he's mislaid it. When I go back I'll drop it behind something.'

'You're going back?'

'First thing the morning. He wants to know if I'm in.'

'And your answer?'

'Depends on you, boss.'

'Your face, what happened?'

'I met a plastic surgeon.'

Churchill's laughter was ghostly, mirthless, but he got the point.

'Thing is,' Malin said, 'I hear you're selling out.'

Churchill was cool, challenged nothing. 'Bits and pieces. I've done it before, Leo. The organisation's too big. Where you think your hundred grand's coming from?'

'Sooner forget the money and be back in with you, boss.'

'We have to adapt, Leo. Time you make it on your own. Who knows, maybe one day you employ me.'

'You want me in or not? This guy is out to bleed you.'

'What's he offering?'

'A share of the take. Plus the blackmail stuff.'

'So *you* will blackmail me?'

'General idea.'

'Why not do it? You don't even want to know what the stuff is?'

'Couldn't do it, boss. I can't send you down. You been my life.'

'Well,' Churchill said, 'loyalty is important, that's very true. One thing is not clear. The spic made you this proposal in return for what?'

'Am I back in?'

'OK, you got a chance to redeem yourself. What?'

119

'The house. He's got this thing about the house.'

Amazed, Churchill said, 'Why?'

'That bit, he won't say.'

'So what's he laying out?'

'He's gonna take the house apart.'

'You told him the arrangements there?'

'I had to tell him some. Or why should he tell me anything?'

'All right. He has muscle?'

'Me, I guess, is all at the moment.'

'Right, I take care of the house. You stay with the brown-skin.'

'Had this idea, boss. I could fix a team watch at the house.'

'No, you stay with the spic. Leave the house to me.'

'Yeah.' Malin paused. 'Right, that's the best idea.'

But Malin knew he had blown it. He had hesitated, thought about it a moment too long. The one thing that had not gone the way Rudi had planned. Get the German to agree to you putting a watch on the house. But Churchill didn't want it that way, Malin had registered the setback, and the German had read it instantly.

Churchill stood up to look at the lights along the bay.

'Return that letter. Talk to our dago friend. Think how we hit the solicitor's. Call me before lunch. Good to have you back, Leo.'

Churchill offered his hand. In spite of himself Malin's eyes moistened. Churchill's thin lips smiled kindly.

As Malin left Churchill gazed at the night-time view again. The other side of the darkness lay Switzerland. Churchill already had funds there. Now, day by day, he had more. In most things Churchill was an old-fashioned man, but the microtech world beguiled his love of efficiency. Money no longer depended on traceable bits of paper, but winged its way gracefully, almost at light speed, across continents. Time for a new life. Switzerland the location. On all the freeways into town happyland signs declared that Edenville was twinned with Unterbogelberg, Switzerland. *Ein gutes Vorzeichen*, a fair omen. It would be good to speak German again.

Next morning Rudi called at the offices of Jacques, Dowson and Walsh, where he retrieved the packages he had left there. The arrangement by which they would be mailed to their addressees if a week elapsed without him calling, he terminated.

Rudi took his envelopes and taped them into one large padded bag which he then sent to Bruce Rabey, registered mail, at Lagoon Close. He recorded himself as sender, care of the Ace Language Academy, where he was still a fee-paying student. Then he told Bruce and Annie not to answer the door in the mornings, particularly to postmen. Rudi had learnt that if the recipient was not there to sign for the package, the postman had to take it away again. After a week they wrote to the addressee inviting him to call and claim it. After another month they returned unclaimed packages to the sender, every stage signed for. Short of burying the papers, Rudi couldn't think of a better way to hide them.

EIGHTEEN

Malin drove up to Churchill's country house. Rudi knew nothing of Malin's visit, the German himself did not know Malin was there. Even Malin did not know why he had gone there. But his guts – well larded with game pie, a whole Camembert which breathed the smells of a Normandy farmyard, finished off with an obscene gateau – his guts directed him out here.

An unexpected figure, not one of the married couple who formed the live-in maintenance, appeared in the drive. Malin stopped, opened the window to a tall man with frizzed hair, body muscle straining a technicolour tee-shirt.

'Leo.'

'What you doing here, Gary?'

'Working, mate. What the fuck's going on, Leo?'

'What about the shop?'

Malin was referring to FLICK.

'Don't ask me about no fucking shop.'

'Get in here.'

Malin reversed away from possibly being seen by the caretakers. He asked Gary, 'What's going down?'

Gary was a Malin protégé. Twenty-two years old, expelled from school for physical abuse of female teachers, his sheet listed petty theft, sexual misdemeanour with minors, and extorting money from elderly residents as payment for 'property renovation'. Gary had done two short sentences, then Malin had steered him towards a positive future. He alternated club doorman with sex-shop minder.

'What's going down is, I don't fucking know, right, but I'm in the shop, right, and some fucking coon walks in. Imagine that, Leo, spades in Edenville. Not one of these rich Africans with a twenty-inch cock wrapped in folding money. Just some blubbery-lipped piece of shit from London, swans in, right, on these high heels, gold chains, the fucking works. Looks at me like I'm standing in the corner having a wank, right, says: hey, baby, under new management, you're outa here. All this cool dude riff, feeling up the merchandise and giggling. Know what the bastard did? Only stuck a big pink dildo in front of me and said: hey, man, we didn't have time for no gold watch. Next thing I'm expecting that scarfaced bastard to stroll back in, guy what took the place apart.'

'He left town,' Malin said.

'Done the right fucking thing. So I'm about to tell this nigger cocksucker to get the fuck out, and who comes in but Mr Lord Shitface Snedker.'

'Snedker?'

'Right, plus some smoothie with a rug job and a camel coat. I mean, a camel coat in summer. Who are these arseholes?'

Snedker was a financial consultant Churchill used. Malin had always avoided him. Gold-rimmed glasses, striped suits, keen jawline, smiling aggressive mouth.

'What that shit want?'

'Only told me to piss off, didn't he? Asked how much I was due, in front these other scumbuckets, wrote the cheque just like that. Cheeky fucker. Give me all this smile crap, then says: right, got another job if you want it. So I'm out here, enn I?'

'Doing like what?' Malin asked.

'Can't figure it. Prowlers about, lot of nob properties get done out here, Snedker says. Back-up for Darby and Joan over there.'

'They got a twelve-bore and a couple dogs live on canned human throat. What support they need?'

'Don't tell me, mate. I met them. But these dogs, right, the old guy snaps his fingers, they lay down, roll over, take their teeth out and put 'em in a glass.'

'Only if he snaps his left fingers,' Malin said. 'He snaps his right, they kill you.'

123

'Shit,' Gary said, 'let's hope he don't forget which is which.'

'You're like pissed off, then?' Malin asked.

'You kidding? I was on a good number, right. You know me, Leo, work my fucking tits off, I like what I'm doing. Then they lay this on me, security adviser Snedker calls it, fucking piss artist. Good earner, right, don't get me wrong. But talk about fucking crazy. Drop a filter tip and I got Cruella De Ville yelling at me. What I do twelve hours a fucking day, watch my pubic hair grow?'

'Twelve hours?'

'Twelve till twelve, late. Some other face does the other half.'

'You were here last night?'

'Right, yeah.'

'Anything happen?'

'Some old guy turned up. Just when I was going off.'

'Old guy?'

'Seemed like he lived here. Who the fuck *does* live here?'

'What you see?'

'What can I tell you? The other shift was coming on, that face, what's his name, everybody calls him Frogman.'

'Scobie.'

'Scobie, right. I just want to get the fuck out. That's what I did.'

'You met the old guy?'

'Not really. The odd couple catered that one. Me, I'm just the meathead, get the picture. They said who I was. Geezer looks at me, says work hard for good money, right. Just like that. Real concentration camp number, know what I mean? Total fleshcreep.'

'Seen Snedker again?'

'No way. Said he'd be round every two, three days. What the fuck's going on, Leo?'

'Trying to find out. Catch you later, son.'

Gary took the cue and got out. Malin drove up to the house and went round to the caretaker's quarters by the kitchen garden.

Malin's appearances here needed no explanation. Unless Churchill had set the MacBryans against him. But Malin found no sign of this in the lined sunburnt features of Andrew MacBryan as he gave him the usual tour of the gardens.

'Greatest food I ever ate,' Malin said. 'And totally organic, right?'

MacBryan pointed to fronds of celery pushing up through a long mound of soil.

'Grown on chickenshit, the best. Give you some when you leave.'

'How things, Andy?'

'Never better.'

'Great life.'

'Great, mate.'

'Yeah, great. Into the hothouse fruit now, then?'

'Don't go away.'

MacBryan came out with a bunch of seedless white grapes. Through a mouthful of sweet pulp Malin said, 'Had the estate agents here, then?'

'Estate agents?'

'Fuller and Broadhead. Seen their van on the road. Thought maybe they been here.'

'No, mate, no way they was here.'

'Just like, a guy was taking pictures. Not inside the grounds, don't misunderstand me. Sort of outside.'

'What you reckon, then?'

'Valuation? Place is a telephone number now. Property out here, you're looking at silly money. Guy out in the sticks had this old thatched place, rats' nests, woodworm, acre of thistles. Went to auction, only took a hundred eighty grand. Some consortium bought it, never even seen it. So what's this lot worth?'

MacBryan fussed with the bird nets over some soft fruit. He seemed troubled, apart from Malin's efforts to disturb him.

'Wife and myself thinking of retirement. Wife's people run a hotel on the east coast, always needing help. Dunno if the old man might sling us a few quid when we go.'

'Absolutely no problem, Andy. Job you done here, you must added five figures on the value. Total class, hits people soon as they drive in. Listen, who's the face on the gate?'

'Old man wants extra security. Lot of break-ins, these big places. Burglar alarms no good, no bugger hears them.'

'See much the old man lately?'

'Joking. Only every night.'

'Don't say.'

'Always a gent. Real manners.'

'Old style. It's all flash now. Poncey tat, who needs it? Sleeping out here, is he?'

'No, no. Just comes for the hour, then away again.'

Notice anything strange, way he behaves?'

'Can't say so. Why?'

'Something's getting to him. Thought maybe he comes here to escape. Peace of mind routine. Am I right?'

'All I know is, he goes down below for an hour, comes up again, drives away.'

'Down below?'

'The cellars.'

'Yeah, I remember it being built. Always figured, air-raid shelter. World War III number. You been down there?'

'Never. Strictly *verboten*, mate, down there.'

'You reckon what, private porno theatre?'

'Beats me. Keep my nose out.'

'Reason I come out here is, is to say your missus, her birthday's soon, right? September, something like that?'

'October.'

'Yeah. She's what, fifty?'

'Fifty-three.'

'Anyway, on me, my treat. Write the menu in person, touch of the night-life scenario. For many favours received.'

'What can I say, Leo? Knockout. Who done your face?'

'You'd never believe it.'

Malin went and said a brief hello to Dolly MacBryan, then made an exit. Along the drive he picked up Gary again.

'Where you kip these days?'

'Split a drum with some skirt, don't I? Real dumper, slag-style, know what I mean? But mucho screwo, can't leave, can I? Every time my legs walk out my dong pulls me back. Why?'

'You know my gaff?'

'No.'

Malin scribbled on Gary's Rothmans.

'Stop off when you finish here tonight. I'll make some eats. Everything goes down, tell me. Bring me something I want to know.'

Malin did what he often did, ate and napped in the early evening and set his clock for the interesting hours. When Gary came by it was two a.m. and Malin was contemplating breakfast.

He fried things while Gary described how the old man had arrived around midnight. Gary had stuck around. Frogman, coming on shift, was even more pissed off than he was, so the company was welcome. Cut it short, the old man was nowhere above ground. Gary did a check on all the rooms. He even found a door that looked to give on to another room, but outside that point there was only a sort of brick built-on bit.

'Built-on bit?'

'Yeah, just poking out. Not a room, right, just a bit.'

'Ordinary door?'

'Yeah.'

'Try it?'

'Yeah, locked.'

'Gary, son, this is worth fifty. Make tracks on that sausage. You got a hungry woman waiting, you lucky boy.'

Malin shaved round the plaster over his wound and reflected that Churchill was worried or he would not be licensing a chrome-plated dickhead like Snedker to employ as security Gary Creed, whose only reasoning organ was the one that punched his underpants every time he thought about sex, which was two out of every three thoughts he ever had.

Malin looked out at the Edenville night. Sheet lightning lit up rooftops as the sky shed its oppression. He could still make the graveyard shift at the Roxy. He liked to be there at four, when the only thing that kept the staff looking alive was their pink shirts, when the diehard gamblers digested the sick fact that dawn was the big zero on the wheel. Like life itself, daybreak worked for the casino.

Sudden rainfall swamped Malin's last few steps to the smoked-glass cube of the Roxy entrance. He signed in and went through, thinking as he went. It had to be metal or ice the German had underground. Money, no, not even as tax evasion. Inflation wiped out cash. Hoarding banknotes didn't gel with Churchill's technique. Gold, it had to be, diamonds, glitzy minerals that leapt ahead when people

127

panicked out of coinage. Maybe all along the country house had been a drop for hot traffic. What was the Kraut doing down there, counting?

One thing for sure, Malin thought, I don't soon get into business for myself, there won't be no business to get into.

In the morning, about ten, Malin drove out to Lagoon Close. Everybody seemed to know about the cellar except him. It was time to kiss and make up to the spic some more.

Number 14 was empty. Malin had not phoned. He didn't want anybody preparing for him. Lagoon Close was one of those open-plan developments, pairs of small houses crammed together to give an illusion of size. The side gate was unlocked. Malin looked around the back, stared in the windows at empty rooms. When he went back out a postal van had drawn up. The postman was at the front door.

'Bruce Rabey?'

'Yeah.'

'Registered.'

Malin went across.

'Three days I been trying to shift this.'

'Yeah. Been away.'

Malin signed. He took the parcel and waited for the post van to leave, then drove out in a hurry.

NINETEEN

Seven days Churchill had given Rudi to take his offer, or not. For Rudi, an active week. He guessed the German had not been holding his breath either.

For two days he had tried to contact Churchill, and failed. The arrangement had been that Rudi would leave, at Churchill's office, a message to simply request a meeting. Rudi gave Bruce's phone number for reply. When no answer came and he called again, the chill-pack secretarial voice said Mr Churchill was busy, please do not keep ringing, they would be in touch at the earliest opportunity.

A cover-up, Rudi knew. The way Churchill had sweetened up with that welcome-on-board deal was a stall. Rudi had been right to act on his suspicion. This incommunicado stuff confirmed it.

Suddenly Rudi felt a bad need to have his parcel back. He went to the local post office and said he was expecting a package, registered, but had been away. Bruce Rabey, he said, 14 Lagoon Close. He had Bruce's driving licence ready. But the clerk told him, delivered. Signed for, the clerk indicated the tab. If you were looking for Bruce Rabey, that was what the illegible scribble said.

Rudi quit the queue and went out to the sunlight, stunned.

Edenville beach had been topless for several years. The cataclysm predicted by the town's decent citizens had not happened. Bare breasts hung loose, nobody dropped dead. Bruce and Annie had been squabbling over how much it was worth for Annie to remove her bikini pants for a whole minute by Edenville pier, and whether lying on her front would count.

The beach was a litter of bright colours, thick with tanning bodies. Game arcades hummed and squealed and rattled money. The air was vital with patchouli, vinegar, frying smells, pungent with salt, meaty with ozone. Windsurfers keeled into the bay like giant gaudy-winged moths.

Rudi squinted through thick sunlight. His mind was like a sheet of paper in which a burn widened. As he steered through the beach's flesh-show, the radios and yelling children, he felt the nihilism of somebody whose life had been snuffed out before his eyes. He recognised Annie's bag and the Lagoon Close towels. At the tideline skittish waves danced in and ran back from the firm wet sand.

Rudi shouted to Bruce. Even above the good-tempered Edenville sea it was difficult to project sound. When Bruce looked Rudi beckoned.

Bruce cheerfully refused. He and Annie were throwing a striped ball and splash-fighting. He waved Rudi to join them.

Rudi went back, stripped to his pants and left his clothes with the others'. Then he ploughed waist-deep into the water. Bruce threw the ball. Rudi ignored it. He kicked Bruce's legs from under him, grabbed his head before it could surface, and pressed him under.

Bruce's face came up purple, gasping, eyes and ears full of water and noise.

Rudi shouted, 'Where is it, you bastard? What you done with it?'

Bruce choked on heavy brine. Lank strands of hair licked his eye sockets. Through his blurred eyes Edenville beach whirled in garish nightmare.

But when he screamed that he didn't know *what* fucking parcel, he meant it.

'Bloody nearly killed me.'

Three pairs of eyes stared over greasy meatballs. None of the inhabitants of 14 Lagoon Close could cook. Dining out in Edenville required resources. On the eve of his insurance bonanza Bruce had become a neurotic tightwad. Rudi claimed to be broke. Annie was broke. Greasy meatballs they could do at home.

'Misunderstanding, man, like I said. Total misunderstanding.'

'What was this bloody parcel anyway?'

'Don't matter, Bruce, not important. I'm sorry, what more do I say?'

'You have to admit, Rudi,' Annie said, 'there's something very peculiar about you.'

Everything about Rudi was very near the surface. He sparked. 'Hey, don't you call me peculiar, baby. I don't take shit from you, not today.'

'Why today?' Annie said. 'Baby.'

'Look,' Rudi said, 'it's out of hand, it's my fault, I've apologised, OK? Can we all get together again?'

Annie looked at Bruce with mobile eyes and a leering smile.

'First he tries to drown you, now he wants to fuck you. Strange guy.'

Rudi said, 'Hey, come on, listen. I mean that other thing.'

'Ah no,' Annie drawled, 'it's smash and grab time.'

Rudi was getting nervous. These two had been talking about it. Something had changed.

'Come on, we had a deal.'

'Actually,' Bruce said, 'we're a bit off the idea.'

'Because I screw up and soak your head?'

'No, before that.'

Rudi looked from one to the other. Then he wagged a finger, clicking like a metronome.

'Got it. You two, right? Uncle Rudi's games are rough, that it? You selling me out, hey? Settle down time?'

Bruce was defensive, starchy. 'Things have to change. No point taking unnecessary risks.'

Rudi looked at Annie. She shrugged. Her shrugs were like thick glass, you could see beyond but you couldn't get to anything.

Bedtime proved it. Arrangement was, Bruce and Rudi had a room each and Annie spent nights with one or other, but always first visited the one she would not be staying with. Tonight Rudi sat in bed, his door half open. But the other door closed on Bruce and Annie. For the night, he knew.

Well, fine. He wouldn't be staying for ever, that was always the plan. Boy had met girl and wanted a future. Life after Rudi. Sure.

His door still open, Rudi woke in the dark at hearing somebody about. From the tread he sensed Bruce. Rudi listened as Bruce went downstairs, peed, flushed, snapped on the kitchen light and poured himself some fizzy water.

Rudi went down, shut the kitchen door behind him. Naked, he confronted Bruce. Bruce wore pyjamas. Specially for the trip, or sleeping with Annie in pyjamas?

'Didn't want to startle you, Bruce.'

'Well, you succeeded.'

'I been thinking.'

'Can't it wait?'

'You don't remember so good, Bruce. I got to keep reminding you of things.'

'I'm not in the mood. I'm going back to bed.'

'Hey, keep Annie waiting a bit longer. Think about your alibi.'

'What are you talking about?'

'Me, Brucie.'

'That's all over.'

'It's never over. I go to the police, say I made a wrongful statement to protect my buddy Bruce. Then they pick your story apart, reopen the case. Suspicion falls on the husband, the horny Scottish chick he moved in here right after the funeral. Man, you see what they'll do with that? The local paper, your place of work? And kiss goodbye the insurance, Bruce. Tiniest smell of suspicion, they freeze that money for ever.'

'You filthy treacherous sod.'

'Another thing, my friend. Whatever set-up you got with Annie, any hassle, she's away. See that dust cloud, it's her.'

Bruce collapsed on a stool and watched the bubbles dying in his glass.

'So that operation,' Rudi said, 'it's back on the agenda. You two help me burglarise this guy.'

In deflated misery, beyond words, Bruce nodded.

'And when you go back upstairs, tell Annie come and be nice to me.'

★

132

Rudi could not get Churchill because nobody could. Malin had him.

Gary Creed had phoned, using the house phone once the German had gone below ground. Malin had driven out and sown the end of the drive with enough tacks to stop a container truck. The Corniche started to bump just after midnight.

MacBryan had done his usual patrol with the dogs before Churchill left. Everything seemed in order. But the caretaker was ageing, Churchill noted. Ill at ease, somehow weighed down. Still, it made it easier to let him go. Imminent, Churchill thought, just as the front offside started to sag. As Churchill got out to check the puncture a knife flicked open behind him.

When you had money, influence, power, you did not go armed, or show panic, fear, loss of dignity. Churchill did not speak or look round, even when someone approached from the road.

Malin said, 'Hello, boss. Need a lift?'

They drove the dual carriageway towards the lights of Edenville, Churchill said, 'What is this, Leo?'

By now Malin had read the contents of the package. Everything had changed. Malin understood why the German had been so scared of Rudi St Paul. He also realised why, what seemed like ten years ago, they had planned to stiff that plastic surgeon Bedell. And why all the companies were now out to auction. All that power had fallen into his own grasp.

'Taking care of business, boss.'

'We could have done this without you damaging my car.'

Churchill sounded hurt, suddenly the petulant hurt of an old man. Malin smiled. No other words were spoken. They pulled into an empty backstreet where downmarket hotels met new road systems and planners argued about what happened next.

Trong shone a torch through rubble to a door which he had forced open earlier. The ground floor still smelt of the Chinese takeaway it had once been. The torchbeam led them up a fake-marble staircase. Churchill obeyed directions. The operation had the rehearsed smoothness that promoted docility in the victim. He knew the technique well.

The room where they stopped had one small window which caught minimal light from below. Churchill understood their thoroughness when he saw a chair and ropes in the torchbeam. Briskly and without respect the Vietnamese tied Churchill to the chair while Malin aimed the light. Then Trong went away.

Even in the dark rotting building, Malin's lack of social poise was a problem. Trussed up, powerless, Churchill still awed him.

'What's the game, Leo?'

Malin leaned on a wall, kept the German in the flashlight.

'See, boss, I got everything now. The papers.'

'Papers?'

'All the shit the greaseball had on you, I got now.'

'He gave them to you?'

'Not exactly.'

'He knows you have them?'

'What you think?'

'Then why are we here, Leo? We should be celebrating somewhere.'

'It's all got to be true, boss, or you wouldn't been so bothered about the guy.'

'Well, if it's true, so what?'

'The Dutch people in the barn, that true?'

'What are you suddenly, Leo, a humanitarian?'

'Just want to know who I'm dealing with after all this time.'

'Get to business, Leo.'

'It says you grenaded and machine gunned over a hundred Dutch people in a barn. That right?'

'Not me personally.'

'Says you gave the order.'

'An officer's duty is to give unpleasant orders.'

'What about the tortures?'

'You had to be hard on those resistance terrorists. To protect your own men. How else do you fight a war?'

'Don't get me wrong, boss,' Malin said. 'It's a long time ago, right? But why we're here is, I don't have to trust you no more. They're putting a concrete ball through this lot tomorrow. Clearway extension. I'm back here about five, and you're making me a terrific offer. Then we go to my place and call your lawyer. Other hand, I don't like it, you get terminal demolition. When they shunt this lot away they'll never find what's left of you.'

With a long piece of cloth Malin gagged Churchill, then torchlit his way back down.

By dawn Churchill's body was rigid and aching. Also he had wet his trousers. In Edenville's main square a clock struck the hours. Soon after five Malin returned, bouncy, refreshed by sex, two hours' sleep, shower and pizza. Fist kneaded palm in the grainy light.

'I take the gag off, or what?'

Churchill nodded. Malin unbound the rag. The German maintained a steely control.

'I'm old, Leo. You show those papers to the media, what you think happens to me? Nothing.'

Malin sensed defiance. Silent, he straightened out the gag and made ready to bind Churchill's jaw again.

'No, wait, wait. My point is simply this. The deal I conclude with you is simply take or leave. You don't like it, leave me here. I've killed people more ways than you can imagine. I'm not scared to die. But then what do you get, Leo? You get a whole heap of nothing.'

'The wrecking crew are here at seven,' Malin said. 'Make it fast.'

Churchill outlined a dual-control arrangement. The money from the liquidated businesses would go into a both-parties-sign account. All new investment would require their joint consent. Four million plus, Churchill said, the properties would double that. He agreed to open all the books for Malin's audit. Furthermore, they would write into the contract a stipulation that the interest of one partner could only be inherited by the other. After a suitable time lapse, naturally.

Malin was slow on these matters. It sounded fine.

'We get your lawyer out of bed to draw things up?'

'Sure. A document in principle. A few days to finalise.'

Malin cut the ropes. He offered to help Churchill down the stairs. But the old man, wet trouser legs, grinding joints, politely insisted on going unaided.

For the lawyer, Malin refused to allow Churchill to clean up and change. Immediately after the transaction was sketched out, back on the street Malin said, 'The cellar.'

Churchill asked what cellar.

'We go to the house. Whatever it is you got under there I want to see it.'

With the strange compliance that had characterised him throughout that night Churchill answered, 'OK, why not?'

Malin drove. In the back Trong nursed his knife.

At the foot of a subterranean stair, fluorescent strip lit a concrete ante-chamber. Via several locks and a lever handle, Churchill opened a big metal door. The room was some ten feet square, carpeted, surprisingly warm, with heating and humidity controls and venti- lation ducts. No ordinary cellar, it might be a fall-out shelter. Along two walls stood cabinets of pale wood.

Malin looked bemused. Churchill smiled and reassuringly patted Malin's arm.

'Sinister, hm?'

Malin asked, 'What's inside?'

Churchill was candid. 'A small art collection. You like to see?'

'Yeah.'

Churchill unlocked and slid out trays. Each contained several fine paper binders which Churchill opened delicately.

'This collection I built up in the days when the work of minor artists didn't cost fortunes. Charming, no? It's something to retreat to, away from all that shit out there.'

'What's it worth?'

Churchill looked pained. 'You're forcing me to sell it?'

'No, just curious.'

'Maybe hundred, hundred fifty. Artists are in and out of fashion, you never know. Find a rich American, maybe two hundred.'

'Grand?'

'Too much, you think? Over-estimate, maybe. What do you think of this one?'

A smudgy work in brown ink on rough paper, it left Malin blank. In his own place, unchanged in fifteen years, he had the chain-store print of a woman with a green face, and two fishing boat pictures in loud oils bought in a tourist bazaar in the Algarve. This bistre sketch could be anything. Malin wondered if Churchill was trying to catch him out.

He said, 'Modern?'

'Interesting, isn't it?' the German said. 'Not everybody's taste.'

He slid the drawer shut with carefully hidden satisfaction. The only time Malin had met the name Rembrandt was on a pack of cigars.

Churchill indicated another case.

'Shall we go on? For me this is great pleasure. For you, I suspect, an anticlimax.'

'Yeah, well, OK.' Malin turned aside and sniffed while Churchill gazed at a picture. Malin felt foolish, upstaged.

Churchill said, 'Now if you don't mind, Leo, you've kept me tied up all night in a derelict building, you've forced me to sign over my wealth to you, I am still in soiled clothes, hungry and tired. Do you mind if I remedy some of these things?'

'Sure,' Malin said. An apology would sound like weakness. He didn't apologise.

'The Roller's OK to go when you want to leave.'

Churchill recalled the Corniche's flat tyre, nodded mildly and said, 'Be in touch tomorrow morning, Leo. Not too early.'

Malin grunted agreement and left. Churchill made the basement door fast. Inside, he slid out more trays, viewing again watercolours on which Malin's gaze had fallen like birdshit. An animal, he thought, Malin. Hogmeat.

From the moment Malin stepped out of the night Churchill's whole being had distilled into hate, hunger for revenge. Now he trembled for its fulfilment. Churchill had submitted to the fat man's humiliation almost with relish, because it fed his appetite for vengeance. Through all the hours at Malin's mercy he had tasted in advance the image of the fat man's butchered body.

Meanwhile, the pictures.

War was about plunder. Nobody would ever know what had been lost to the Nazis, or where it had ended up. The collection of aquatints with which an old Dutch Jew had bought his life from *Sturmbannführer* Emil Goltz was only a microscopic part of it. But such a collection. A family of collectors going back generations, hoarders of *objets d'art* and pictures outside the trawl of the big markets, amassing for amassing's sake the way those old European

Jews did. Insurance, and it worked, it bought life. Until one night when two SS troopers entered the loft where the old Jew was hiding and dragged him away, because Emil Goltz saw a German defeat looming and did not want the Dutch or the Jews combing Europe for these paper treasures.

They were easy to move, too. Churchill contemplated a drawer Malin had not seen. Easy to hide, protect, move, guard as a secret unique pleasure whose value had outstripped money a thousandfold. Beautiful, *beautiful*. Fifty-eight works spanning four centuries. A collection no price could be put on. It mocked the crudeness of money. If ever Churchill wanted to buy his life, one of these pictures would be enough.

Goltz himself had an art background. He had been one of those cultured Nazis whose contempt for other humans was put to work by the SS. Style plus violence equals history. He was expert enough to know the pictures were not forgeries. The perfection of styles was too diverse for them to be phoney. Anyway, forgeries always homed in on galleries or the vaults of investment funds. Not some rat-eaten backstreet of a town like Grootendahl. And these aquatint sketches, the bed of irises, the landscape whose version in oil was world famous although inferior to its watercolour draft, the cypress beyond the meadow – these were things nobody could fake.

Churchill had never dared seek authentication of his art. In fact Malin was the first person to see them, and here Churchill was counting on several factors. One, Malin was a cretin with no idea what had been in front of him. Two, preparations for the pictures' removal were almost complete. Three, as of last night Malin had only days in which to kiss himself goodbye.

Malin felt cheated. The German was fooling. He had been too laid back about this. Malin said, let's go to the cellar, they went to the cellar. For some naff collection of old pictures.

There had to be something here. The dago was hot shit about the place. Churchill guarded it with Dobermans. Malin sucked his teeth and mangled his facial flesh, in thought.

Frogman was on duty. Less of a mouth than Gary Creed,

Frogman was thick, unpleasant, a griper with big ideas and Cuban heels.

Malin said, 'How things, rocker?'

Frogman, not bright enough to be bored, said, 'Quiet, Leo, quiet.'

'Still shifting with Gary?'

'Yeah, yeah.'

'Time drag?'

'Well, we got radio in the kitchen, some books Gaz got from the shop.'

Frogman held his hands flat below his chest and jiggled them up and down.

'You and Gary here all time?'

'Most, yeah. Bum pain, but dosh, right. Can't be choosers.'

'See much the old couple?'

'Every few hours they go round with the dogs. Gives you the fucking creeps. Still, end the week.'

'For what?'

'Job cops out. Snedker's paying us off.'

'Finished here?'

''Sit.'

Malin went to his pocket for the bankroll he always carried.

'Fancy an extra earner?'

'Sure, every time.'

'Bit of physical?'

'No sweat.'

'Anything comes out this place, I want. I don't care what you gotta do. Hijack, conk the driver if he gets silly, all that number. Best thing is, blindfold job, take the truck somewhere, empty it, drive somewhere else, let the boys have their wagon back. But get me quick, right?'

Malin scribbled some numbers and flipped out four £50 notes. The money humbled Frogman.

'That again for a good job. A bad job, you give it back and get your legs broke. I'll give it to Gary as well. Right?'

Malin pointed to Trong, distant by the car.

'I'm leaving him here. See he gets fed, he won't bother you. I'll clue him in, he's on your side. Know him?'

'Seen him around.'

'He's mean as shit. But any aggro, he's like your own private atomic weapon, right?'

'Right,' Frogman said.

TWENTY

Churchill paused only to clean up and change. Then he phoned Rudi, made coffee and was drinking it when Rudi drove along the overcliff. The apartment door was open. The German sat looking out over a glittering early sea.

Rudi was confused and nervous. Churchill had got him out of bed. More precisely, off Annie's half awake, reluctant body. Bruce had taken the call.

'He won't give his name and he won't hang up.'

Rudi scrambled down. It had to be Churchill, and it had to be that he knew about the package. Churchill's voice was formal, polite. But all the way there Rudi knew the old Nazi was going to say he knew Rudi no longer had the package, then maybe take his revenge. Unshaven, with the kitchen knife that had slashed Malin's face taped inside his sock, Rudi waited to find out.

They started with coffee and the view. Ultra-civilised, *über-menschlich*, all that Nazi shit. Then pulp him. Rudi played along. No option but.

Churchill watched him. Below the softening lines of age the raw, savage cut of the SS officer still strutted. Tighten the skin, darken the hair, back came the arrogance, the leather and steel, the naked power.

'So,' Churchill said, 'when do you return to Colombia?'

Rudi said, 'I don't get it.'

'I think you get it perfectly well, my young friend. Your visit here no longer has a purpose.'

Rudi found nothing to say.

Churchill added, 'Your hold over me has gone. Now you go too. Back to your stinking shanty town.'

Churchill smiled. Rudi waited for a door to open, some heavy-weight goon to step out. Instead Churchill got up.

'Something I wish to show you.'

Somehow, Rudi did not catch the trick, Churchill activated an electronic device. A gilt-framed landscape swung out to reveal a combination-lock safe. Churchill twiddled it open.

'I want to give you a present.'

He indicated they should sit down. The album he displayed contained a photographic record of his art collection. As he turned the pages Rudi felt sick with the knowledge of being right too late.

'Choose one.'

Rudi said, 'What is this?'

'Providing you are willing to earn it.'

'Doing what?'

'In twenty-four hours I want Leo Malin dead. Can you take care of this?'

'For one picture?'

'Whichever you like.'

'This one?'

'We both know what that's worth.'

Rudi looked at the Van Gogh aquarelle. Even in a photograph the colours were heartbreaking. A private sale in Colombia, he would be rich for life.

'Upfront,' Churchill said, 'I will give you one thousand pounds. This is to cover your travel expenses. You must get out of the country immediately. But also take it as a token of my seriousness.'

'Twenty-four hours isn't enough,' Rudi said.

'Why?'

'I need time.'

Churchill's reply was crushing. 'If you can't do it in twenty-four hours you won't do it. All you have to do is book a flight to somewhere in the Americas. This time tomorrow Malin is dead, you are away, I will have the car picked up from the airport.'

'How do I get the picture?'

'No problem. Make your choice, I will have it here. You bring me proof, then collect and goodbye.'

'Proof?'

'Malin wears a ring with a small ruby inset. I know this well, it was many years ago a gift from me. It has grown into his flesh. There is only one way you can bring it to me, and only one way you can take it from him. This ring is the proof. One other thing also, if you accept.'

'OK, sure, I accept,' Rudi said, rattled by Churchill's spiderlike approach. 'What's this other thing?'

'He has to know, a moment before it happens, who sent you to kill him. You will tell me how you arranged this. You will also bring me everything you find on the body, notably his key ring.'

With which Churchill would immediately enter Malin's flat and retrieve the package. Malin was not sophisticated enough for lawyers or bank vaults.

'The body,' Rudi said. 'What I do about that?'

'Your problem. But use his car, not the one I lend you. No trails back to me, understand? I would suggest, do it by darkness and use the forest.'

'*Nacht und Nebel*,' Rudi said. 'Night and fog.' He tried to grin.

Churchill said, 'You don't need to translate. I remember.'

Money was like blood, Edenville a placid sea through which dark shapes glided at its faintest smell. Churchill's pay-off scared Malin more with every day that passed. Above street level, Malin had no financial skills. A hundred grand would melt in a year. He would end up a disco bouncer again, a debt collector with sore feet and bad armpits. But now that he had new leverage over the German, millions sloshing around, some face in a club had offered Malin an in to Edenville's sexy money. Just like that, a dealer's town.

Barbecue smoke drifted across a big outdoor pool. Around a ceramic terrace people with ha-ha voices clinked ice and laughed forcefully. A warm, hazy afternoon. On sun-loungers basked still forms of tanned bikini-clad bodies who did not look like anyone's wives. On some of them spectacular breasts sprawled across skinny ribs. Tits like a tiler's nailbag, Malin thought. At bashes like this, topless advertised ambitious.

Malin focused on them not for beauty but for their homeliness. Boobs you could always relate to. Wobbly flesh made Malin feel secure. Everything else there made his hands sweat.

Malin had dressed up for the occasion, but somehow his outfits always came out the same. Thick-stripe shirts, check jackets, soft-soled shoes, trousers whose waist–ankle taper got more triangular by the year. The public-school barracudas were pricing him up. They knew he had money. His appearance instantly told them there was no other reason he would be here.

By the time the thunderstorm broke Malin had been smiled at and then ignored by almost everybody round the pool. The contact who had introduced him seemed to have vanished, and Malin had lost touch with why he was here.

He didn't trust these people, the wet-trumpet laughter, their talk of havens, offshores, futures. To them money was a code of good manners designed to keep the outsider totally but totally out. But to Malin money was like food, full of grease and vital juices, to be rolled in the hand, to fill the guts. He could never meet these people even halfway. When the thunder crashed he decided to leave. Vertical rain whipped the pool. The tan-skinned lovelies rushed for cover. The smart-suited money-boys ducked indoors with their cocktails. Malin headed for the drive.

Somebody came after him. Malin looked round.

'Not going back to town, are you?'

He pronounced 'town', tine. Malin feared an attempt to make him stay. He grunted the beginnings of an excuse.

'Cadge a lift? Urgent client call. Car-share problem.'

Malin, relieved, said sure.

It was a short journey, the passenger bending Malin's ear all the way. When he got out he handed Malin a card. Driving away, Malin learnt he had just met Rodney Pinkroot.

For Rudi it was a bad day. For once he believed Churchill. The German could have taken all sorts of revenge, but the brilliance of men like Churchill was that they always located the positive energy in a negative situation. For a small incentive, Rudi's weakness was going to make Churchill stronger. Even on the receiving end of the manipulation Rudi had to admire it.

Churchill had calculated on the fact that Rudi had declared himself a killer. That and his desperation. But Rudi had never killed. And this was no time to practise. He would need more than desperation to waste the fat man.

Still sweating on the theory, the knife still taped to his leg, Rudi sought Malin out. He found him at the Roxy late afternoon, looking powerful but pissed off, throwing lilac chips at the only roulette table in play so early.

Rudi flashed Bruce's card and signed in as Bruce Rabey. Weird things were happening to Bruce, sitting round the house like a zombie. Even using his membership card gave Rudi a sense of bad luck.

The last meeting of Rudi and Malin was to bull up some kind of partnership. Since then everything had changed.

'The fuck you want?' Malin muttered.

The table girl watched them nervously as she flicked ball into groove.

Rudi said, 'Gotta talk.'

'Too late, pal. Who needs you?' Malin leered sideways. 'You're nothing. A naff little spic with a busted arse. Just fuck off before I pay you out for this.'

Malin touched the plaster on his face. Rudi tensed his leg tendon so the knife pressed. He hated Malin. Maybe he could kill him after all.

'Listen, tough man, I ain't here for laughs.'

'Just what you ain't gonna get.'

'Like your life, better hear me.'

'Threaten me, greaseball?'

'Educate, fat shithead. You don't survive tomorrow, who cares?'

Malin's number had come up, but he ignored the heap of chips the girl pushed towards him.

'Better be good.'

'End the pier,' Rudi said. 'You're not there fifteen minutes, forget it.'

On the paved area between pier-head and flyover kids were performing stunts on skateboards. A burger stall shaped like a Big Mac oozed fried onion and meat. Rose-grey powder, weary with thousands of imprinted feet, the sand awaited the massage of breeze and tide. At the end of the pier the wind blew Rudi's hair about and cooled his skin. Malin was waddling towards him.

Along the planks of the pier Malin thought he should never have felt more confident in his life. That he didn't, worried him. He was about to get out of his depth. All the ways he had Churchill by the nuts were somehow one short. Seven-digit numbers, the big time, were beyond his depth. When it was dangerous to swim off Edenville, the red flags went up. The sea looked the same, just that invisible currents would suck you away. Malin felt like that.

'OK, what?' he said to Rudi.

The striking blue of Rudi's eyes stared into the glossy mud of Malin's. Fantasies of knifing Malin in a dark car were receding.

'Our friend Churchill, you really upset him.'

Malin was aggressive. 'How's that?'

'You want to hear this or not?'

'What's in it for you?'

'Like I said last time we met, it's you and me against the German.'

'Crap,' Malin said. 'What you mean is, you are out of it, Pancho. You ain't got clout no more. What you bleeding me for?'

'Shouldn't worry,' Rudi said. 'In one day, you're dead.' He prodded Malin's chest. 'Twenty-four hours, is all.'

He walked away. Malin was soon after him, hauling his shoulder.

'Explain fast.'

'I just tell you this, OK? Churchill gives me a contract on you. Terrific pay-off. Wants you real bad. Part one is, you gotta know why you're dying.'

Malin's face showed fear. He backed off at the sudden thought that this scene out on the pier was the hit. He looked round for somewhere to run to.

Rudi grinned. 'Relax, man. This was it, you'd be dead now.'

Malin said, 'It's such a good deal, why don't you go ahead?'

'Figure I can get more without I kill you. So why kill you?'

'Got alternatives?'

146

'You're screwing the old man for cash, OK? Better level with me, 'cause if I don't kill you by tomorrow, he gets some other talent do it. Stranger, ice job, don't make plans the weekend. He's that mad. You're taking his money, right?'

'Not your fucking business.'

'My business, Leo. Some other gorilla hits you, I get shit. I hit you, I get one picture. I help you keep breathing, I get lots of pictures.'

Malin pondered. Slow, shrewd, the hedgehog with one big thought. Sea wind chapped their faces.

'You reckon what, we blow Eric away?'

Rudi said, 'Why not? He dies, you richer or poorer?'

'I wouldn't complain.' Malin was catching on. He looked at his watch. 'I got a meet. Let's do this. Call me early tomorrow, say eight. I'll tell you where to come. Bring ideas.'

It seemed months, but it had only been days since Rudi had paid another visit to Churchill's country house, unknown to anybody other than the MacBryans.

The caretakers were rural people who had found a nice number. The place was used little. They kept it shiny, in good repair. The grounds and gardens were paradise to this retiring, feudal couple.

'A war criminal,' Rudi repeated.

His face was familiar from when he had been there with Churchill, so when he arrived and asked to speak with them the MacBryans were receptive. Then, gentle-voiced, Rudi proceeded to smash up their world.

Between getting his package back from the solicitor's and feeding it into the registered mail system, Rudi had brought it out here to show the MacBryans. Their shock was pitiful. What he told them dishonoured their loyalty, made their future suddenly a nightmare.

For added sincerity Rudi spoke about himself. The video, which he would not show them unless they insisted, was a film of his own father, who had been Churchill's wartime comrade and admitted his own share in the guilt. Rudi explained his need to expose Churchill as a way of living with his own shame.

147

Andrew MacBryan had been one of the liberators of Belsen. Mrs MacBryan's brother had been found dead in an abandoned prisoner-of-war camp.

'So what you're saying,' MacBryan ruminated, 'is for twenty years we been working for a Nazi war criminal.'

In different words Rudi repeated it again.

'Think about it, make your own arrangements,' he advised them. 'Once the news breaks the press will be after you. If you quit before the story's out, nobody can blame you. I'm waiting for the Dutch and the Israelis to give the word, then I release my evidence. I'll keep you informed every stage. Just one thing I'd ask you to do for me.'

The MacBryans were eager to comply.

'Your employer keeps something hidden here. Is there some high security room, a cellar maybe? Anyway, it's important we know when he moves stuff out of here. If you warn me the first sign of action, I'll return the favour when things get hot.'

Rudi cautioned the MacBryans against any approach to Churchill. If he discovered their knowledge of his secret they would never draw a safe breath again. He left some spare xeroxes from his file, keep them uneasy.

A long shot. But you never knew.

The once-fashionable shopping street declined from short-lease take-aways and ethnic groceries, through consumer hi-tech stores, imported quick-turnover clothing, second-hand gold and jewels, finally to places like Pinkroot Galleries, opulent interiors that stood immaculate year after year with no sign of doing any business, while the short-lease places worked their butts off and sank without trace.

The door notice said Closed. Pinkroot's card gave a private number. Malin returned home and rang it. The time was now around eight p.m. He reminded Pinkroot of their earlier meeting and said he had some art to discuss. Pressing, had to be instant. Pinkroot was politely unwilling. Malin gruffly insisted. Pinkroot gave an address.

In clifftop pine groves, seaside mansions had been replaced by exclusive apartment blocks solid as fortresses, blind to landward and gazing hungry-eyed at the sea. Malin had to declare himself at a barrier, then again at the house door. Exotic plants postured in the temperature-controlled atrium. Faint perfume and soft decor, it was like walking over a woman's body.

'My dear Mr Malin, come in.'

Pinkroot wore a crimson velvet jacket. He was oily and menacing at the same time. Gay, Malin was sure, and didn't like it. He hated benders. Edenville had them like crabs.

'Well, a drink before business?'

Movement came from another room. Malin anticipated a youthful male in pastel pyjamas. He was surprised at the young blonde with a vacant smile and nothing on beneath the cotton slip that only just covered her crotch.

'Don't mind Nikki,' Pinkroot said. 'She'll make herself scarce, won't you, like a good girl.'

Pinkroot had been following Malin's eyes.

'You a connoisseur, Mr Malin? I suspect you like life's finer things. Here, darling.'

Pinkroot lifted the mottled cotton and exposed Nikki's flawless buttocks.

'Feel for yourself.'

Malin had no use for nuances. He wanted the lot. Nikki quivered slightly as his large beefy hand clutched the pale rounded flesh. Pinkroot smiled and gave her a brush himself as if to wipe away Malin's touch. Nikki breathed 'Byeee' and disappeared into another room.

Pinkroot went behind his built-in bar and with mock deference, eyebrows minimally raised at the choice, served Malin a vodka and pineapple.

They sat on leather so soft it looked synthetic. Pinkroot had dark crinkly hair, alert eyes and moist lips. His face had a permanently flushed look, through which black razor shadow showed. He had a lethargic arrogance. Malin felt him waiting for something to laugh at. You couldn't live in Edenville and not know the type.

Languid, Pinkroot said, 'Something about pictures, was it?'

'You buy and sell art?'

'My dear chap, what else do you think I do?'

'You valuate things?'

Pinkroot twisted his lips and looked doleful.

'Your auntie died and left you a hideous oil painting?'

'Look,' Malin said, 'don't prat around with me. This town's full of art dealers. Reason I'm here is, exactly what do you handle?'

'If there's a seller and a buyer, my dear chap, I'll always provide the necessary lubrication. What had you in mind?'

Malin emptied his vodka.

'You bothered where it comes from?'

Pinkroot's eyebrows moved. The rest of him was totally still.

'I was ten minutes in a car with you, and I just got a feel for this. I figured the source of origin wouldn't be a problem to you.'

Pinkroot's eyelids dropped. 'Hypothetical question, old boy. Can't really say.'

'I might have some gear to unload, the conditions being very quick and no guts all over the place.'

'Well, I think I know what you mean.'

'Interested, right?'

'Mr Malin, are we talking pictures?'

'You got it.'

'Can you give me the teensiest clue as to what they might be?'

'No.'

Pinkroot caressed his bow-tie. 'Are you sure you've come to the right man?'

'Yeah, I reckon. All you got to know as of now is, the whole deal is bent. So when I come to you again with a solid proposition, it's got to be handled in a totally bent way. You understand?'

Sound erupted from behind an ornate gold-on-white door. Synthesiser funk, some hit they were always playing at the Roxy. Pinkroot went to the door.

'Nikki darling, *please*! And if that Pomeranian shits on the carpet again I'll take him out on the yacht and sling him in the bloody Channel.'

The sound diminished slightly. Pinkroot beamed.

'Well, Mr Malin, let's have another drink.'

★

At Lagoon Close the phone rang at seven a.m. Rudi had been awake for hours, stomach and mind eaten up by thoughts of what he and Malin had to do to Churchill, before Churchill could do it to them.

He ran for the phone, limbs trembling. Andrew MacBryan was equally tense at the other end.

'I just got a call. Somebody's coming to clear the cellar. When? He said immediate.'

TWENTY-ONE

Rudi ran to his car. He always left it some way from Bruce's house to avoid the jealously guarded parking spaces of Lagoon Close. When he turned the key the engine kicked once then died. After that it refused to squeak. The dip lights had been left on.

Bubbling with adrenalin Rudi sprinted back to the house. Bruce was still in bed, staring livid-faced and wide-eyed at the ceiling. The other side of the double bed Annie lay face down, asleep, the bedding below her shoulder blades.

'Bruce, I got borrow your car. Where the keys?'

Rudi had already failed to find them in their usual place. He hadn't intended to ask permission.

Bruce stared mutely at the ceiling. Annie stirred.

'Hey, Bruce, please.'

'I want you out of here,' Bruce said.

'Anything, Bruce, but I got to have the car now. Mine won't start, man. Come on.'

Bruce pouted like a haggard old drag queen. That was it. Rudi grabbed him by the pyjama top and started hitting him into the pillow.

'The car keys, Bruce. I got to have the car keys.'

'I'm not giving you my fucking car,' Bruce shrieked. 'Get off.'

Annie woke up and yelled in protest. Rudi cooled down.

'The last thing I'll ask, Bruce. Then I'm gone. Tonight, maybe.'

Rudi held up his hands in a gesture of peace, feeling Bruce weaken.

'Well, I'm driving,' Bruce said. 'Not trusting you with my bloody car.'

Ten minutes later, after a lot more shouting, the three of them were in Bruce's Metro heading off the estate, Bruce at the wheel. Rudi gave terse directions. These two bimbos were the price of making it. Dump them later.

In the kitchen, Gary Creed slept. He passed the time with girlie mags, the odd drink, slept all he could. The van woke him. When he stared out the Corniche was there too, but the smooth Roller engine hadn't penetrated. Gary shook himself up, tried to look on duty. People in the house, Malin's words, Malin's money and threats, reflooded Gary's mind.

He better show. He opened a door. Two men, one the old guy who owned the place, clearly in command. His eyes drilled Gary's skull.

'Outside. Watch the gate.'

A voice you didn't buck. Gary muttered compliance and went out. He shivered, drew deep on a cigarette. Knocking off a van, sure. But this old guy with the accent was no average wanker. Just the sight of him scared Gary. The prospect of screwing up for Malin scared him even worse.

Gary went back inside. The two men had disappeared. Gary grabbed the phone and dialled Malin's number. His eyes bulged as he prepared to drop the receiver at the slightest noise. Finally it answered.

'Leo, Gary. They're here. A van.'

Malin was grunting and cursing. 'You know what to do.'

'The old man's here. The owner.'

'On my way,' Malin said. 'Just stop that fucking van.'

Movement in the house. Gary got outside quickly. He started in horror at the jaws of the Dobermans, held on tight leashes by MacBryan.

'They're getting to know you now,' MacBryan said.

'Yeah? Looks like hunger to me.'

Pale, trembling, he backed away down the drive, reaching for cigarettes. The caretaker and the dogs, that was all it needed. He prayed for Malin to get there before anything happened.

MacBryan and the Dobermans continued out of sight round the building. From a distance Gary watched the other men carrying what appeared to be plates of cardboard, hardboard, about a yard long. The van was sign-written 'Maltby – Craftsman Joiners'.

Gary needed to piss. Not just nerves, but nerves made it unbearable. He slipped into the shrubbery near the gate. Then the van's rear doors slammed.

Gary finished off as best he could. The van was rolling gatewards. Gary stepped out into the drive. His only idea was about to be tested. From the house he had brought an axe handle. With all the talk of security risks it seemed a good investment. It lay on the tarmac now, driver's side. Gary waved his arms as the van approached.

The Mitsubishi slowed. Gary stood in the way. No messing, the van had to stop. He flagged the driver down. The window slid back. An angry countryman's face demanded, 'What's the trouble?'

Say anything, Gary thought, just hang him up.

'Can't go that way, pal. Something in the road.'

'What you talking about?'

In one action Gary dipped down for the unsighted axe handle, reached for the door and opened the cab, got on the footplate and hit the driver across the shoulder.

Gary's young muscles and air of obscene menace terrified the middle-aged carpenter. Sudden pain finished him off. As he cowered away his foot slipped the brake pedal. The van started to roll. Gary pulled the handbrake tight and forced the driver out the other side. Hand clamped to collar bone, the driver stumbled to the ground.

Gary revved the van and rocked out into the tree-shaded road. Panic and instinct made him take the Edenville route. The van at sixty, Gary considered this might be stupid. Also as the snaky road unwound he saw the Rolls in his mirror.

He fumbled a cigarette into dry lips, lungs so choked he could hardly inhale. The Roller could match the van's top speed at a stroll. And what did he do about Malin?

Road signs cued in the expressway that bypassed the original bypass and fed the Edenville–London motorway. As Gary approached the slip road Malin's big red Ford came very fast towards him. Gary flashed the van's lights in a frantic sequence. At eye contact, Malin stomped the brake. His Granada slalomed down the narrow road. Just then the Rolls came in sight. In the rear-view, Gary saw the Ford slither round and force the Corniche on to the verge.

On the flyover roundabout, Gary took the van right over and forced it past seventy. On the other side of the carriageway early commuters were heading for Edenville. Gary had picked up another car, but maybe that was accidental. No time to check who was in it. Malin's Ford was closing. The Roller seemed to have been left.

Gary slowed, waited for a signal. All he got was Malin's headlights flashing. He surged the van again. There would soon be traffic, and the filth were up and down here all the time looking to put their sirens on. Gary swung right where a minor road cut across the carriageway, U-turned across the NO U-TURNS sign, went back to another junction, exited off.

Along this stretch of original country route there was a derelict roadhouse. A once elegant long low building, for trippers in bull-nosed Morrises and square-topped Fords, Gary didn't know what he would find there. Only wanted to get out of this fucking van.

Two cars followed him off, Malin's Ford and a grey Metro. Gary's limbs were pleading for release from the van. Past two disused petrol pumps he lurched to the side of the roadhouse, through a barrier balanced on two petrol drums and a KEEP OUT sign which somebody had already smashed down. He drove across an area of crumbled tarmac which grass had partly reclaimed, a former tennis court whose perimeter fence was a broken mesh of rusted iron. Gary braked, the slewing van scattered grit.

Gary jumped down. Beyond the fence was only pine trees. A burnt-out single-decker bus stood over against the roadhouse's boarded windows. A cold fearful sensation made Gary's limbs jelly. He lit another cigarette and waited. Something would happen soon.

Churchill felt satisfied with the conservative shrewdness of it all. This craftsman furniture maker would replace panelling in the luxury caravan Churchill would then pilot to Switzerland himself. The panelling would be in thin hardboard layers carefully sealed and veneered after certain 'private papers' had been concealed inside them. The carpenter was flattered by Churchill's appeals to his skill. A four-figure sum assured discretion.

The panels would be part of the caravan by the end of that day. As they carried the 'private papers' out to the van Churchill thought how his money had already found untraceable sanctuary in Switzerland. The money which that very moment, no doubt, Malin was dreaming about, Malin the garbage-eater who in a year's time would have lost every penny. But Malin had no money and no year ahead of him. They would find — if they ever found him at all — his decomposed body and a very cold trail. Not a man whose death would stir police efforts.

Rudi, then. His old comrade's son. Some comrade, Churchill reflected. Some son too, a half-breed *indio*. If he went ahead and killed Malin, Churchill would keep the bargain and deal honourably with him. If he botched it or failed to front up for the job, other talent would come to take out Malin *and* the spic. Churchill had it fixed up already. He could always rescind it later.

After the van was hijacked the first thing Churchill did was stop. Maltby, the carpenter, was more shocked than injured. Churchill helped him in. The last thing he wanted was an outraged yokel calling the police. He would take care of this himself.

To the bewildered craftsman Churchill said, 'I regret what has happened, but we stick to our plan. I know I can count on your silence.'

Churchill kept the van in sight making no attempt to catch it. When the other cars appeared on the scene his face creased in thought, but he controlled the Corniche with the same steady will.

He parked across the gap at the side of the roadhouse. With a gesture he ordered the carpenter out. From the back of the car Churchill took a silver-chased shotgun. It dated from years when he had found a country-gentleman image good for business.

'Remember,' he told the carpenter, 'you are seeing nothing.'

Maltby had seen too much already, and nodded helplessly. Churchill told him to wait there till he was called for.

Two cars and the carpenter's van stood out on the derelict tennis court. Churchill quickly noted the presence of Malin and Rudi. The security man and two other people kept well back. As he came out of the shadow of the roadhouse Churchill had already done the human arithmetic. Now he would call the account.

He crooked the shotgun in his arm and levelled it so a single blast would kill Malin and the dago. These late summer mornings had an autumnal coolness. Churchill felt the deep inner chill of total power. Breath came tight in the cold air.

'My property, I think.'

He advanced on them. For two people in collusion Malin and Rudi looked somehow detached, surprised by everything. Incompetents.

'You will stand against that fence.'

Churchill indicated the back fence of the court, rusted uprights and rotted netting. The five people backed away, Malin last.

To Malin Churchill said, 'You I trusted.' And to Rudi, 'You also.' He smiled in thin-lipped satisfaction. 'It seems you prefer each other. You will now, all you five people, empty your pockets and throw the contents on the ground. And you' – Churchill addressed the tall, lank, horrified figure of Bruce Rabey – 'you will collect them and hand them to me. One stupid move, I fire. I am an old man with little to fear.'

Key rings and wallets clinked on the ground. At a signal Bruce gathered them and held them out as if officiating at a religious rite. Churchill took them. Once back in town he would go straight to Malin's apartment for the papers.

'Now turn your backs. Hands on the wire.'

Churchill was about to call the carpenter to reclaim the van. Sensing movement, he thought the carpenter had come of his own volition. For that short moment Churchill was irritated at the detail. Then the sharp blade on his neck told him he was wrong.

Malin's head turned on its thick tyre of flesh.

'Drop the gun, Eric, or my boy's gonna carve you. Now, or I give him the word.'

At great speed Churchill reviewed the options. He could riddle Malin with birdshot. At these quarters it would leave a real mess, the kind of death shit like Malin deserved to die. But in his mind he saw his own severed neck. His eyes would gape and his tongue thrust out as the blood spurted. How many times had he seen it happen? In other days. But he was old now, comfort had overtaken toughness. And anyway in Switzerland a fortune awaited him.

Churchill turned the gun and put it down sideways. The steel blade stayed with his neck as he bent forward. Malin got the shotgun. His coarse rubbery face beamed. He waved Trong away.

'Well then, Eric,' Malin gloated. 'End Round One. Let's have all the gear back.'

Churchill threw the things on the ground. A gesture of contempt. Malin treated it as petulance. Even the German, in the end, was a sore loser.

Trong, who had observed Churchill's arrival from the cover of the roadhouse outbuildings, spoke out.

'Other man in car.'

'Who?' Malin said.

Churchill answered, 'The van owner.'

Malin told Trong to fetch him.

The carpenter had remained in Churchill's Rolls, too shaken and afraid to run. Trong brought him at knifepoint.

'Whatever was loaded in the van,' Malin said, 'load it out.'

Minutes later the portfolios lay at Malin's feet. He told the carpenter to open one, and checked that it contained art, neatly held in place with tape.

'Right, you,' Malin said. 'Take your van. Piss off. Forget this ever happened, enjoy a long life, know what I mean?'

The van moved off across the pitted tarmac.

'Your turn, Eric.'

Malin smiled arrogantly. In a strange way he resented the fact that the German didn't look proud of him. Sore loser.

Churchill walked away, a diminished figure. The van was waiting for his car to unblock the exit.

Nobody moved. Malin and the shotgun, Trong and the knife, somehow didn't invite anybody to relax. Malin beckoned Rudi over.

'I don't know how come you're here,' Malin said. 'Maybe I don't want to know. But I want you off my back, right. So when I got this lot sorted out, I'll call you and we reach an agreement. Then we don't ever want to meet again.'

Rudi said, 'Anything you say.'

Rudi didn't believe it, couldn't. This was just to put him on ice. Malin was already thinking, take care of business then a couple of boys work the greaseball over so bad he'll go back to chili con carne land on his knees.

'Been quite a summer, hasn't it?' Malin said.

Rudi weakly attempted a laugh.

'You better get back to the other two musketeers.'

Rudi rejoined Bruce and Annie, Malin called Gary forward.

'You done brilliant. You and Trong get this stuff in the car, I'll drop you off and square the dosh then, OK?'

'Great, Leo. Thanks, mate.'

Malin's curiosity was increasing all the time. Before they loaded the portfolios in the Granada he knelt down and opened one up. In the cellar the old man had put him down. Malin hadn't appreciated the art. Now it meant money, his, it gave him an itch.

He undid a tape, leafed through. Pictures were separated by transparent sheets. Indistinct shapes, smudges of colour, they meant nothing to him. But Malin was getting the message. If there was one ballsier thing than owning a woman, it was owning a woman other men wanted. He sniffed, impressed. He had cracked the secret of art.

Impatient, he flicked them over. It was windy on the disused tennis court. One sheet of paper spun away. Malin grabbed for it, but the wind beat him.

Annie ran and caught the picture. Some fifty yards from Malin she stood looking at it.

'Oi,' Malin called. 'Bring it back.'

She was planning a quick run. Malin nodded to Trong. With his knife still open the Viet walked towards Annie. Annie's arms immediately made a sign of surrender. She held out the picture. Trong took it and with his free hand pushed her upper arm. Annie stumbled but was careful to do nothing but smile.

Trong returned the picture to Malin, and the last portfolio was bound up and put in the Ford.

'Would one of you boys,' Annie said, 'mind telling me what that was all about?'

It was an hour since she had been dragged from bed. Rudi's unshaven jaw was clenched tight. Bruce, shoulders and neck rigid, drove through some imaginary tunnel.

When Rudi ignored Annie, Bruce shouted, 'We could have been killed. You realise that? We could have died back there. Jesus Christ!'

Bruce pounded the horn at an elderly driver who refused to let the Metro force him on to the central reservation.

'Poor Brucie,' Annie said. 'Dead as a fucking dodo and never even touched the insurance money.'

Bruce gripped the wheel and wove between lanes, overtaking cars on both sides. The traffic was suddenly thickening.

'You bloody slag,' he said. 'I'm not taking that from you. As soon as we get back, pack your stuff and get out.'

'Oh sure,' Annie said. 'But don't tell me, you just want me to spread my pussy for you one last time. Sentimental old thing. But how you going to stand the loneliness, Bruce? 'Cause I guess Rudi's on his way too.'

Rudi was silent. Annie prodded the back of his head. He didn't like it.

'What was all that back there, Rudi my sweet? How come we were there anyway? Whatever little plan you had, that fuck-up can't have been it, am I right? Big Leo screwed us all once again, eh?'

'Shut your fucking mouth, bitch.'

'Sorry, pet, your edgy time of the month, is it? Anyway, don't worry, 'cause Bruce is going to wrap us up in twisted metal any minute.'

'Yeah, Bruce,' Rudi said, 'don't drive like that.'

'It's all these bloody cars,' Bruce said.

'The idea,' Rudi said, 'is avoid them.'

'You get to the end without bleeding,' Annie said, 'you win a big prize.'

Bruce was still touching seventy into a tailback moving at fifty-five. He began flashing lights at cars slowing in front.

'You can do it better, you cow, climb over here and try.'

'I want to go to the toilet, Bruce,' Annie said. 'You do that again, I'm going right here in your car.'

Red tail-lights came on down the line ahead. Bruce slowed to a crawl, swore, made flouncy gestures of frustration. Then they stopped. After they had been stationary for five minutes Bruce admitted defeat and killed the engine.

Of all the mistakes I ever made, Eric Churchill thought, it was on that boat I erred furthest.

He had made few of life's bad judgments. When the Reich, that perfect machine of plunder, had collapsed, brainpower and nerve had seen him through. And even when the past caught up with him in this genteel flesh-and-money-pot of Edenville, even then he had steeled himself to the task of survival. He did not make false moves.

But on the boat that night he had killed the wrong man. The night they had sent that *minderwertig* con-man Deacon to the bottom, Malin had behaved like a neurotic woman. Better to have deep-sixed Malin. Churchill had forgotten the one lesson the war had taught him: the one man you think you can trust is your greatest enemy.

So Fat Leo had his hour of triumph. Driving back to Edenville Churchill tried to calm himself with the assurance that this hour had already come and gone. The spic was clearly another vermin to be rubbed out. Suddenly everything possessed a lucid orderliness. Churchill urged himself to believe that from now on it would be easy, a final solution. If it wasn't final, it wasn't a solution. Everything was fixed up. He began to laugh at the one thing these dumb bastards did not yet know.

The Corniche wandered. In the fast lane somebody hooted, staccato, and squeezed past, gesturing. For a few seconds Churchill knew that he was master of everything. His will and his contempt they would never conquer. Even the car was steering itself. A tidal wave seemed to crash through the car windows, then subsided again to that calm Edenville sea he had watched so many years. Churchill sagged forward.

At sixty, with Churchill's foot jammed on the accelerator, the Corniche spun into another car, bounced it aside, then performed a swerving backward dance, pinball-like, into two busy lanes. To avoid the Rolls cars hit each other or ploughed up the grass of the central reservation. The Corniche was only halted by the concrete strut of an overpass, which it struck diagonally from the driver's side, a concertina of bronze paintwork, walnut and leather.

Inside the car, Churchill's body leaned forward as if inspecting a fault. On the carriageway a dozen cars, ranging from the scarred to the destroyed, had come to rest like scattered playing cards. Behind them the early commuter traffic, packing both lanes, ground to a stop.

Malin, Gary and Trong returned to Edenville by the old country road. Less hassle, Malin said, miss all the mad punters burning rubber.

TWENTY-TWO

Breakfast TV described Eric Churchill as a 'local businessman'. In Lagoon Close, Bruce Rabey watched the helicopter film of the multiple smash in morose silence. Annie smoked, said 'Jesus!' and smoked some more. Rudi, in an attack of temper which the other two did not understand, threw a cup down on the table and walked out.

Rudi went and sat in the car, Churchill's unreturned loan. He would not need to return it now. The news of the German's death pushed Rudi close to tears, his only emotion was frustration at the end of his dream.

Annie went upstairs to pack. This morning had been one too many. She had always wanted freedom, but freedom seemed to mean your life got chopped up into scenes that turned out either squalid or crazy. She got her clothes together. Even if Bruce forgot his threat to throw her out, he was cracking up and it might be best to go anyway.

Any case, summer in Edenville was over. Daily the sun was declining, the air had a pleasant haze, the crowds had left. Boutiques were dumping the seasonal remnants. This year's mad fling was over. Moving-on time.

She looked out at Lagoon Close, the no-through road, the whitewashed starter homes. Some irony, to wash up in exactly the situation she had always been running from. It had got her, too.

Annie shook her head as if brushing off an unwelcome reminder. She was sharing an overpriced box with a jerk who had been programmed to feel good about a life with all the colour and dimension of a bin-liner. Ten years ago this life was going to claim Annie. Fate had proved that however hard you ran you still ended up in Lagoon Close.

Even the two-way sex thing, with its 'After you, Rudi', 'No, after you, Bruce' aspect, was gruesomely suburban. But Rudi would go, Annie knew her own kind. One day he would just not be there any more. Bruce was the problem. He would throw her out, then on his knees in the street, beg her not to leave.

Annie swore under her breath. She couldn't do it. She put the clothes back before the others saw signs of packing and asked questions. She had no money, no job or home. The only good thing about the jobs and the rooms she would get was they couldn't last long.

Maybe one day, when she was thirty, for instance, her brain would cut out and she would zombie through like the no-hopers you saw everywhere keeping the world afloat. But being in the shitholes of the world was one thing. Making yourself go back to them was something else. She couldn't do it.

Even the knowledge that today Bruce was due to receive the insurance payout was to Annie like part of her own personal fortune. Money like that, she could live on Bruce for years. Affluence had got her like cancer. Wherever you probed, there it was.

'Ah fuck,' she muttered to herself. 'After all this, I'm *married*!'

She went downstairs. Maybe she would make Bruce a cup of tea for laughs. Or call him dear. Bruce met her in a state of rage.

'I'm not going to take this for another second. And you're the principal offender.'

Annie made a face of exaggerated horror, as if they were talking about a third party.

'Come and look at this. I mean, come and bloody look at this!'

Bruce led her into the walk-through area he and Emmajane had called the lounge.

'Look at it. Just bloody look at it.'

When the English middle class got mad, they signalled it by stating something reasonable, then repeating it louder with the word 'bloody', to let you know they were really cross. Annie looked then shrugged. She couldn't see anything.

'Newspapers!' Bruce shouted.

'Och, I'm sorry, Bruce. I'll tidy them.'

'Tidy? You think that's the problem? Look, these Sunday supplements – I haven't finished reading them yet and they're all over the bloody place. Mixed up, folded any bloody way, pages sticking out. This is how it should be.' Bruce grabbed a handful of newsprint and slapped the double pages open flat on the carpet. He aligned corners and drew fingernail creases down the papers' bent spines. Then he read the numbers to himself as he put them in the correct order. When he looked up, a rational sweetness lit his face.

'You see? Is that too much to ask?'

Annie said, 'That's the least you can ask, Bruce.'

Bruce was too far gone to react. As he tidied the out-of-date supplements the recurrent TV newsbreak again zeroed in on the automotive carnage on the Edenville carriageway. It was still not known what had sent the driver of the Rolls Royce out of control.

Bruce appeared to be ignoring the item. Then he said, 'It's nothing to do with us.'

'Absolutely,' Annie said.

'I mean everything that happened this morning. I didn't even know who most of those people were. Much less what was going on.'

'Me neither.'

'Just so we've got our stories straight.'

'Nothing to fear,' Annie said.

She was starting to wonder about Bruce. She was still wondering when he said, 'I'm supposed to go back to work tomorrow.'

Annie quickly dredged up a line of defence for herself. She would look after the house, shop, study cookbooks –

'I'm not up to it. I'll see the doctor later.'

'You haven't shaved yet,' Annie said.

Wasn't that the kind of remark wives made?

Before business hours Leo Malin was on the step of the office where the previous day he and Churchill had drawn up their new contract of operations. To the sharp-suited woman who approached the door he said, 'You work for Buttergill?'

The woman said, 'I beg your pardon.'

'I got to see him immediately.'

Undoing the three locks, in a toneless voice she said, 'Mr Buttergill's diary is full for the next four days.' She flexed immaculately glossed lips. 'Full.'

'This is something he'll want to know about.'

Malin shoved his way in after her. She said he was wasting his time. She fussed about the office as a way of excluding him. Malin said she should ring Buttergill.

'My name's Leo Malin. Just tell him that.'

'I don't care what your name is. But if it's so important perhaps you'd better tell him yourself.'

She looked beyond Malin. The tanned, silver-haired solicitor filled the doorway.

Malin was not taking crap today, but Buttergill also was not oozing charity. Pretending he didn't remember Malin. 'Yes?'

'You catch the news?'

'I heard the national headlines. What of it?'

So Eric hadn't made it nationwide. A stealthy fox to the last.

'Eric Churchill's dead. Car job, two hours ago.'

'Indeed.'

'We fixed some papers yesterday –'

'Ah. You better come through, Mr –'

'Malin, Leo Malin.'

Buttergill had not waited for the answer. In his office he drew Malin's attention to two clauses.

'First, the time lag. The contract becomes valid seven days from draft, subject to no change in circumstances of the parties. To allow for more specific valuations to be made, as you recall. Second, I call to your notice the clause relating to death. The contract is invalidated by the death of either party in circumstances which could be construed as accidental, during those seven days. To ensure, if you recall, that neither party had an immediate interest in the other's death. A detailed account of Mr Churchill's last twenty-four hours is a precondition for any further action.'

'You mean I don't get the money,' Malin said.

'Well, if I were you, Mr Malin, I would not order my yacht just yet.'

Bruce went to the doctor and got some diazepam for insomnia and depression, and a note for another week off work on account of persistent trauma. Living from minute to minute, he went to the Ajax and Achilles to say hello and keep them informed.

In his absence they had remodelled the office to accommodate new terminals. The corner where Bruce's desk had been didn't exist any more. Everything else had changed position. Bruce felt hurt that no empty space waited for him to occupy it. He went to see Ardington, who was up to his ears in paper and phone calls and seemed almost relieved that Bruce would be away for another week. Everybody was very sweet. But they all looked at Bruce as if he was a ghost. Two of the girls were talking about that terrible crash on the local news. In a moment of panic Bruce wondered if his Metro had been spotted. Even now the police computer could be printing his name and address.

'Sorry, I've got to get on,' Ardington said. 'It's been murder today.'

Bruce smiled weakly. Mortgage rates had gone up for the third time in a month. The front office was seething with builders and customers picking their way through the tools and materials. Nobody had time to talk. Before he was even out the door, Bruce realised they had forgotten him.

At Lagoon Close a brown envelope waited. Bruce cut it open with the souvenir of Ibiza paper knife. The cheque was for £19,136.27. Bruce lit a cigarette and sat down. This was his eighth, on a day when he had vowed to smoke only five, at regular intervals. The cheque had drained all his strength.

The covering letter stated baldly that the sum was in consideration of the policy on the life of Mrs Emmajane Gloria Rabey. At the sight of the name tears rolled down Bruce's face. In his hyper-tenderness the financial detail pained him too. What hurt was the £136.27, the small change by which an actuarial computer assessed to the nth degree what somebody's life was worth.

Bruce had seen it plenty of times at the Ajax and Achilles, the dark side of building societies, the homes split by divorce or clawed back in repossession orders. The machines calculated to thousandths, rounded to the nearest penny, and people learnt exactly what their lives were worth. His poor Emmajane had come back to him as a capital sum.

Bruce decided not to touch a penny. He would give it away. There were always brown people starving on TV. He would quell his guilt with a fund in Emmajane's memory. He would go right now into Edenville, find one of those charity shops, and look into the procedure. He hid the cheque in his usual place under the carpet and went straight out. It was raining.

Normally the streets of Edenville, shops full of goods and a wallet of charge cards, gave Bruce a lift. Today it failed. He blamed the rain. But it wasn't the rain. His taste buds were numb. The non-stop disco and broiler lighting of the clothes stores nauseated him. Either he had what they were selling or he didn't want it.

Bruce thought of the cheque under the carpet. Always when life's chickens came home to roost they turned out vultures. A first for mankind, he had discovered *unspendable money*. A new idea took hold of him. He would give it to Emmajane's parents. If it hadn't been for him their little girl would still be with them. It was time to make things right.

Partly for shelter under a convenient awning, partly for other reasons, Bruce was staring into a long unostentatious window which displayed skimpy and garish erotic lingerie and packaged but explicitly labelled sex aids. It was a respectably fronted shop whose sign still proclaimed Surgical Appliances although the concern had gone cross-market. The scarlet and black garter belts, together with his confused thoughts of Emmajane and Annie, made Bruce loathe himself.

He became aware of someone else to one side, also gazing at the window. Like when people stood too long next to him in public toilets, Bruce automatically shifted along. Only the rain stopped him walking away.

'Hello, Bruce.'

Under the rain-darkened check trilby, the face of his father-in-law looked at Bruce almost pleadingly. A Wayce-Dockerell, pleading. Bruce was still awed by the surname.

'Reg.'

They both turned so their eyes could not accidentally light on a filmy pair of split-crotch panties.

'Bit of a stranger.'

'Yes, I've been – busy. Busy.'

'Course, of course. Mother and I, we're both retired, we never stop. Talk about putting your feet up. Always on the go.'

'Pace of modern life,' Bruce said.

'The nail on the head. No time to stop and stare.'

'Been meaning to phone.'

'Course, old son, we know you have, Mother and I. You were mentioned last Thursday, it would have been, and I said, I should think Bruce'll get in touch soon. How's work, all right?'

'Oh, fine.'

'House prices buoyant. One thing they'll never sink, the property market. Backbone of the economy.'

Bruce's eyes nervously roamed the rainwashed street. He looked at his watch and said, 'Got to meet somebody.' He broke into the fatuous smile which had once been the answer to everything. Now it made him feel like an anxious rat.

'Wonderful seeing you again, Bruce,' Wayce-Dockerell said. 'Don't forget to give us a tinkle.'

Bruce hurried away through the rain. Just below the surface, hysteria bubbled. This was the moment he had dreaded all his life. He was going to snap in the street, a howling gibbering mess they would have to come and take away while sneering crowds stared.

He went into a pub, recently renovated to look the way they said it had looked a hundred years ago. Through a wall of stereo, electronic games gurgled like hungry stomachs. Scrums of customers hid the bar. The interior steamed from the heat of damp bodies.

Repelled, Bruce walked hotel-lined streets, pastel fronts blurred by the rain, kerbsides parked solid with cars. From the top of a zig-zag path he watched, distant below, a bulky grey tide hurl froth like boiling milk over the deserted sand.

Out at sea the sky was clearing. A white-sailed three-master drifted through a patch of shining water. So near, it seemed, he could cup it in his hand. Bruce knew it would crumble away, an eggshell-fine symbol of something he would never have – grace, glamour, style, class. It was always out there, gliding across horizons you could never reach.

Self-hate trapped Bruce in a panic. Wet through now, he felt that every time he bumped up against life he was proved a loser. In one of the steep narrow streets that sloped from the cliffs into the town he looked at a window full of tabloid headlines – astonishing scandals, stories to shock, revelations to sicken. HOW I WAS SUCKED INTO A LIFE OF CRIME. NYMPH BRIDE SLAIN BY MANIAC ADDICT SPOUSE. NIGHTS OF TERROR AND SHAME.

Suddenly Bruce knew what he had to do. The cloud broke overhead into an outburst of baroque sky. Upbeat music throbbed from a shop doorway. Bruce's eyes shone with a happy born-again relief.

He was going to tell everything.

Depressed and stripped of plans, Rudi watched Bruce drive out of Lagoon Close. For a few minutes more he sat on in his car, angrily drumming the wheel. Alcohol was too slow. Other stuff he was off and wanted to stay off. Only sex could blot things out at the right speed.

He left the car battery on Bruce's charger and went back in. Annie was playing some beanbag music loud and ironing. Ironing in bra and pants, looked like she knew how to do it too. Rudi went behind and traced a nail down her spine. Annie's body twitched to the airhead music but ignored his finger. Rudi went for the bra clasp but she hunched away. Rudi wrenched it open. As the bra cups flew loose over succulent flesh Annie turned to him with the hissing iron.

'Touch me again, I'll burn a hole right through you.'

Rudi backed off and smiled.

'Hey, come on. What a day. Let's liven it up.'

'I'm all right, thanks. All that gangster shit was enough for me. What are you really into anyway?'

Innocently, Rudi said, 'Into?'

Annie put the iron down, rehooked her bra and moved one of Bruce's shirts round on the ironing board. 14 Lagoon Close was low on power points, and the iron was plugged into an extension lead. Rudi touched his foot on the switching unit and the light went out.

'Just one thing,' Annie said. 'Whatever that pig Malin told you,

you better not believe it. 'Cause I'm only a stupid wee girl, but the way I read it he's got all the cards, and the only party he's inviting you to is the one where he chops your prick off. What the shit!'

She examined the underside of the iron, which had failed to steam. Rudi made to leave the room. Annie put the iron down to check the lead. As she came away from the board he turned and grabbed her. Annie yelled and tried to hit him. Rudi gripped her arms and hustled her across the room.

They stumbled and grappled on the synthetic velvet of the two-seater settee. Annie cursed and Rudi laughed, playfully hit her savage face and well-tanned skin. His hard-on was unbearable as he pinned her writhing body down and pulled at her underclothes.

'Come on, Mrs Housewife, be Rudi's little hooker again. You forgot how to do all them things?'

To free her panties he twisted one of Annie's legs so she cried out and spun round on the settee. He slid them half down, then quickly got his trousers open to expose a penis like a baby's forearm. Rudi pulled the pink nylon over her feet. Annie rolled over and hung her knees over the velvet arm. Compliant now, she was coming round. Pity really, because he liked a struggle.

Rudi was pushing his jeans down when Annie flung her arm out to the glass-and-gilt occasional table. He saw the gesture as a sign of wanting. Until she seized the onyx ashtray.

Full of ash and crushed filters, it collided with Rudi's chest as he moved to intercept it. Dead butts and ash blinded, choked him. The glossy agate's impact stunned his body. Annie leapt up and slammed it into his back. Rudi lurched forward into the cigarette waste, then tried to go after her. The jeans round his ankles tripped him. He staggered to the floor, his strength wasted by the echoing pain in his chest and the confusion in his mind.

'You fuck whore, I get you for this.'

'Come near me, Rudi, you better kill me.'

'Maybe I do that.'

'Aye, or maybe I kill you first. Or I have a word with Leo Malin.'

Annie left the room, flat-footed, her buttocks a mocking wiggle. Rudi pulled his jeans back over his crotch with an angry tightness.

When Bruce returned Annie was ironing again. He said a brisk hello and went up to the spare bedroom, where Rudi lay smoking. Bruce towered in the doorway.

'Downstairs.'

Rudi looked up wearily.

'What?'

'I want you downstairs. I've got something to tell you.'

'Tell me here.'

'Five minutes.'

Eventually Rudi appeared in the lounge, resentful, scowling at having to face Annie again. Bruce had changed into casual clothes and sat on the settee with a dead-eyed stare. When he roused himself his manner became snappy, nervous.

'Right, I've got you both here to make an important announcement.'

Annie gave a derisive fanfare. 'Da–daa!'

'This affects you both. I thought it only fair to give you a chance to make suitable arrangements. This has been the worst year of my life. I can't change things that are done. But I want to set the record straight and take the consequences. I need to look myself in the eye again.'

'Sounds like Picasso,' Annie said.

Apprehensive, Rudi said, 'What you talking about, Bruce?'

'I'm going to the police.'

TWENTY-THREE

Hours after he had stripped Churchill of everything – including brains, because he had out-thought the old Kraut bastard – Malin felt cheated of the lot. Lawyers with bits of paper had crucified stronger men than him. Suddenly all he had was the pictures.

Malin's apartment needed decorating. More, it needed the services of a designer. But Malin liked a home that didn't need him and made no demands when he was there. Things were where he left them, was the basic decor. The file on Churchill still lay on top of the music centre. The pictures were under Malin's bed. He checked and breathed again.

To collect himself Malin washed down half a slab of burnt almond chocolate with a glass of armagnac. Then he got on the phone and tracked down Rodney Pinkroot.

Pinkroot was in magenta bow-tie and paisley silk robe. His eyes had that unnatural sparkle, his full lips a much-licked moistness. He seemed well hyped for the time of day. The prospect of business? No, Malin thought, cokehead.

'Join me for a late breakfast, Mr Malin.'

On the table was white linen, silverware, antique cut glass and freesias in a slender vase. Seeing Malin's face Pinkroot laughed mirthlessly, each syllable like a bouncing ball.

'Oh, it's all right, don't do this myself. My fellow residents and I use a catering service. They wheel in whatever hour of the day one orders, set it all out, come and take it away again later. I do a lot of work over breakfast. All deductible, of course. Do grab a pew.'

Malin sat and accepted a glass of Bollinger and a bowl of coffee. To Malin's taste the table looked unnaturally healthy – the fruit and cereal routine. Throw in some smelly shellfish and a gateau, he would have felt more comfortable.

'Now,' Pinkroot said, 'what business was so urgent? Talk hard art at me.'

'I got the pictures. I want to unload.'

'Sounds revoltingly like defecation. You were very secret last time. What species of pictures are we concerned with?'

'Hot pictures.'

'You mean erotic Japanese woodcuts?'

'I mean I'm gonna show you this stuff, then after a period of time that better be quick, you're gonna make me an offer for them.'

Pinkroot said, 'Where *is* this merchandise?'

'Wouldn't you like to know?'

'Well, I don't know, Mr Malin. You tell me.'

'You want to see it or what?'

'I think I'd better, don't you?'

Pinkroot watched from a window as down in the courtyard Malin unpacked the portfolios. The tooled leather cases suggested something unusual. In Pinkroot's office, Malin put the portfolios on a Louis Quinze escritoire.

'Feel free.'

The dealer unlaced the top portfolio. Other flaps inside opened on to layers of tissue. Malin's eyes rested on Pinkroot's face. The first picture was some brown and green watercolour, a landscape sketch that did nothing for Malin. Cover a damp patch, was its limit.

Pinkroot's expression telegraphed something else.

He tried to disguise it. A downward pout of the chubby lips, a bored crinkle of the eyebrows. But too late. A con-man was a con-man, however high class. After twenty-five years on the Edenville streets Malin could peel their minds like onions.

Pinkroot slid the pictures out reverently, inspecting them against the light, checking the reverse for stamps of provenance or ownership. Malin toyed with his earring and impassively pretended he knew as much about this stuff as Pinkroot did.

'Interesting collection. Where did you get them?'

'Don't ask.'

'Do I take it they are not legally yours?'

'Much mine as anybody's.'

Later Malin would realise this remark was a mistake. But for the moment he was enjoying Pinkroot's losing battle to retain his frozen-turd manner. An indefinable chemical reaction, maybe a heightened odour of Pinkroot's musk-oil body rub, conveyed that at gland level the dealer was biting. By the end of the second portfolio, returning to some pictures in awed disbelief, Pinkroot had gone pale and quiet. His upper lip was sweating nicely.

'An exceptional group, Mr Malin. Wherever did you pick them up?'

Malin smiled slowly, didn't reply. He clamped a hand on Pinkroot's shoulder. Through the rich silk, Pinkroot's physical frame, for all his plump well-being, felt puny and crushable. Malin led the dealer across to a large acrylic abstract. A multi-coloured daub, to Malin's eye. Its prominence on the wall argued otherwise.

'What you cough for that?'

'When I bought it? Or what would you pay now?'

'Whatever.'

'An original Conrad Lush? You have to be talking four, five.'

'Grand?'

'Well, I don't mean pesetas.'

'What you got in mind for that lot?'

Pinkroot said, 'Are you aware exactly what you're asking me to do?'

Since he arrived a register in Malin's mind had gone on racking up the figures like a taxi meter, from a modest five-digit start, as he watched Pinkroot survey the collection.

'Sure. I'm asking you to get me a fast one and a half million. Quid.'

Pinkroot said, 'You jest.'

'Read my face,' Malin said.

'Unbelievable, Mr Malin. You come here, off the street as it were, with a most peculiar collection of art. Some of it, I agree, interesting. You admit that the origin is best not looked into. You wish me to dispose of it in a hurry. Do you have any idea how complicated it is

175

to arrange a private auction? In which the bidders never see each other and nothing becomes public? Frankly, in a position like this you don't name figures. You take what you can get.'

Malin said, 'You don't want to know, fine.'

He began lacing up the portfolios.

Pinkroot protested. 'I might go three or four hundred. But at this stage I couldn't commit myself further.'

'Can't say fairer than that,' Malin said indifferently. He continued to pack.

They both looked round as somebody entered the apartment.

'Rodney, that bloody car —'

It was Nikki, the girl-possession Malin had been invited to fondle on his previous visit.

Pinkroot purred, 'Not now, darling —'

'I'll be late. Can I take the Jag?'

'Out of the question, my precious. I've got a pig of a day.'

'Oh Christ. You're not going into town, are you?'

She gave no sign of having met Malin before.

'Yeah.'

'Could I hitch a ride?'

'Right.'

'If Rodney-poohs won't be too jealous —'

'Really, Nikki darling, why should I care?'

'Meet you downstairs,' Malin told her. Nikki left. To Pinkroot Malin said, 'Call me between ten and midnight tomorrow, or I go somewhere else.'

Nikki was a gabby blonde with a perky chest and, to Malin, an unforgettable firmness of buttock. The mould of his hand still felt the impress of that cream-cheese rump. She wriggled into the Granada and said Rodney was a nasty old sod she was trying to leave but the way he spent money, where else could she get that lifestyle?

'Grateful for the lift.'

'No problem.'

Malin joined a line of cars heading on to the expressway like drops of water along a drainage channel.

'It's just my electro appointment. They're really good, but dead fussy about time.'

176

'Electro?'

'Oh, you know, hairy legs and things. Bikini line. You know what bikini line is?'

Malin said, 'I'm gonna think about it while I drive you there.'

'You're not the sort of person Rodney usually has at the flat.'

'I bet.'

'I really like your hair, the way it sort of tufts out at the back. And the earring. Rodney's friends all have wavy hair, looks like it came out of a whippy ice-cream machine.'

'Ice-cream daddies,' Malin said. 'Edenville style.'

Nikki giggled and said, 'He's not ripping you off, is he? He usually rips people off.'

'No. No way.'

'I could tell you a few things.'

'Why don't you?'

'Better be your place.'

'I'll be back tomorrow evening.'

'Great. I'm going out, he won't know where I am.'

'I'll do dinner.'

'Not nouvelle, *please*. Rodney always does that, three slices of courgette in some orange yuk.'

'You name it,' Malin said, 'I deep-fry it.'

'Or,' Nikki said, 'we could just skip the food.'

'Right.'

'You help me relax and I'll tell you about Rodney. I better have your address.'

Nikki wrote it in a reptile-skin pocket-book.

'Rodney charms people, you know. That's how he screws them.'

'I'll be OK,' Malin said. 'With your help.'

'People feel safe with him. But dealing with Rodney is safe as oral sex with a cannibal.'

Malin laughed so violently he almost sheared the trim off a Montego in the inside lane.

In his apartment Malin ate and drank while his suitcase-size Wharfedale speakers groaned out the dirgelike rock-soul music he favoured.

Like a crematorium, somebody had said. Music for burning bodies to. An hour later Malin was driving through rising countryside north of the Edenville plain. The best idea was hide both himself and the pictures, the two things he refused to trust to anybody else. He headed for a village forty miles inland, through landscapes smoky from stubble fires.

Malin's parents, old now, tottering around their bungalow and feeding their chickens, were always glad to see him. His room was kept much as it had been twenty-five years ago, when Leo had taken the county bus for lodgings and a hotel porter's job in Edenville.

Malin parked, the portfolios locked in the car, on a blank bit of ground between asbestos garage and chicken runs. Malin always began his returns here with a walk around. Apart from a few secluded luxury developments in the outlying pastures, the village retained the look and feel of his childhood. It brought out a strange sentimentality in the fat man. A good place to grow up.

Funny though, you didn't see kids about any more. Too much fast traffic steaming through, too many child molesters up alleyways. Now the kids were all bussed to school twenty miles away, or sat indoors watching the horror videos which had become the village store's main source of profit.

In Malin's day there had been a gang of rag-arse kids in handed-down clothes, wandering the country like out-of-time tribesmen. The place had been tarted up since the smart money had moved in and got the place short-listed in a nationwide Beauteous Village contest. A committee got the stream cleared of the watercress which choked it, but already the cress was fighting back. The orchard remained where Malin's gang had scrumped unripe apples, the fields where they had followed combine harvesters, faces and clothes black with chaff, and where they had piled up pyramids of loose straw which boys and girls crawled into for a do. Malin always revisited the spot on the edge of the wood where for the first time he had put his hand inside a girl's clothes, found coarse hair and gooey flesh, and discovered the secret of the universe.

Malin's mother kept him up to date on all his former playmates as she maintained the supply of food in front of him. Malin grunted, nodded, ate. As adults his old friends weren't that interesting, their jobs and divorces and illnesses. Their best time had been when they were all kids together around this village. His too, Malin always thought when he came here.

As Malin ate and listened, his father, a quiet man with an anxious smile, limped about the bungalow, limped as he had always done in Malin's recollection, crippled by repeated kicks to the spine by a German prison camp guard.

'There's nothing to discuss,' Bruce said. 'I'm going to the police.'

Annie asked, 'What for?'

'Clear everything up. My life's a mess. I want to put everything straight.'

Gently, Rudi said, 'Bruce, let's talk about the problem.'

Bruce was obdurate, a martyr to obsession. 'The only reason I'm telling you two is so you're prepared for what may happen.'

'So what do you expect us to do?' Annie asked.

'We've all got to make our own plans.'

'When is this great event?'

'Tomorrow.'

While Annie and Rudi, still reluctant to be in the same room together, thought about this, Bruce crossed the lounge like a sleepwalker and lifted the edge of the carpet. They watched in disbelief as he took out the insurance cheque and left the room.

After some agitated movement upstairs, Bruce came back in and took the portable cassette recorder, then left the house. Only when his car pulled away, Annie and Rudi's eyes joined in hostile meeting.

'Seems to mean it,' Annie said.

'Fucking crazy,' Rudi said. 'He won't do it.'

'No? Just make your plane reservation.'

'I didn't break any laws. Why should I worry?'

'Up to you, sweetie, but whatever it is you're into, you're into it right up to your furry little balls.'

'You don't know shit.'

'When Bruce goes in the police station and says "Leo Malin", you just watch what happens.'

Rudi shut himself in the spare bedroom, away from the Scottish bitch's taunts. He was almost out of money. Only Bruce paying the bills and restocking the fridge had kept Rudi going this far. He couldn't collect on Churchill's cheque for ten days. Of his own money, the plane fare would empty him. His plan in Europe would fail, embitter the rest of his life.

Colombia, too – in Colombia they kidnapped public figures, left-wing guerrillas blew up pipelines and power stations, death squads murdered unionists and anybody who opposed the coke barons. Peasants protested and soldiers sprayed machine-gun rounds into them. The main cause of death for men under forty was homicide.

Rudi had seen a way out of all that and tried to take it. No other chance, ever. Back in Colombia he would live again with that tunnel vision, blinding himself to the roadside corpses, the butchered torsos in the Margarita river. A life of praying not to join them.

If Bruce told the police the prelude to Emmajane's death, Rudi would either be gaoled or deported. In self-extenuation he would have to incriminate Malin. The last thing he needed was another enemy, specially that enemy. After a long spell of depressed blankness, interspersed with painful clarity, he went to find Annie.

She was lying on the double bed reading glossy magazines. On the floor a transistor radio played tinny pop. Annie took no notice of him.

'Hey look,' Rudi said, 'I know you hate me, OK? Just want to ask you one thing.'

Only Annie's eyes moved, upward, derisive.

'This guy Malin. You know his address or number?'

'You're such a big shot, how come you don't know?'

'I'll do anything to have them.'

'You're so cheesy,' Annie said, 'I'm gonna give it you for nothing.'

She had been to Malin's once, on an errand for the kebab-house owner. The only reason Malin left her alone was, he already had someone else there. Annie wrote the information on a torn-off magazine margin. The door-frame rattled as Rudi slammed out the house. Annie's plucked, peroxide eyebrows rose.

Malin was out. Rudi had no phone number. The book didn't list the fat man. Rudi checked the Roxy. Just open, the club sheltered a few solitary drinkers and hollow-eyed addicts waiting for the roulette. Rudi stopped a man in evening wear who happened to be the restaurant manager. Don't know the name, he said. A pink-bloused girl setting up the blackjack didn't know it either.

Rudi felt too visible looking for Malin, so he slid a note under the fat man's door. But tension kept him around Edenville's centre, the way a ten-time loser haunts the gaming tables, eats his heart out over fugitive wealth only a silver ball away. Drifting through the crowds, Rudi periodically returned to the shady, over-the-hill block where Malin lived.

By the time Rudi quit he had been parked six hours on a half-hour limit. He tore up the ticket and scattered it on the road. When he wondered who the car number would eventually be traced to, Rudi remembered Eric Churchill and again sweated at the thought of Bruce and the police.

He would go back to Lagoon Close and talk Bruce out of it. Or beat him out of it.

Annie was watching TV and eating baked beans. Their eyes shared an unspoken message.

It was Bruce's Safeway night. In a state of ritual monomania he went to Safeway at seven p.m. every Thursday. He traversed the supermarket by an identical route and loaded his trolley with the same things. It was always a bad week when they reorganised the shelves.

Maybe he had done the shopping and gone out again?

Annie shook her head.

'He never came back.'

TWENTY-FOUR

In the Shalomar hotel, a modernised rococo villa originally built for the mistress of a royal duke – its economically remodelled space and wipe-clean surfaces a disappointment – Bruce started his cassette machine. Outside his window, slanting pines lashed each other. Beyond the cliffs the sea bellowed.

'My name is Bruce Rabey – twenty-nine years old, six feet one, white, male, caucasian. Shit!'

He jabbed the Stop. Why had he said that? Of all the stupid things. Too many episodes of *Miami Vice*.

Bruce rewound and played. Unease tingled his skin. He sounded hesitant, a weak nasal voice riddled with guilt. He recorded again to clean the tape.

On a student pad, Bruce started to write. At least that way he could keep track of the confession. But written English gave Bruce a different problem. Incapable of the most mundane business letter without endless redrafting, he felt nausea and despair as he stared at the sentences he had just written. He scribbled down a few phrases and tried alternatives, then crumpled the paper and threw it aside.

Bruce solved the block the way he had often overcome the tough situations in his life. He pretended he was in a movie. He played himself as a lean, rangy good guy who had never quite got life's breaks, the victim of his own good nature and drive for self-fulfilment. Gradually the words came.

Bruce ended up with a rambling account of that summer with Rudi and Annie, Emmajane, Reece Deacon and Leo Malin and Eric

Churchill, in compromised entanglement. He wound up the tape with the words, 'This is for you, my poor Emmajaney, because I'm guilty of your death.'

After speaking this line Bruce sobbed for a while in the warm tobacco-fug of the room. Then he thought of what the police might do with that sentence, rewound and erased it.

The following afternoon Bruce had still not returned and Rudi had still failed to raise Malin.

'He's with the cops,' Annie said. 'Whatever he's got to tell them, he's telling. Do you look sick.'

'Hey, bitch, they'll come for you too.'

'But I, Rudi darling, have done nothing. Whereas you are walking around like your shoes are full of shit. Once they tie you in with Malin you're down the toilet.'

Taunt for taunt was senseless. Rudi concentrated to harness his dwindling energy. The police arrived, he was finished. Could happen now, any second. His only hope was find Malin and warn him and get a deal on the pictures. No other future. Rudi left Lagoon Close, determined not to return till he had seen the fat man.

In Edenville he wandered the new mirrored shopping malls and the retouched glass-roofed Victorian arcades, kept clean of beggars, where even the buskers played concert-standard Vivaldi on violins and flutes.

Rudi had never spent so much time around Edenville. He walked the pleasure gardens, the seafront. Across the bay the nude beach was now a long sliver of bleached lonely sand. Edenville had worked its seduction on him – the laid-back hedonism, the effortless beauty of the place, where money had charm and everybody could feel a winner. Apart from wanting to stay alive, Rudi didn't want to leave.

Bruce walked back in with his portable recorder as if he had just been sitting on the lawn playing the meaty ballads he enjoyed.

Annie asked, 'You all right?'

'Yes. Why?'

'We thought you'd gone to the police.'

'Not yet.'

'But you are going.'

'That's what I said.'

'Can I get you some lunch?' Annie looked at Bruce's face. 'No, maybe not. I think we ought to have a wee chat.'

'Re what?'

This is creepy, Annie thought, the poor sod thinks I'm Emmajane. No wonder he looks so scared.

'Come and sit down, Bruce, I'll pour us both a' – Annie rattled her way through the drinks cabinet – 'sherry.'

She popped the cork. 'A fine golden oloroso' sounded about right. Docile, Bruce took it.

'Rudi's gone looking for Malin.'

'So?'

'All that stuff yesterday morning – you know what it was about?'

'Why should I?'

'Bruce, for Christ's sake, I'm not the police.'

'I'm not afraid of the police.'

'Snap snap,' Annie said quietly. She waited a minute then said, 'Somebody was stealing something, and we were standing there.'

'Nothing to do with us.'

'Nobody's saying we're guilty. But you realise what it was all about?'

'I don't want to know any more.'

Annie lost patience. 'OK, Rudi's ripping you off the way he's ripped you off all along. Didn't you see those pictures Leo Malin was stealing?'

Bruce shrugged, beginning to fear life had made a fool of him again.

'One of them blew away, and I ran after it. You know what it was?'

'*Whistler's Mother*.'

'A Van Gogh.'

Bruce's laughter was a shrill nervous hoot. 'You're insane. I've always known it. You're out to lunch. Totally crackers.'

'Bruce, you know anything about art?'

'Yes, quite a bit, actually. I know that Van Goghs don't blow around the country waiting for lunatics like you to pick them up.'

'Yeah, well I do too. That piece of paper was the work of mad Vince. You better believe it.'

'You're winding me up. What do you know?'

'In my earlier life, Bruce, before I realised the world's not run by people like me, or even people like you, but people like *them*, I went to art school. Van Gogh was my special study. I didn't study much else. What you might call a passion. I followed that guy everywhere, Arles, Auvers, St Remy, every place I could see his pictures or walk around where he'd lived. Yesterday morning I held a piece of his work in my hand. If somebody hadn't had a shotgun on me, I'd have run the fuck out of there.'

'Got to be a forgery,' Bruce said.

'Aye well, there are some things you can't forge. That was the realest thing I ever held in my life.'

'I just can't accept it. Got to be rubbish.'

'You think all that business was about forgeries?'

Bruce asked, 'There were more Van Goghs?'

'There was a lot of something.'

'What was the picture?'

'A watercolour sketch for one of the famous landscapes.'

'Van Gogh only painted oils.'

'Not right. Anyway, a lot of his work was destroyed. Nobody bought it, people found it lying around and put it over their cucumber frames or used it for target practice. Who knows what the poor guy painted? But that sheet of paper I held, he painted.'

And now, Annie remembered, in Arles you could buy Van Gogh gateaux, Van Gogh deodorant, Van Gogh throwaway cocktail trays. Bruce was looking pale around the lips.

'What do you think it's worth?'

'Christ knows. You remember the irises? First the sunflowers went for twenty-five, a Japanese insurance company. Then the irises went for twenty-seven. Million pounds.'

Secure your future with the Van Gogh Multigrowth Hyperfleximegabond. If ever the poor mad Dutchman had known!

Bruce looked stupefied. 'This might be worth – a few hundred thou?'

'It's worth what some rich arsehole is gonna pay for it. I guess that's what Rudi and Fat Boy Malin are discussing right now.'

'That's why he's been here,' Bruce said. 'That's what he's been after.'

'Congratulations, Bruce.'

'He fucking ripped me off!'

Bruce was like every other man Annie had ever met. Feed him a good idea, he ignored it, then two minutes later it came back recycled as his own.

Bruce's mind sparked red warning flashes. Rudi had played him for a moron all along – with Emmajane, Annie, Malin, using his house, his car, his money. He had brought excitement, but he would leave nothing. Perhaps he had already left.

Bruce asked, 'Is he coming back?'

'I don't know.'

Bruce went upstairs fast. Rudi's things were a functional travelling kit and a heap of dirty washing. Decoy, Bruce concluded. With a million in his pocket Rudi could leave all this behind. He just wanted them to think he was coming back.

Bruce shut himself in the bathroom. As he splashed bubble bath into the hot jet he wondered why he was shaking.

Downstairs Annie spun into what felt like a bottomless confusion. The next thing she would do was pack, then leave. Goodbye, Lagoon Close, it was about time. If she ever got that far. All the signposts of her life had been uprooted.

The problem was the Van Gogh. She was right, she knew it. As sure as if the sky had lit up like a gameshow backdrop to tell her she had handled a work by the depressive genius. Nobody could fake that power. Mighty Vince couldn't have painted a toilet wall without the world gathering in stunned silence. For the first time since she had had a pet as a kid, Annie had loved something. Christ, it made her weak.

Annie decided to leave right then. The Van Gogh was a fantasy. Van Goghs were for the super-rich or those who would kill for them. Maybe Vincent shot himself because he sensed that. After all, the peasants didn't want him. Unrequited love, always a disaster. Annie couldn't afford it. Leaving Lagoon Close meant being hard again.

She packed in a hurry, blindly stuffing things into her frayed holdall. The bathroom door was closed, she passed it with relief. Then, she couldn't do it to Bruce. Another moment of softness. Fuck, what was wrong with her? She went back.

The door was locked. Annie couldn't believe it. Bruce always left it open, hanging around in there hoping Annie would walk in half-undressed or something. The bathroom turned him on like nothing else.

Jesus, he's suiciding! Annie pounded the door.

Bruce jumped in the neck-deep water, his trance shattered.

'What? What?'

'Are you all right?'

'Why, what's happened?'

Through the door, 'Nothing's happened.'

Bruce's heart threatened to bruise his ribs from inside. 'Why are you knocking the door down?'

'I came to say goodbye.'

'Hang on.'

Bruce's words echoed. The water froze. He was limp meat inside a block of ice. If he stayed, she would wait, he figured, then no, she'd seize the moment and run . . .

Bruce leapt out the bath, taking some of the water with him. He had locked the door to protect his personal space. Now his wet fingers slipped on the tight key.

Annie was sitting on the stair. Bruce stared down at the back of her cropped blonde head. The tap-root of his body dripped on to the berber-style carpet. In his usual way when under stress, he barked, 'Do you know where Leo Malin lives?'

Annie whispered, 'Yeah.'

Again Bruce barked, 'Right.'

The carmine Granada was Malin's. Rudi cased it hard with hollow eyes that had looked into a zero future.

Every time he had visited the building Rudi had checked the parking area at the rear. This time, as the sky darkened between the working day and the emergence of the evening people, it came up. Malin's car at last.

Rudi entered. The one-time luxury block was dowdy now. Big pot plants at the corners of the stair failed to offset the cracked plaster and scarred surfaces.

Nobody answered. Rudi rang again and again. The buzz in the apartment, he wasn't imagining. He jabbed repeatedly till it sounded like a demented flesh-fly in there.

No way he was leaving. He tried the door, opened it, walked in.

Annie and Bruce had already been and gone, two hours earlier.

On the way to Malin's Annie got nervous. Bruce on one of his highs would make anybody nervous. Plus she knew how ugly Malin was, all through.

Bruce was fearless. 'He can't hurt me. I've got power over him.'

'Aye, till he twists your balls off.'

'If I go to the police, Malin's a dead man.'

'Get out of here.'

'He blackmailed me into killing somebody.'

'Bruce, they'll put you in a straitjacket.'

'Malin got somebody lured out into the country. My job was to run him down in a car. Make it look like hit-and-run.'

Lured out into the country. The blood drained from Annie's face as she remembered a long-ago phone call she had made, to a nameless customer at a number Malin had given her.

Bruce found the street. Apart from pointing out Malin's block Annie didn't speak again. Bruce left the car on double yellows. He got a ticket, so what? Hadn't he just put £19,136.27 in the bank?

'Let's go.'

'I'll stay.'

'I need you there.'

'No chance. I'll smile at the traffic wardens.'

Within a minute Bruce was back.

'He's out.'

'You should have phoned.'

'I don't want him to know I'm coming. Surprise gives me a tactical advantage.'

Annie rolled her eyes. When Bruce wasn't being a screen lover, he was a general of the army.

'What now?'

'I'm going to show you the place Malin set up for me to kill this guy.'

'Must you?

'It's all right, I didn't kill him. It all went wrong. The guy I was meant to kill, I think Malin killed him later. He certainly disappeared all of a sudden.'

Annie said, 'I can't believe this.'

Bruce was riding a tide of manic cheerfulness.

'Surprised you, eh? You thought I was a wimp.'

'No, you're not a wimp, Bruce. You're a raving fucking madman.'

Bruce took it as a compliment and laughed. They drove through the outer reaches of Edenville, roads lined with housing estates and factory units, litter-choked streams and eroded heathland over which pylons marched. Bruce drove fast but succumbed to a growing mood of indignant rage.

'That bloody Rudi's probably with Malin right now, sharing out those pictures and splitting the take. What I wouldn't give to get my hands on that bloody thief. I've got this feeling we won't see him again.'

Annie said, 'I think we might.'

'Why?'

'Because he can't go anywhere without his passport.' Annie took it out of her handbag and held it up. 'See?'

TWENTY-FIVE

On the music centre deck, a disc still turned. In Malin's living room the lights were on. No signs of disturbance. The record stylus, tracking the terminal groove, pulsed quietly through the outsize Wharfedales. Rudi felt chill.

A narrow corridor led to kitchen and bathroom, maybe another room. Lights were on beyond the door, which swung back to reveal Malin's legs, big shoes with chunky corrugated soles.

Rudi stood numb. From the floor Malin stared at him, propped against the wall, head to one side as if listening, eyes in shock. Rudi saw the blood first, then the bullet hole on the hairline above Malin's right ear.

Slowed by terror, Rudi looked round. The killer could still be there. Malin was not long dead. When Rudi had called less than an hour before Malin was out. Now, dead, he looked fresh, the word half-formed by his parted lips might still speak itself.

Rudi tried to think. What was there to think? If he left he gained nothing. He might be seen anyway, that was tricky enough. But to get clear with *nothing*, what was the point?

So be cool. No portfolios, Rudi saw none. Malin hadn't gone into this room to look at pictures. The apartment ran along the back of the block. A door gave on to the fire escape. Lever marks showed the crushing of the softwood jamb to force the deadlock. They had entered and left this way.

Rudi searched the rest of the apartment. No hit man, no art. One had taken the other, had to be. Rudi snapped his fingers as he thought, *keys*. Not by the entrance door, on the shelf with the junk mail. Not lying around anywhere. Rudi went back to the bedroom. The fat man's expression was one Rudi had never seen there before. Above the scar his own knife had made Rudi saw outrage, disbelief, the realisation of a fatal mistake.

A superstitious dread prickled Rudi's veins. He had linked his fate with Malin. Faced with the slaughtered body, he feared the partnership still ran.

Rudi crouched down, touched Malin's clothes, ready to recoil if the body slumped over. His nerves were alert for signs of breath or worse, the fat man coming back to life, jumping up with those glaring eyes. Rudi fingered the hairy material of the jacket. From the pocket he fished out a key ring.

The doorbell buzzed.

Rudi met Malin's dead eyes. Guest-to-host reaction, reflex. Rudi kept still, his only chance. The buzz again. Then somebody did what he had done, let themselves in.

A voice called, 'Mr Malin?' Well-bred English, a touch uncertain. The voice then muttered, and another answered, low and unclear. At least two people, the door between Rudi and them barely shut. Rudi's palm sweated around keys which he dared not move. He stood like his foot was on a mine, eyeing the fire-escape door, paralysed.

Rudi hoped the deadlock hadn't jammed back into the wood. He took a step alongside Malin's body. Out in the street, police sirens did a shrill two-tone.

Rudi got nearer the fire-door. The sirens got louder, then stopped. The action was all at the front. Rudi shouldered the door. The fire escape was old, rusty, but solid. Rudi had to get off that floor. They would burst into the room, see him through the glass, bingo. Steps soft, delicate, rapid, he zig-zagged down. The iron rattled slightly, but no police came to the back. Once they found Malin they would pause for breath. On the ground Rudi was just another innocent citizen.

One more corner, and down. How were the police there anyway, roaring in like prime-time TV? Rudi clicked his tongue at the question as he went to Malin's car.

He bared his teeth, awarding himself a big congratulatory grin. Whoever had killed Malin had not come for the treasure in the car boot. Rudi disregarded the sounds of police action round on the street, the penumbra of flashing blue lights, as he lifted out the portfolios. He whistled softly, eased the boot lid down and left it unlatched not to draw attention with the slam.

Rudi felt cheerful and at peace. What he had got sick wanting, almost given up wanting, was suddenly sitting in his hand like an Easter chick. He didn't stop to ask how. Miracle, right?

The car park area had a high wall, only the one exit. Rudi didn't want to lurk and get spotted. The cops hadn't blocked the way out. Rudi decided to go. It wasn't dark yet, but big purple clouds were blotting the sky and the streetlamps were off. His car was half a mile away. But fifty yards down the street would be heaven.

Rudi went. He whistled gently, that was the way to do it. Not sing loud and shout like he wanted to. About to come out on the street, he saw a car cruise up looking unsure whether to stop or get away from the police. Then a window wound down and it was Bruce waving him over.

Rain started, big splashes. The angels pissing miracles. Rudi bundled in the rear seat and Bruce drove past three flashing blue lights, sensible speed, nothing suspect.

'What the hell's all that?'

'Hey,' Rudi said, 'I thought you were with them.'

Bruce, uptight, said, 'No.'

'You didn't bring the cops here?'

'Absolutely not.'

'We got lots to talk about. Like how come you're here, for instance.'

'You too,' Annie said.

Malin had told Trong to go there around six. The fat man had an idea Pinkroot might call with company. When Trong got no answer and saw light under the door, he went in. If he ran from the sight of his patron dumped on the floor with a hole in his head, it was only because Trong knew that a body would bring people in uniform.

They would put him on a boat again and cast him out into that ocean that began where Edenville ended.

Not because he was running but because he was yellow-skinned, the passing police car hooted him in. When Trong sprinted away they gave chase. The weapons amnesty had just expired, it was illegal to carry knives on the street. When they caught Trong and searched him they found his customary switchblade. After twenty minutes' deadpan silence in an interview room, Trong realised that if they found Malin's body without his help they would simply tie it to him. So he helped them.

Malin was right about Pinkroot. The dealer came early, planning to get into the flat, and if there was nothing worth stealing to jump Malin when he arrived. Pinkroot had double company, one muscle, the other to let him into a secured apartment. Contract labour, they had no interest in the job, only the exercise of their own up-for-hire skills. When the police sirens hit the street both men were fast out of the building. Rentacrowd faces gathered at the sudden hysteria. Pinkroot repeated Rudi's actions of a minute before – glimpsed Malin, paused to get a hold on himself, thought about the pictures, quickly, sickly scanned the apartment. On the stairs he walked into the police.

As they hustled him into a police Escort, Pinkroot saw a young man he did not know slip out of the driveway and get into a car which that moment drove up. An organised snatch it must be, innocent, slick. Through the whirling blue light Pinkroot saw clearly what had obsessed him for twenty-four hours. The portfolios, no mistake.

Pinkroot's muscle man was standing near, helpless but still ready for work. Pinkroot stepped towards him, told him, 'Get that car.' Then he gave the WPC a big smile and climbed into the police vehicle. Pinkroot was composed, silken, assisting the police with their enquiries. In the hassle of the murder scene, his instruction on the street went unnoticed. Except by the muscle, who dived into his Cavalier and fizzed off along the rainy tarmac.

Only Bruce, as driver, could see the rear-view mirror. If he spotted a car taking the same route behind, he had other things to do than worry about it. In the tight world of suburban Edenville, motorists often followed identical rat-runs. A car turning the same corners was normal.

Inside the Metro it was tense and silent. In the house Rudi played for control.

'Some coincidence, police being there. Just a fight, a domestic. Woman yelling, guy waving a knife. Guess somebody phoned the cops. I just finish my business with Leo, out the back way, the blue lights come flashing. Then you turn up. Only thing is, I left my car parked. When you came I forgot. Maybe take me back later?'

Bruce said, 'Certainly.'

Rudi gave a broad smile, winked at Annie, and went upstairs with the portfolios, from which he had not removed his hand. A minute later he was back.

'Somebody been at my stuff?'

They both ignored him.

Rudi said, 'Come on, my passport's gone. What you know about it?'

Bruce said, 'Are you making an accusation?'

Rudi looked at Annie's face. Expert at the dead stare as she was, Annie gave it away. Maybe the coolness did it.

'Hey, you bitch.'

Rudi dived at her handbag, shook it on to the floor. Annie let him. Rudi scrabbled through the contents. No passport. He was about to attack her physically. Annie was ready to grab something heavy and respond. Then Rudi registered that Bruce had gone upstairs. The portfolios were upstairs.

In the bedroom Bruce had already unstrapped one set of pictures. The one personal expertise Bruce had in life was an uncanny feel for the market value of things. Show him a watch, jewellery, designer clothing, he could state the shop price within ten per cent up or down. As he began inspecting the tissue-protected sheets of paper something troubled Bruce. After some moments he got it. These things were *priceless*.

The definition of priceless was that people died for it. Bruce was thinking this, and simultaneously thinking it was the break he had waited for all his life, when Rudi appeared.

Rudi had calmed down and worked out his line. He gave Bruce a friendly touch on the shoulder.

'So now you know,' he said.

'Do I?' Bruce said. 'What?'

'Time I got straight with you, my friend.'

'Bit late for that. Go ahead and lie to me anyway.'

'Hey, Bruce, no lie. You know what this is? Private collection of a rich Colombian who employed me to get it back.'

'From a ponce like Malin?'

'Malin was a thief, man.'

'Was?'

'Listen, everything belongs to somebody. I got to return these to their rightful owner.'

'What's this one worth, you reckon?'

'Worth nothing, Bruce. Not for sale.'

'I'll have it.'

Bruce laid it to one side. A landscape sketch in sepia wash on paper creamy with age. Rudi pretended to laugh.

'Joking, Bruce. Listen, I'll let you in on this. You know why the cops were there? Ready for this? Malin got blown away. That's right.'

Rudi prodded a finger at Bruce's temple. 'Bang bang. Other people gonna be after me. Trap me here, they'll come here. Keep these pictures, they get you.'

Bruce refused to hand over an advantage. But his lips felt tight and drained. Rudi was lighting a cigarette. Bruce took one from the pack unoffered.

He said, 'You know how it is, Rudi. Lately I've been hitting moments of truth like a pinball. You know what the biggest was?'

Humouring a maniac, Rudi said gently, 'What, Bruce?'

'The building society where I work. I can't go back there. If I look at that counter and those desks again from the inside I'll start screaming. I can't face that future any more. A few days, I'll snap, wreck the place.'

'Need a change, Bruce,' Rudi muttered.

Bruce went on, 'All this year I've felt life was about to make me an offer. Something big, the sort you only get once. If I failed to take it, I'd never get another chance. I'd spend the rest of my life staring at that bulletproof glass and counting other people's money.'

'Good secure job,' Rudi suggested.

Bruce was unamenable. 'That moment has come. If you want my help getting out of here, we split this lot two ways.'

From the doorway Annie said, 'Make that three.'

Rudi said, 'Hey, this is ridiculous. They ain't my pictures to share around. Sorry to trash your dreams –'

Annie said, 'You want dreams, sweetness, let's trade. How you going anywhere, except in your head maybe?'

'The other day you wanted to borrow money,' Bruce said. 'You can't buy tickets with Van Gogh originals. What do you think travel agents are, stupid?'

'How about this,' Annie said. 'Your passport and travel exes in return for a three-way split?'

Rudi protested, 'It's a collection, come on. All the value of this stuff, it's because it's *together*. Break it up, all you got is pieces of paper. People won't pay nothing for that. Few hundred, not worth looking at.'

'How much as a collection?' Bruce asked.

'I don't know, thousands, hell of a lot.'

Annie said, 'OK, we sell it as a collection and split the money.'

Rudi screeched. 'You wanna *die*? You any idea how many people want this stuff? They don't buy, they kill you for it.'

'But they don't know you're here, Rudi,' Annie said.

'One day, two days, they find me. Market this stuff, rats to meat, man. They're here, we're dead.'

Annie said, 'I've got a great idea.'

She said it to Bruce, who was now the poised man-of-the-world, supercilious, *comme ci comme ça*. A drop of sweat appeared from the black hair by Rudi's ear.

'Why don't we do what you were gonna do? Rudi darling? I mean, flee to safety. I had a hairdresser's appointment but I'm sure I could cancel.'

'Ace suggestion,' Bruce said.

'We don't want dead bodies in Lagoon Close, do we?'

'Ruin house prices.'

'Where do the ROROs go from here?'
'Cherbourg. Every midday.'
'France the right direction for you, Rudi?'
'Fucking asshole, stinking cocksucking bitch.'
Annie said, 'Somehow I knew you'd love it.'

The roll-on roll-off ferries shipped container trucks and tourists daily across the Channel from a natural harbour terminal west of Edenville, remnant of the commercial port that had preceded the seaside paradise. As Rudi sat in his room with the portfolios, he considered the plan. The next day the three of them would go to the terminal and embark.

He grasped at the fragment of hope. They would have to return his passport. Bruce would have money. Once on the water Rudi could bust these two amateurs. By the time they reached France he would find a way. Quit England was a good idea too. Rudi started to feel better, headed for the lounge drinks cupboard.

Bruce stood with his back to the room, making anguished noises and gesturing like a victim of motor disease. Head clamped into personal stereo, he remained unaware of Rudi. If Bruce clicked tongue and fingers it was reggae. If he bellowed and wailed, Wagner. If he cried out sharply and punched the air, Springsteen. Tonight he was scooping armfuls of space and groaning deeply, which meant Wagner. Things were always worst when it was Wagner.

In the kitchen Annie was frying something and singing along to a disco tape. Rudi took a bottle of supermarket scotch and returned upstairs to decode the message of Malin's executed corpse.

All he could bring to mind was the shrewd emotionless face of Eric Churchill. Maybe it was the German in him that revealed to Rudi the trick the old man had pulled. And then Churchill's unexpected death on the expressway made it perfect. Just when Malin and Rudi thought themselves clear, free of the German's revenge, the machinery Churchill had already set in motion took over.

Churchill would have set up a hit timed for a specific date unless countermanded. Somehow Churchill would get into the flat and remove any material that linked him to Malin. The incriminating papers and videos, Rudi recalled painfully. Payment for the hit would be made through some remote contact untraceable to Churchill. Proof would be simple, the body left on display, a report in the next day's *Edenville Clarion*. A job done, a credit transfer to a foreign account.

The body? The bodies.

The killing of Malin was neat and swift. The hit man had come in from the fire escape, disturbed nothing in the flat, waited. Hours, a day maybe. Cool, he had waited there while Malin put a record on, maybe heard him fix some coffee, sing along to the music. That *was* cool. Until Malin entered that room, then he shot the fat man, and left. When Rudi got there Malin was still warm. Only that broken door and the bullet hole in his head indicated that anybody else had been there.

Rudi thought hard, and remembered. Once when Churchill was toying with the idea of making Rudi a partner he had asked, 'Where, if I need to, can I reach you?'

It meant, show that you trust me. At that time there had been nothing to lose. Rudi had given the phone and house number of Lagoon Close. Churchill had called him there once. It was all known.

The hit man was out there, coming for him. No other conclusion. If Churchill wanted Malin dead, he would not leave Rudi walking around. The operative would telescope the killings as finely as possible. Malin had been shot about six. It was now eleven. Rudi was full of scotch but not drunk. Empty milk bottles rattled as Annie put them out on the step.

Bruce came in, headset round his neck, music still crackling from the foam earpieces.

He said, 'I think we should split the pictures tonight. One each, pick in turns.'

Rudi objected, 'Sure, and tomorrow I find you two creeps disappear with all this art? No way.'

Annie came upstairs and said, 'Just shut up and look out the curtain.'

Bruce went first. 'I don't see anything.'

'A car, people in it.'

'Somebody saying goodnight.'

Annie noticed that Rudi's handsome brown face had turned grey.

'On the step just now I felt them watching me.'

'Them?' Rudi said. 'How many?'

Bruce snarled, 'What does it matter how many? What have you got us into?'

'You wanted in,' Rudi said. 'Remember?' Deriding, he mimicked, 'I wanna change my life, I wanna be a big-time person instead of a shitty little bank clerk. Well, Brucie, you got it.'

Annie said, 'The question is, Rudi, do they want the pictures, a cup of malted milk, or your balls on a plate?'

'There a back way out of here?' Rudi said.

''Cause if all they want is you, maybe we can fix them up.'

'Don't get any dumb ideas,' Rudi said. 'They'll kill you too.'

Annie peeked round the curtain.

'I think we're about to find out.'

TWENTY-SIX

'Don't answer it,'

   'Put the lights out.'

   'Leave them on.'

   'How do we get out the back way?'

   'A footpath the other side the fence.'

   'We'll go that way.'

   'Why don't we call the police?'

   'You crazy?'

The doorbell rang again.

   'Sit tight, let it go.

   'For Christ's sake, I live here. I'm not going to be a prisoner in my own house.'

   'There's somebody at the back. How many you see?'

   'Two.'

One at the front door. The other had gone through the side gate and was behind the house. Knuckles rapped the picture window of the lounge.

   'They know we're here.'

   'Stay cool, what can they do?'

Rudi motioned them down. They sat on the bed.

Bruce said, 'This is ridiculous. I can't live like this.'

Annie said, 'Bruce, shut up.'

With a finger at Bruce's forehead Rudi said, 'You open that door, bang!'

It was the finger that did it. Bruce snorted and took the open-plan stairs two at a time. Perhaps they saw him through the frosted glass. The bell chimed again.

Bruce called, 'Who is it?'

He instinctively responded to the elegant, assured voice. 'My name is Rodney Pinkroot. I'm afraid I don't know yours.'

'What do you want?'

'I deal in pictures. Can we talk?'

Bruce started as the letter flap sprang open and a card leapt through. The engraved curlicues of Pinkroot Galleries were impeccable. And why take instructions from a pathological liar like Rudi? Bruce pocketed the card. Leaving the security chain on, he flicked the outside light and opened the door.

The well-groomed, plumpish man in striped suit, brown hush puppies and bow-tie hardly fitted Rudi's nightmare. If Bruce ever had to choose, he wouldn't choose Rudi.

Pinkroot smiled. 'I apologise for the lateness of the hour. Had to help the police. Witness to a ghastly accident. Is that your car?' Pinkroot flapped a wrist at the Metro in the close. 'If not, could you kindly tell me which of your neighbours is the owner?'

'Why should I?' Bruce asked.

Pinkroot said, 'Some property of mine was stolen, and this car was seen driving it away. There may have been a misunderstanding, so before I bring in the police I'd like to talk to the owner of that vehicle.'

Every signal Bruce got from Pinkroot rang true. The accent, the assurance, the expensively unattractive clothes, spoke of honesty, honour.

'Wait,' Bruce said. He shut the door and went upstairs.

In whispered dialogue they established that none of them knew who Pinkroot was or how he had come there.

'But he knows about the pictures,' Bruce said.

The air got cold.

Annie said, 'Anybody with him?'

'No. Maybe you were wrong.'

Rudi said, 'There's somebody else out there.'

'He says the pictures are his.'

'Crap,' Rudi said.

Bruce quivered with incipient fury. 'If he says they're his, why the bloody hell shouldn't they be his? They're not yours.'

Grimly Rudi said, 'They're mine. This guy is a con.'

Annie asked, 'So who was the old man in the car smash?'

Rudi was about to explain everything. Then nothing. All he said was, 'They were his pictures. Now he's dead they don't belong to nobody.'

Bruce brandished the card. 'So how come *he's* here? How did he know?'

Rudi shook his head angrily. Before he could speak, glass broke below.

A hand reached through the frosted pane of the kitchen door, undid the Yale. Heavy footsteps traversed the ground floor. The front door was open. Before the three upstairs could shake off their postures of fear, Rodney Pinkroot was on his way up.

'I'm sorry I couldn't wait, but the night's getting on and I felt conspicuous out there. Perhaps you'd care to discuss this downstairs. Oh, and my friend's armed, so behave nicely.'

The bull-like man with the stubby automatic had followed Bruce's car to Lagoon Close. Once he saw the cul-de-sac sign he stopped and walked far enough to see which front door the three went in. Then he drove to the police station and waited for Pinkroot to finish making his statement. Now as they gathered in the lounge he said to the three people, 'Sit. Down. Don't. Make. Trouble.'

Like a child at Christmas, Pinkroot brought the portfolios in and inspected their contents. As he gazed on the pictures again his face enacted a mountain range of feelings – excitement, love, greed, ecstasy, power.

To Rudi he said, 'You. It was you I saw, stealing these articles. You stole them from a person called Malin, with whom I had an appointment. And who had just been very nastily murdered. I have just made a statement to the police saying that I saw nothing. But as I recover from the shock my memory will no doubt clear, and I can identify you. The convenient arrival of your friends here makes them accessories. Motive? They'll find one. You must have left a fingerprint somewhere. They'll find that too.'

'Or, am I right,' Rudi said, 'we keep quiet about this?'

Pinkroot's pulpy lips turned down in mature consideration.

'I am only reclaiming my property. Unorthodox means, I admit. But yes, we could proceed on that basis.'

'Screwed again,' Annie said. 'Hello, life.'

Pinkroot beamed. 'No point being bitter, my dear. You've been the victim of a cruel joke. Let's all be glad it's over.'

While the man with the gun stood in immobile guard, Pinkroot made ready to leave.

'Please,' he said, 'forget this happened. For all our sakes. The back way, I think.'

Pinkroot went through the kitchen. The gunman backed away from Bruce, Annie, Rudi, who remained inert in their chairs.

Portfolios under his arm, Pinkroot opened the kitchen door. Out in the dark a soft, amiable voice asked, 'Rudi St Paul?'

Pinkroot's face was fishlike with surprise. In the lounge they all heard. Annie shuddered. Suddenly she *knew*. From the other side of the dimly lit kitchen she called, 'Rudi? Who is it, Rudi?'

A silenced automatic hissed. The faint popping noise staggered Pinkroot back against the breakfast bar. Pinkroot's assistant reacted instantly to the art dealer's crashing fall through the lightweight kitchen furniture. His big silhouette blocked the hall light long enough for the automatic in his hand to become visible to the man outside. The unseen gun spat again.

The huge body collapsed into the kitchen. Annie realised the idea of calling Pinkroot 'Rudi' was not so bright. She felt her limbs wither. The killer knew someone else was in there. Someone with a female voice.

She felt sick, she wanted to wet herself. Bruce was bug-eyed, lips trembling. Only Rudi acted.

'Come on!' An urgent whisper through gritted teeth. 'The fuck, come on!'

Rudi scrambled back upstairs. Annie and Bruce shook themselves to go after him. They got into the bedroom, locked the door, moved a chest of drawers against it. First sound on the stair, Rudi said, they would get on the carpet and stay low.

Annie watched from behind the curtain. She saw a man in a flat cap briskly disappearing along the close.

'I think,' she said, 'we've survived this one.'

Rudi looked, but the man had gone. Annie didn't think he had been carrying anything. Rudi went down to the kitchen.

The portfolios still had Pinkroot's besotted arm across them, and the crooked right knee of the other man. Rudi drew a breath deep with relief. A trail of blood and brain matter had jetted over the kitchen floor within millimetres of the portfolios. A little further and the pictures would have been part of the carnage, their removal the first thing the police would notice. But now Rudi slid them out of Pinkroot's protective clutch. The evidence of these two corpses, whose identity still mystified him, was left intact for the forensics.

After three hours of individual questioning, cross-referring of stories and statements, Annie, Rudi and Bruce were allowed a few hours' sleep in the Edenville Central cells while the police team got what it could from 14 Lagoon Close. At dawn a police car drove them back. Splinters of broken glass and unobtrusive bullet marks were the only signs of what had happened. They had left the portfolios in a storage drawer under Bruce's bed. They figured that with the police there the art was safe.

The police warned them to expect further questioning. But the three stories had stood up. What the police couldn't answer – how Pinkroot, only hours after giving evidence in the killing of Leo Malin, had died himself in the same way, in a house he had never visited before – the residents of 14 Lagoon Close could not answer either.

Their alibis were unshakeable. For the afternoon and evening they had all been together, some odd bits of shopping, a drive. The police had to let them go. Weird they were, victims maybe. Killers not.

Annie braved the kitchen, in which a closer look still revealed blood smears and splinters of damage, to make coffee. Like a man who has viewed his own death enacted on a screen, Bruce hovered just beyond the door. The coffee smell was the first thing in the last few hours that didn't terrify him.

Annie said, 'Where's Rudi?'

'I think he went in the bathroom,'

'With the pictures?'

Haggard, Bruce still bristled. 'Oh Christ!'

Annie went upstairs and came down again.

'He took them in there with him.'

'So bloody what? I can't live with this paranoia.'

'Listen, Bruce. He keeps them with him even when he takes a crap. He is going to *rip you off*.'

'Me? Me? What about you?'

'A few hours, I'm on my way. You've been very sweet, Bruce, but people getting their heads blown off for things I don't understand . . . Time to get the fuck out, pardon my English.'

Bruce's throat swelled. 'You don't have to leave. I won't stay here now, of course, but as long as you want –'

Annie's voice fell. 'It's all over, Bruce. Cold mornings, the punters all gone, people like me on the road again. Over.'

She poured coffee and handed a cup to Bruce, who beneath his pallor looked badly churned.

'Rudi came to Edenville to con people,' Annie said. 'The point is, do you let him walk away with all that money?'

'What can I do?'

The bathroom cistern gushed water.

Annie said, 'Listen fast.'

'Face it,' Annie told Rudi, 'whoever shot you last night is gonna read somebody else's name in the paper. Then he'll try again.'

Rudi shrugged, 'I don't plan to be around.'

'Bruce sounds manic.'

Above the bathroom splashing rose a long crescendo of wordless music, the uncorked anguish of Bruce's soul.

'What you want?' Rudi said.

'Bruce is gonna screw you.'

'Bruce couldn't screw a doughnut.'

'Look, he phones the police and accuses you of something – theft, maybe, something to make them hold you. While you're out the way he gets your pictures.' Annie grimaced. 'Not bad. After all, you're the foreigner without the passport. Also he can tell them we lied to cover you after we met you at the place Malin was killed.'

Rudi said, 'See me trembling?'

'Bruce is a prat. Why not help him win a prize?'

'What you selling?'

'Answer this. The Channel trip is out, yeah? No reason why you should want to go to Normandy.'

'Places I'd rather be.'

'Go along with it. Bruce wants to put you on the boat and drive away with the pictures.'

'The pictures are in the car, I get out the car, he pisses off. That it? You're crazy.'

'If he thinks he can, he will.'

'He can't, so he sure fucking hell won't.'

'Let him think he can. You and me get on the boat. By the time Bruce finds out he's got shit, we're away.'

'What's in it for you?'

'Come on, I want a share of the money. Not a lot, just a little bite, OK? I might let you have your passport back, you agree.'

In the bathroom Bruce ploughed ever deeper oceans of unstoppered emotion.

'Deal?'

'How come I never found any balls on you?'

'Sweetie, you never looked in the right place.'

'OK, bitch, deal.'

In Annie's purple lipstick Bruce had written on the bathroom mirror, EVERY STORY IS A LOVE STORY.

Annie shook her head. It really was time to leave.

Downstairs Bruce said urgently, 'We better go.'

His face flashed silent messages at Annie, who confirmed them likewise.

Rudi jangled car keys on to the hall table and called up, 'Pictures locked in, Bruce.'

'Right, let's go.'

'One more thing.'

The two men passed on the stair. Bruce began to pace between kitchen and front door. Rudi found Annie in the spare bedroom with another suitcase, an ugly case in grey nylon with leather-look vinyl trim in red.

'What you doing?'

'Just wanted one last look.'

'OK, you had your look.'

'Why you so jumpy?'

'Do the bag up, let's get out of here.'

Annie zipped and strapped the pictures in.

'May I?'

Rudi shrugged as Annie took the case. They went down. White-faced, Bruce said to Rudi, 'Would you step in here a moment?'

Annie said, 'Christ, Bruce, we'll miss the boat.'

'Keep out of it, you cheap cow.'

Rudi followed Bruce into the kitchen.

'Come on, man, what? Let's go before any more shit comes down on this place.'

'Right, that's it! You insult my house, you seduced my wife – yes, I know all about it, don't worry – you've laughed at me ever since you got here –' Unequal to shouting, Bruce's voice shot up an octave. 'You've treated me like dirt, you've brought murder into my house. Once you're out of this country, stay out, because as soon as I get back I'm going to the police. I'll hang everything on you.'

Rudi said quietly, 'OK, Bruce, sure. Understood.'

In the hallway Annie had opened the door to the understairs cavity which held household maintenance equipment and power meters. From it she took a grey nylon bag with red leather-look vinyl trim, exchanging it for the identical bag she had carried downstairs. There was a lock on the door. She turned the key. Smooth, so silent, she had oiled it specially so it didn't even click. The key in her pocket.

Bruce had regained his cool. Before we leave the house, Annie had told him, lose your temper with Rudi, so he's glad to leave. Rattle his judgment.

'Fuck's sake, boys, can we get going?'

Rudi took the bag. Defiant, contemptuous, German-Hispanic, that was how he would go out. The three of them were pale and drawn, each for their own reasons.

Whenever alone in the house Annie had searched everything.

Know your environment, survive. The double bed had sliding drawers built in beneath, full of linen, winter bedding, travel stuff. Annie had suggested they put Emmajane's clothes there. To spare Bruce the daily torture of seeing them. Desperately relieved, Bruce said yes.

Bruce and Emmajane had been into his 'n' hers, for instance matching travel gear. When Annie took from under Emmajane's clothing a nylon bag perfect for transporting the pictures, she left its twin packed to the same weight buried below the double bed. Easy enough to shift this to the utility cupboard.

A final touch.

Bruce indicated the nylon bag Rudi carried. 'Put it in the boot.'

'No way it leaves my hand.'

Bruce got worked up again. 'Are you saying you don't trust me? Put it in the bloody boot or the trip's off.'

Assert yourself, Annie had said. He's suckered you long enough. Inside his blue eyes Rudi's pupils dilated into black gun barrels of menace. He waited long enough to make it look like his decision, then complied.

They didn't want him checking things on the way. Annie climbed in the back. Bruce ground the gears and aimed the car at Edenville.

They had to get British and French money. In the car park behind Bruce's bank Rudi said, 'Let's get the bags out.'

For Bruce this whole issue was a flashpoint. It put the stature of his car, therefore himself, in question.

'This is a bank,' he said. 'People rob banks, not bloody car parks. The bags stay.'

Annie quickly said, 'I just have to go and buy a few personal things. I'll meet you at the ferry terminal.'

Bruce and Rudi were still arguing as she left. In her handbag Annie had Rudi's passport, recovered from beneath the carpeting of Bruce's Metro. Rudi's idea was to get into France on the day-return trip, no visa required, head for Paris, do business, fly back to Colombia. He claimed he had confirmed all the details. Annie suspected they might not let him on the boat. Maybe he wanted it that way. She didn't care now.

And in the boot Annie's tartan holdall carried, Bruce thought, the pictures. Annie had flashed it open, revealing two modest water-colours, before she locked it. A moment would come when Bruce would be alone in the car with the tartan bag. Annie had told him what to do when this moment came.

Annie went to the taxi rank by the shopping complex and got a cab back to Lagoon Close. She had a spare key. In seconds she was nursing two bags, one with the pictures, the other personal things. She told the driver the RORO terminal.

The trucks were lining up along a potholed service road. Some cranes climbed the sky above timber warehouses, but the once busy port showed little other activity than the daily horde of container lorries. To make way for the terminal, old houses and commercial buildings had been torn down. Foundations still sketched their sites in waste lots behind heavy-duty wire fences badged with guard-dog signs. The remaining warehouses had been converted to prestige offices and heritage exhibitions.

Annie paid off the taxi and followed the truck line through the morass of diesel exhaust from idling engines. These truckers could smell a hitcher blindfold. Some shouted offers down to her. Annie waited till she saw one who didn't look like a lonely, smelly, apelike psycho. She asked where he was going. Tours, Bordeaux, Toulouse, but wherever he said was fine.

Annie held up her bags. 'Can I leave these in there?'

Sure she could. He was Scots too. Clean, nice, he would jump her, then take out photos of his kids, one gaptoothed, one blond, all smiling for their dad. She had met him a hundred times. He stowed the bags rear of the cab, unobtrusive.

Annie said, 'I just got to get a ticket and stuff. Can I see you on the boat?'

In the bar, he said, we'll have a few drinks. Annie hoisted a boot on to the footplate and retied a lace. As she leant forward he could see right down to her navel. Annie let him look, then smiled up. His eyes had gone into business on their own, magnetised by what they had seen. With a little wave Annie walked away, feeling his gaze riveted to the vortex of tight fabric at the back of her crotch. If it wasn't him it would be somebody else. In Cherbourg she would give him the slip.

With what she had left of her own money Annie bought a one-way ticket. In theory they were all broke, waiting on Bruce's bank account. But freedom meant having the right bits of paper. Freedom was the one itch you had to scratch.

The convoy had started to roll into the mouth of the truckliner when Bruce and Rudi drove up. The Metro pulled into the terminal forecourt, on the double yellows. Annie realised what Bruce was doing, and it was smart.

Bruce was twitchy, about to go hyper. Rudi looked sullen, impatient. Bruce finally unlocked the boot and tossed out Rudi's luggage, a shoulder bag and the grey nylon. He handed over some banknotes which neither he nor Rudi bothered to count.

'Get the tickets. I'll find the long-stay car park.'

Bruce met Annie's eye, and froze. An amateur to the death. Annie smiled and nodded weakly. Rudi made a great show of interest in the trucks crawling into the guts of the ship.

'Back in a minute,' Bruce barked.

He pumped the gas with the handbrake still on, then released so the car squealed and shot forward. Rudi scowled and exhaled like a tyre noisily deflating.

'OK, that it?'

Bruce's car skirted ranks of parked vehicles and was heading along the wire to the exit gate.

'Guess so.'

Annie already had the passport in the back of her jeans. She handed it over. Rudi flicked the pages then stooped down and began to unstrap the grey nylon bag.

'Ah Christ, come on. They'll close the barrier soon.'

Rudi ignored her, clawing at the straps. Annie decided now was the time to run. Before she could move she looked across the traffic areas and gaped. Bruce was driving back.

'What the fuck . . .?'

Rudi had got to the towels, and inside the towels the newspapers. He shook the bag out on the tarmac. No pictures. His bewilderment and rage were turning on Annie when he also noticed that Bruce was back.

It was Bruce Rudi targeted. Annie wondered if Bruce had stopped and ripped the lock off the tartan holdall. Expecting the whole collection and finding bedlinen. But there had not been time for this.

In the Metro Bruce reached forward to switch off the ignition. The car died before he touched the key. His foot was down on the clutch, but he dismissed the cut-out as a stall and unslotted the key. Honesty had brought him back, and fear. He would come clean, let the others take the pictures and go. Otherwise he would never sleep again, knowing that Rudi would come for him, or somebody like Pinkroot, or Pinkroot's faceless killer. Bruce couldn't just disappear like Annie. Edenville wouldn't let him. The treasures of this world belonged to those who would kill or die for them. In life's caste system, Bruce admitted, he was a *shopper*. He could only have things other people let him buy. So he had swung the car round.

To Rudi, advancing on him in a homicidal fury, Bruce raised open palms of atonement. The blast of the RORO hooter filled the space between sky and water. The trucks were all on, passenger cars boarding in separate lines. Smoke was coming from Bruce's car.

Annie was transfixed. Both men thought the pictures were in the boot of the Metro. Rudi wanted the pictures first. Then he would kick Bruce round the parking lot. The smoke trickled from the front wheelspace. For a moment it could have been stray fumes from an exhaust, but the small cloud thickened. Gunmetal grey, it drifted up over the windscreen, almost obscuring a tongue of orange that licked the steering wheel then withdrew again.

Bruce and Rudi stared at each other, then ran for the car. The same thought possessed them. At that moment the strange glow in the car interior flared into ripples of vermilion. Everything stopped as people crowded the ferry rail or came from the admin centre to watch. Before hundreds of eyes the Metro torched.

Rudi refused to stop. He grabbed the keys from Bruce's hand. An arm crooked across his face, he struggled into the heat and the nightmare of his own fear. A window shattered. Rudi sensed it coming, threw himself down. Some paces back Bruce cringed from the blaze. Rudi scrabbled along the tarmac.

Annie lost the conflict going on inside her. She ran after Rudi till her face burnt on the wall of heat.

'They're not in there! They're not in there!'

From the ground beside her Bruce looked up, eyes terrified. Perhaps he understood. Rudi heard nothing. Uniformed men were running to drag him back.

Then the petrol tank exploded. Rudi barrelled along the ground. The shower of flaming debris just missed him. His skin scorched, he stood dumbly watching the car burn out as people sprayed it with dry powder.

Bruce went over and put a hand on his shoulder. After a moment Rudi shook it off.

The boarding gate was about to close. Annie's papers were fine, she got through. Before they locked the vehicle deck she spotted her container driver and persuaded him to fetch her bags from the truck. She took the bags and arranged to meet him in the bar after a trip to the ladies' room.

Engines rumbled deep within the RORO. The ship bumped twice then was away from the quay. From the deck Annie saw the burnt-out skeleton of Bruce's car.

Why she would never understand, but she took the explanation with a smile on its face – Bruce had staged it himself, had dumped the tartan bag somewhere then come back and arsoned the car. So Rudi would think – and Bruce could live happy ever after with his bunch of dreams. Smart thinking, and in a way very Bruce to have pulled a thing like that.

Another version went: whatever reason for Bruce's return, it had produced his regular tacky luck. The car had caught fire because wiring faults didn't ask people first. And shit, Annie knew that had to be it. Whatever Bruce's plan, the real world just hadn't played along.

One day she might come back and ask him.

From beyond the barriers Bruce and Rudi watched the funnels pull away as the truckliner headed through markers to the deepwater channel. Annie moved along the side of the boat to escape their field of vision.

She would go to Arles, St Remy, Auvers, take mad Vince's babies home. Then see. Maybe she had got lucky: every story a love story. Or maybe unluckier than ever before in her life. That was all *Edenville* now. Worse or not, the future had a different name.

For Rudi Edenville had been a blackjack table. For Bruce it was a fate. For Annie a stage on a journey.

The harbour floated away. Wharves, hoists, the skyline of warehouses. The truckliner veered along a shore of rambling mansions with private mooring jetties in the dark embrace of rhododendron and pine. Then luxury apartments overlooking boatyards and marinas. Then past the chain ferry into the open sea.

Now the truckliner glided parallel to the empty windblown dunes of the nude beach. The boat carved the sea like liquid marble. Annie narrowed her eyes, bit her lip at the wake widening to miles of bright sand, sunlit clifftops, the glamorous landfall of Edenville.